Romancing the Billionaire

Ashley Zakrzewski   Darby Fox   Ida Duque
Anne Lange

All individual story copyrights remain in control of the individual authors over their own works:

© Fling with a Billionaire by Anne Lange © Bidding on The Billionaire by Darby Fox © Inn Love or Money by Ida Duque © Obsessed with my Boss by Ashley Zakrzewski

No part of this book may be reproduced in any form or by any electronic or mechanical means, including information storage and retrieval systems, without written permission from the author, except for the use of brief quotations in a book review.

Cover & Formatting by Zakrzewski Services

Fling with a Billionaire

Anne Lange

Chapter One

Kaitlyn

It's been one hell of a long week, and I can't wait to get home put my feet up on the worn coffee table, and chow down on some cookie-dough ice cream.

Everywhere I go in this small-ass town, I see or hear about Brandon and Tiffany's wedding. God, I'm sick of hearing about Brandon and Tiffany's wedding.

Like every small town in America, the cozy, personable, welcoming atmosphere of Hailey draws tourists and those looking to live a quiet life. But also, like in every other small town, everybody knows your business, and you know theirs.

I need to move to a city. Somewhere far away, where there's lots to see and do, lots of people I don't have to know – and most importantly who don't know me. Where I can be lost in a sea of faces on the street. A place where I won't run into my neighbor, my dentist, and my mother's hairdresser all in the same morning on my way to the local café to grab a coffee, where I'll undoubtedly run into at least twenty others I'm on a first-name basis with. Did I mention my ex and the new love of his life? I don't want to run into them, either.

"Kaitlyn, have you seen the drawings for the retirement home project?"

I glance over at Margo. We've been working together for four years at the town's one and only landscaping company and have become good friends both in and out of the office. While I grew up here, Margo is a transplant and two years older than my thirty years.

"I just filed them. I can pull them out again if you'd like?" I'm sure the paper cut I received putting them in there won't have a problem reminding me of its existence.

"No, that's fine. If you stick them in my hands I'll feel obligated to look at them. And on a Friday afternoon, the first weekend of June, I have no desire to dig into something that can wait until Monday. We have," she glances down at her Mickey Mouse watch, "exactly twenty-three minutes left of this work week. I want to get out of here on time tonight. It's supposed to be a beautiful weekend and I have gardening of my own to do."

"Then forget I said anything." I tidy up my desk, return samples from the small conference table to their rightful spots along the wall, and water the plants. I like to keep things clean and organized so that when customers or clients visit, it looks like we have our shit together.

"Have you decided what you're going to do yet?"

The dreaded vacation conversation. Again. "No."

"You should go on a trip."

"I don't have the money." All the money I had went towards my boyfriend's education. Sorry, ex-boyfriend. I worked so he could finish med school. Some people thought I was quite the martyr for supporting him like that. Others thought I was an idiot.

I wish I'd listened to the latter group.

"Do you have any relatives or friends out of state you can

visit? Getting away would be so refreshing. It might give you a different perspective on things."

Oh, my perspective is just fine. My boss is forcing me to take time off. Time I don't want to take. "I have no money and nowhere to go."

"If you *had* the money, where would you go?"

"New York," I say without giving it a millisecond of thought. "There's so much to do there—plays, concerts, museums, shopping." Brandon and I had always talked about New York, or maybe it was just me. I had high hopes of spending our honeymoon there one day.

I hear he's taking Tiffany to Las Vegas.

"Why won't they just let me work?"

She sighs, and it's a 'we've-had-this-conversation-many-times-already' sigh. "You know why."

"If I've earned it, and it belongs to me, I should have a say in when I take it."

"You do, honey. But you haven't taken any vacation days since you started four years ago. Sam has been very generous in letting you carry it over. But it's costing him money." Margo is the accountant slash planning person. Our boss, Sam, is not the only one hounding me.

"They can just give me the money."

"You know that's not how it works. It's a mental health thing as well. We all need time to recharge. You have been working non-stop."

That's because it's the only place I can go in town and not be bombarded or reminded that my ex-boyfriend and my ex-best friend are getting married in two weeks.

Did I forget to mention my ex-best friend? She's a nurse. He's a doctor. Guess what game they were playing during the night shift?

"Margo, Kaitlyn, let's go. We're cutting out early tonight."

I glance up to see our boss standing in the doorway. "Why?"

"We're celebrating," Sam says with a wide grin. "We just landed a huge contract with the school board. I'm treating everyone."

That is excellent news for our small landscaping company. It will require travel to nearby counties for the grounds team, but it will keep us in the black for the next couple of years. "Let me finish up, and I'll join you."

"You can finish on Monday. Let's go." He turns away, but not before giving us the 'I'm-the-boss-do-as-I-say' glare. He really is the best. Unless he's trying to force me to take vacation, that is.

We follow Sam out the door, wait for him to lock up, then cross the road and walk up the street to one of the two pubs in town. At five o'clock on a Friday evening in June, the sun is not quite as warm as it was mid-afternoon, but hot enough bare arms and shorts are more than adequate.

Not surprisingly, the restaurant is packed. We shoulder our way through, stopping to say hi to everyone we know. By the time we make it to the bar, my throat is dry, and my face hurts from smiling. The rest of the crew is already there waiting for us.

Sam leans over the bar and calls to the server. "Free round for my entire crew, Lindy."

The young blonde gawks. "Wow, must be celebrating something special." She takes the orders and gets to work.

While we wait, I look around the room, taking in the heavy wood décor, the square four-seater tables, and the green vinyl booths. The overwhelming scents of grilled meat and fryer grease swirl through the air. They make the best burgers here. Partner it with deep-fried pickles and a banana shake and yum —my favorite meal.

Lindy places our drinks on the bar. "Hey, the fifty/fifty draw closes tonight. You still have time to get tickets. Half the money is going towards a pool table for the back room and some pin ball machines if we make enough."

"Oh, I'm in." Margo fishes her wallet out of her purse. "Come on, Kaitlyn, fork it over. This town could use a good games room."

I request three tickets from Lindy as she works her way down the bar collecting for the cause.

Two hours, two drinks, and a mouth-watering burger later, Lindy rings the bell to quiet everyone down so she can call out the winning ticket.

"Call my number, Lindy and I'll buy you something special."

"Call my number, Lindy and I'll ditch my wife and take you on a trip."

"Call my number, Lindy and I'll ditch my *husband* and take *you* on that trip."

We all laugh at the comments from the peanut gallery in the back.

"Okay, guys. First, thank you to everyone who contributed to the draw. We managed to raise twelve thousand, six-hundred and fifteen dollars over the last month. I am *so* amazed. Thank you. That means somebody in this town, maybe even one of you here tonight, is going to walk out that door with an extra six thousand, three hundred and seven dollars and fifty cents in their pocket."

Oh, that would be such a healthy start to my new savings plan.

"And the winning ticket number is five, three, seven, two, two zero."

She repeats the number.

I dig my tickets out of my back pocket. Five, three, seven,

two, two, two. Five, three, seven, two, two, one. And the last one, five, three, seven...holy fuck. I double and triple-check the last three digits.

"Anybody here have that number." She repeats it a third time.

"Me."

Nobody hears my squeak. I raise my voice and my arm, with the tiny white ticket clasped tightly in my fingers. "I won."

Beside me, Margo jumps up and down. "Oh my God. Oh my God. Seriously? You won?"

I hold out the ticket for her to confirm.

She screeches.

People pat me on the back as I make my way to the bar, where Lindy congratulates me and hands me a check. I glance down at it, and my mouth goes dry.

"Now you can go on that vacation." Margo, God love her, refuses to give up.

I'm shaking my head. "This money will resuscitate my depleted savings."

When I unlock the door to my tiny apartment in our town's one and only apartment building and close it behind me an hour later, the shock has almost worn off. I remove the check from where I had tucked it in my purse and lay it on my two-person kitchen table. I'll deposit it on the way to work in the morning. But for now, as somebody who's never won a thing in her life, I want to look at it for a while.

The weight of the day, and the beers, hit me, so I grab a cold bottle of water from the kitchen, pick up the week's mail that's been piling up, and plop down on the sofa.

I flip through bill after bill and a bunch of marketing crap but stop dead when I come to a pink embossed envelope. My heart lodges in my throat.

Oh no. No. No.

I recognize that handwriting. Anger and disbelief wash over me.

Are you freaking kidding me?

Are they that bold? Or that clueless?

I don't even have to open it to know what it is. I've seen enough people in town rip the seal on theirs.

My eyes burn. My hands shake.

I drag my eyes away from the wedding invitation, looking anywhere but down in my lap. My gaze lands on the table.

Standing, I let everything on my lap fall to the floor. I stroll over to the table, pick up the check and stare at it.

New York, here I come.

Chapter Two

Elliott

Reaching over, I smash the alarm, hitting snooze for probably the tenth time before scratching my chest and yawning widely. The nice thing about being me is I don't answer to anybody but the man in the mirror. If I want to be late, I'll fucking be late. And after a long night of sitting at a bar talking with a woman more interested in my bank account than me, and then realizing I wasn't even interested in having sex with her, I deserve a few extra hours of sleep.

I roll my head to the empty side of my bed. Fuck. You'd think I would be used to waking up alone at age thirty-four. It's not like women ever flocked to me. This is my norm and has been my entire life. And yet, disappointment settles like a lead balloon deep in my gut.

As a young man, I'd foolishly thought cash would bring them in droves, regardless of the ugly scars on my face. While they don't tease or call me names these days, they only stick around for the gifts. Once they get to know me, they decide staying for the long haul isn't worth it.

Story of my life.

Swinging my legs over the edge of the bed, I jerk the covers aside and sit up. First things first. I pick up the phone and dial the kitchen.

It rings three times before it's picked up, a cheerful voice on the other end. "Mr. Carrington, Sir, good afternoon."

"Afternoon, Gus. Are you having a good day so far?"

"It's a beautiful day, Sir. The sun is shining. The city is bustling with activity. What can we get for you this afternoon?"

An advantage to living in a hotel—I never have to cook. Or clean. And I have a constant supply of top-of-the-line bathroom products at my disposal. I have a place I can stay in all of my hotels, but I prefer living out of my New York location, so this penthouse suite is mine, and mine alone. It's never rented out. I keep personal items here. I work from here. It never made sense to me to own an expensive apartment when I already own an expensive hotel.

And I like New York.

I can afford nice things, and I enjoy traveling. I won't apologize for that. Still, I've grown tired of making those trips alone, sleeping with random women I don't remember two weeks later.

"I'll take two eggs over easy, bacon, whole wheat toast and some strawberries, please."

"Coffee, Sir?"

"Absofuckinglutely. And some ice water, please." I'll need to hydrate anyway.

"What time would you like it delivered, Sir?"

I glance at the clock on the bedside table. "Give me thirty minutes."

"Of course, Mr. Carrington."

I hang up and strut over to the bathroom to take care of business before I jump in the shower.

The downside to living in a hotel is there's no sense of

home. It's not cozy. There's no warmth, no feeling of family. My suite is two levels and includes a kitchenette and dining room. But there's no photographs or papers stuck to the refrigerator with a giant colorful magnet. There's no personal artwork, no lived in look.

Then again, I never had that growing up, either. So, really, this is like home for me.

From birth, I've been surrounded by household staff—cleaners, cooks, landscapers, drivers, hell, we even had a butler once—a phase my mother went through. No hugs, no birthday parties with friends from school.

And nothing changed no matter how much trouble I got into, just begging for them to lift their heads and take notice. At least they allowed me to attend public school.

I'm wandering out of the bathroom, hot mist trailing behind me like a ghost, when there's a sharp rap on the door.

"Room service, Mr. Carrington."

Securing the fluffy white towel around my waist, I stroll out of the bedroom, down the stairs and across the living area to the door. After I disengage the deadbolt and lock, I swing the door open.

Gus is delivering it himself this morning. "Must not be too busy in the kitchen."

"We had a quiet moment." He rolls the cart past me. I let the door close on its own steam as I follow him into the main living area, waiting while he positions the cart near the chair where he knows I like to sit. He pours the coffee but leaves the dishes covered. "Anything else, Sir?"

"Nope. I'm good, Gus. Thank you."

We make small talk as I walk him out, and then I'm alone again in my room, the smell of crisp bacon sneaking out from beneath the silver warming lid.

I doctor my coffee, then sip the hot, fresh brew. My eyes drift closed, and a sigh falls from my lips. Only the best.

Okay, time to scarf down some breakfast, and then I need to run downstairs to grab a few reports from the main office before I tackle a little work.

An hour later, dressed more casually than typical for a work day, I step off the elevator and reach for my phone in my back pocket. While descending from my penthouse suite, I listened as guests chatted about their trip to the city.

One young couple gushed about their imminent honeymoon. Their excitement to visit Maui got me craving some warmer weather and sand myself. I should head to an island for a few days. I'm sure I can find a beach bunny wherever I land to keep me occupied. All I'd have to do is buy her a few trinkets in exchange.

I scour through my phone contact list for the pilot I use as I push open the door to the hotel office area. I send off a quick message to confirm his availability.

At the last second, I remember why I rarely come down here. Two feet over the threshold, Celeste is right up in my personal space, her heavy floral perfume clogging my nose, a sneeze already building. Today she's in white leather, and are those handcuffs in her ears? Little handcuff earrings. I can't contain the eye roll.

Holding the phone to my ear, pretending I'm mid-call, I take two steps back. One night with this woman was more than enough. An hour into our date, I knew I'd made a terrible mistake giving in to her suggestion we go for a drink. She set her sights on me and has not backed down. She even followed me to a club one night, and used that information to try and worm her way between my sheets.

The woman is constantly propositioning me. She'd have me

tied to a bedpost if those cuffs were authentic. Not that the idea is abhorrent, on the contrary. But she's not my type.

While I may want a life partner deep down, I'm not interested in somebody who's only interested in draining my bank account or who's twenty years older. It's too bad she's so fucking great at her job. This place would fall apart if it weren't for her. As my Hotel Manager, she runs a tight ship, but she's fair. She knows what she's doing and came highly recommended. They just never warned me she was a starved cougar on the hunt. I can trust her in every aspect of my hotel business. I can't trust her behind *any* closed door.

"Elliott," she purrs. "I was over the moon when I heard you were here. I've missed you the last few weeks."

That would be by design. "I don't know what you mean, Celeste. We talk almost every day." I push past her and head to my office. Not that I work from this desk too often, but the hotel's records are here, so unfortunately, I have to make an appearance occasionally.

She's right on my heels as I circle my large glass-topped desk. She's tall for a woman, only a couple of inches shorter than my six-three, so in heels that puts her at eye level. I can feel her hot breath on the back of my neck. Even my dick is trying to shrink into hiding.

"Listen, I'm really sorry, Celeste. But I just came down to grab the quarterly reports I sent to the printer last night." When I return to my room, I'm putting in an order for a printer to be delivered to my suite. "I'm heading out of town for the weekend and wanted some reading material for the flight."

"Don't you want company instead?" She dances her fingers up my arm.

Did she just squeeze my bicep? I jerk out of her hold, desperate not to be rude. My mother instilled impeccable manners in me. Still, I don't want to spend my morning dodging Celeste's blatant sexual innuendos and grabby hands. "Um, no, not this time."

"You're looking very casual today. Do you have time for lunch before you leave? We could dine in your room."

Stepping out of her grasp, I put the desk chair between us while I quickly grab the pages from the printer and spin around, not wanting to give her my back for any longer than necessary. I've made that mistake before.

"Sorry, Celeste. No time today."

For the record, a pout isn't attractive on a woman in her fifties.

I tuck the pages under my arm while walking around the opposite side of the desk, heading back to the door. "I'll be available by email if anything urgent comes up." Giving her a hasty wave, I beeline for the lobby, stopping at the reception desk to use a stapler or find a folder for this report, and to check my phone to see if the pilot has responded yet. I can't even do the simplest of things in the office when Celeste is around.

"Excuse me?"

What now?

Pink-tipped toes in white sandals enter my line of vision. I slowly lift my eyes and come face to face with the most fresh-faced, naturally gorgeous woman I've ever seen. Shorter than me, she's got long brown hair hanging straight down her back and beautiful dark chocolate brown eyes to match. Looking much younger than she probably is, *than I hope she is*, she's dressed in light blue denim overall shorts and a baby pink tee shirt. Her toes match her shirt. Her skin is flawless, smooth, and has a pretty blush tone to it. Like she spends a lot of time in the sun.

Something about her, something in her eyes, draws me in. She looks a little scared, a lot hopeful. I suddenly want to know everything about her. I *need* to.

"Can you help me, please?" She points to her bags.

The bellhop is probably assisting guests outside, so my gaze wanders over to the front desk area. Everyone is busy and doesn't notice her talking to me. Otherwise, at least one would rush right over to intervene. Before that happens, I fold my papers in half and tuck them into my back pocket along with my phone. I reach for the extended handle of her luggage.

"Of course. Which floor are you on?"

She glances down at the key card in her hand. "Twelve. Room twelve fifteen."

Nodding toward the bank of elevators I stretch out one arm in that direction. "This way."

I relieve her of a backpack, and take charge of her larger suitcase. We make our way across the lobby, her juggling a coffee in addition to her carry-on, and a purse that keeps slipping off her shoulder. I notice some of the staff look at us with questions in their eyes and confusion on their faces. A few appear as though they plan to intercept, but I stop them in their tracks with a slight shake of my head. The pretty woman, oblivious to the undercurrent, is chatting away about her trip from the airport and the weather as I follow her to the elevator and then press the up button.

"Where are you coming from today?" I ask. With only a few minutes to spend with her, I intend to discover everything I can.

"Idaho."

"Is this your first time to New York?"

"Yes. It was a last minute decision. My boss is forcing me to take vacation time, not that I need to. I would have preferred to save the money I won because I've depleted my entire savings account, but you don't need to know that story."

I want to know that story.

"You're travelling alone?"

"Yup. It's not something I do often, well at all, but I *desperately* needed to get out of town and didn't have time to beg my best friend to drop everything and come with me."

The elevator arrives, and we load in, stepping to the side as others join us. She tells me about her flight during the trip and then I lead the way down the hall to her room.

"My friend thought it would be a good idea for me to get away, especially right now. And I have to admit, while I really can't afford to waste my winnings on this trip, I *really* need it."

"Here you are."

We stop in front of the door to her room, and she pauses to take in a breath. She uses her access card to open the door. Once she's crossed the threshold and flicks on a light, I hand over her luggage. Now *I'm* eager to find something, *anything* to say that will delay me walking away and possibly never seeing her again.

"Thank you," she says. "Oh, wait!" She fumbles in her purse.

I hold up my hand. "It not necessary."

"Are you sure?"

"Positive. How about instead, you repay me with a date." I can't believe I suggested that. She's going to think I'm nuts. If I'm lucky, she won't call the front desk and complain to security.

I watch as she bites her lip, then twitches her mouth as though deep in thought. She's probably wondering how to turn down an ugly-assed bellhop who just hit on her. She might even be questioning her decision to visit New York thinking we're all over confident assholes. I'd prefer the latter since I don't give a damn about my scars.

And then she surprises me.

"Well, I did come here looking for an adventure. I promised Margo I'd do something out of the norm." Her eyes are locked on me, and she's mumbling loud enough for me to hear. "Besides, I deserve it. Brandon and Tiffany can go to hell."

I'm siding with Margo. I don't know who Brandon and Tiffany are, but if them going to hell will get her to go out with me, I'll send them there myself.

"Okay."

I can't believe she said yes. "Meet me downstairs in the lobby at seven pm."

"Seven it is. Um, what's your name?"

I grin at her awkwardness because she's so darn cute. And because I can't help it. "Elliott. Elliott Carrington."

"Hi, Elliott Carrington. I'm Kaitlyn Moore."

"I'll see you at seven, Kaitlyn."

She gives me a shy smile before she closes the door.

Chapter Three

Kaitlyn

Margo would be so proud. I, however, am mortified that I accepted a date with a stranger. But he works for the Fairchild. He can't be all bad.

I know I shouldn't have splurged on such a swanky hotel, but when I glanced down at that pink wedding invitation, my fingers brushing over the gold embossed flowers at the top as my brain flooded with memories of all the planning I'd done, I decided I deserved something good in my life, for me. At least once.

The man I thought *I'd* be marrying this weekend with my best friend since high school by my side was getting ready to walk down the aisle with said friend. They even used my venue. To be fair, there are few prime locations in our hometown to have a wedding, but still. They could have at least picked one of my least favorites.

While Brandon may not have cared, Tiffany knew every aspect of my dream wedding, from the color theme to my flower choices, even the clothes I planned to pack for the honeymoon. And then, to send me an invitation at the last minute was a slap in the face.

I decided I could save my money again *after* my trip to New York.

And now, here I am, about to spend the evening with a man I know nothing about. Probably not my smartest move, but I like to give people a chance. Besides, he's very handsome. Tall, dark hair, scruff. I didn't know I liked scruff on a man. He has a rugged face. I'm guessing he had acne as child and it left its mark on him. Nothing serious though, just a handful of faint scars. And who doesn't have scars from our teenage years? I think it adds to his appeal. He also fills out a polo shirt very nicely. I do find it odd that the Fairchild hotel allows staff to dress so casually, though. Not that he was in dirty jeans or anything, but all the other staff I saw were dressed in uniform.

As the elevator descends to the lobby, I do a mental check. After a quick shower to freshen up from the flight, I unpacked before doing my hair and make-up. I chose a simple maxi dress for tonight with my white sandals and kept my hair down.

The doors slide open, and I step out, look around, and head toward the seating area in the lobby's center. There's a ring of two sofas, four single chairs, a large square table in the middle, and a massive display of colorful summer blooms.

The registration area to my left is hopping, and the lineup to check is lengthy. To my right, I can see the bar and what I assume is the entrance to a dining room behind it.

"What do you think?"

"Oh!" Elliott surprises me, coming up from behind. I turn, feeling my face flush, but I don't know if it's because he caught me off guard or because he's even more handsome tonight than earlier.

"Spontaneity isn't my strong suit," I blurt out.

He arches one dark brow. "Is that your way of telling me you've changed your mind about dinner?"

I put a hand on my chest. "Oh, gosh, no. Not at all. I've been accused of being overly cautious. This is all so new to me. New York, on my own, dinner with a man I don't know." I'm blabbering and can feel the redness creeping up my neck onto my cheeks.

His smile softens his angular jaw. His stormy blue eyes twinkle as though he has a joke he's not sharing. He takes my elbow and guides me out of the traffic flow and over near the back of one sofa. "What would you like for dinner?"

"Um, I don't know. I guess the options are endless in New York." My gaze darts around the expansive room but is quick to zero back in on Elliott. I love his name. It's so rich sounding. I wonder what he does. Tonight he's wearing dark jeans with black loafers, and a black dress shirt with the sleeves rolled up to below his elbows.

"What are you favorites? Let's start there."

"I love Mexican and Chinese. Oh, and Italian. You can also never go wrong with a good American burger."

He tosses his head back and laughs, and it just rumbles out of his throat, sounding like I imagine whisky might if it had a voice. Other people turn to stare.

"If you can find us something where Mexican and Chinese are in the same place, even better. I can mix and match."

He smirks. "I know just the place."

We walk out of the hotel, where he directs me to a black sedan idling at the curb. A man is standing near the back door and opens it when we draw near.

Elliott simply smiles and offers me a hand to help me inside. "Well, this is fancy." How can he afford this on a bellhop's salary? I should tell him he doesn't have to spend his hard-earned money to impress me. "We could have taken a cab or the bus."

"This is easier."

We don't talk much during the drive, but that's my fault. I'm too busy ogling everything in sight. I'm sure my neck will ache come morning with all the side-to-side action it's getting so I can see what's happening out of each side of the vehicle.

The car pulls to the curb about twenty minutes later and comes to a stop. I dip my head to look out the window, curious to see what restaurant he's chosen for us. But I don't see one.

"We'll get out here and walk the rest of the way," he explains.

"Oh, okay." Before I can open the door, the driver is there, helping me out.

Elliott climbs out behind me. He nods to the driver. "I'll text you when we're on the way back."

"Yes, Sir."

I'm not sure what to think, but I am impressed.

Elliott holds out his hand, as though we've done this a thousand times. I take it after a moment's hesitation. His warm fingers wrap around mine, encasing my small hand in his bigger one. Following his lead, we stroll for about a block before approaching an intersection blocked by barricades and a police car.

"I guess we can't go this way."

"We're not crossing." Elliott takes us around the corner, and I come to a complete stop.

I inhale deeply, feeling the excitement of the street fair before me in the evening air. The sun is setting, painting the sky in beautiful shades of red and orange. Shouts of laughter and conversation fill the air, and the smell of the food trucks, so many food trucks, wafts through the crowd. My stomach grumbles with anticipation as I peer up at Elliott. "This is perfect.

What a great idea." That he's brought me to such a public place, alleviates my fear of being with a stranger—no matter how handsome he is. "There's so many choices. What do you think we should get?"

"I think we should we try a little bit of anything you want."

We weave our way through throngs of people, admiring the various offerings. I can't help but feel drawn to the Mexican food stands with their bright colors and inviting aromas. Zeroing in on one truck, I increase my pace, eager to get some delicious Mexican food. As we draw closer, the delightful scents of carnitas, tacos, and spicy salsas fill my senses. My mouth waters.

"Do you want to get a few tacos? Or maybe some enchiladas?" Elliott suggests, pointing to the dishes displayed on the menu board.

"Enchiladas sound great."

He places our order, and we step out of the line and to the side to wait until it's ready.

Small picnic tables are scattered everywhere. Some have pretty gingham patterned umbrellas, other are solid colors. "Should we find a table?" I ask.

"If you'd like to grab one over there, I'll wait for our food."

I find an open spot near the truck, in Elliott's line of sight, and settle in. He joins me less than ten minutes later with our spread; he's even added a couple of cold water bottles. I snatch up and unwrap one enchilada, taking a bite, savoring the spiciness on my tongue. "This is amazing. It's so good."

When I open my eyes, Elliott is staring at me, or rather, his gaze is locked on my mouth, his eyes dark pools I could drown in. He nods slowly in agreement though he hasn't even unwrapped his yet.

He clears his throat, and his eyes rise up to meet mine. "I'm glad you like it."

Heat floods my body in response to the deep sexy timber of his voice. I shove my food into my mouth and smile back, feeling an early connection with this man I don't even know. It's far too soon, and besides, my gut instinct regarding men hasn't worked in my favor. I pull my gaze from his and look around, noticing a Chinese food stand a few feet away. "Time for the next course. How about some dumplings? This time, my treat."

"I invited you out to dinner."

"Yes, but I want you to save your money."

He gives me a funny. "Okay."

"You wait here."

I trot over to the other truck. Glancing back to see Elliott watching me, a lightness in his eyes and I wonder if it's always there or just for me.

It takes about seven minutes until my turn, and I can make my selection. Playing it a little safe since I don't know what Elliott likes, I ask for an assortment of dumplings with some rice.

When I'm back at our little table, he glances up at me after taking a swig from his water bottle before tackling his food. "Do you have plans while you're here?"

Shrugging, I sweep my gaze around the picnic tables surrounding us. Most are filled with families or couples enjoying the evening fair. We have community events back home, but it's not the same. I can hear traffic a street over. People are shouting. Occasionally, a car honks its horn or squeals its tires. There's a buzz amongst the activity that doesn't exist in a small town. "Nothing specific. I didn't have time to make any reservations for shows, and I'm sure all the best ones are sold out. I decided to book a flight and hotel before I could second guess myself."

"You mentioned winning money for this trip."

I nod. He waits patiently for me to finish chewing. The pork-filled dumplings are delicious, and I can't hide my enjoyment, which seems to amuse him. "Yes. A fifty/fifty draw at one of the pubs where I'm from to raise money for their games room."

"And what made you choose New York?"

"I hoped to come here for my honeymoon."

He rears back. "You're married? Engaged?"

"I was."

He leans forward again. "Should I say I'm sorry?"

At first, I was hurt. Then embarrassed. Then pissed. Pissed lasted a long time. I'm back to embarrassed. "No. I'm getting over it." Once I got beyond the anger, sadness hit. I lost my best friend in the breakup, and I could have used her shoulder. "So what about you? I know you're a bellhop, but what do you like to do for fun?"

Elliott squirms on the bench and tucks another bite of food into his mouth. I hope he's not ashamed of his job. He gets to meet so many people every single day. It must be exciting.

"I travel a lot."

"You can afford it?" I want to slap myself for being so rude. "I'm sorry, I didn't mean it like that."

"It's alright. There are Fairchild hotels all over. I spend time at each of them every year."

"Wow. That's an odd thing to do in your job, but I guess it's a great way to see different places." I sigh heavily. "If I had all the money I saved over the years, I'd be able to do more travelling. I want to see so many places."

"What happened to your savings, if I may ask?"

"It paid for my ex-boyfriend's education."

"That was generous of you." He looks skeptical.

"At the time I thought *I* meant as much to him as his

medical degree." I also thought I meant more to my best friend than he did. Guess I was wrong on both counts.

"Why don't we focus on what you plan to do while you're visiting? I can show you around if you'd like."

"What about your job?"

"My schedule is flexible."

"You must have a nice boss."

He grins, and, oh my, it's a devilish grin that, on his chiselled face, is sexy as fuck. "The best."

The sun is setting, and the crowd is thinning out. The street fair is wrapping up. Elliott stands and holds out his hand again for me to take. On the walk back, he calls the driver to meet us.

"This has been a fantastic evening. Thank you, Elliott."

He casts a look over at me, giving my hand a gentle squeeze. "You're welcome."

The sounds of laughter and conversation fade away as we walk farther up the street back to that first intersection where the barricades are now being removed, and vehicular traffic admitted.

The drive back to the hotel is quiet, as is our walk through the hotel, to the elevator, and up to my floor. When we stop in front of my door, I turn, my back against the dark wood grain.

Elliott is standing close.

An awkwardness descends on me. I haven't been on a date in years. I don't know what to do. Do I kiss him? Say goodnight? Invite him in?

Thankfully, he takes the decision out of my hand when he places a finger under my chin and gently tips my head back.

A marching band could parade their way up the hallway right now, and I couldn't drag my eyes away from his. I'm falling into their depths as he lowers his face, his warm breath caressing my skin.

My nipples harden beneath my dress. My thighs quiver and my pussy tingles.

But he doesn't kiss me.

Is he waiting for permission?

"You can kiss me," I blurt out.

His nostrils flare, the only sign I get before his mouth crashes down on mine. It begins as a clash of teeth and tongues. But before I can suck in air, he changes course and becomes tender, exploring. He rests his other hand on my waist and jerks me against him. His hard erection presses into my belly.

The man kisses like a God.

My lady bits want to party.

A door slams shut down the hall, and I break our connection, touching my forehead to his.

"I want you, Kaitlyn."

Wow. I've never had a man say that to me. Brandon never said that to me. "We can't. I don't want you to get fired."

"I can't get fired."

I place my hands on his chest intending to gently urge him to step back. But the pounding of his heart under my palm has me curling my fingers into his shirt, keeping him in place. "I won't let you risk your job, especially when I'm only here for a few days. There must be rules about fraternizing with the guests. I would never forgive myself."

He closes his eyes. "Kaitlyn, I own the hotel."

Chapter Four

Elliott

I didn't plan on telling Kaitlyn that last night. I would have eventually, or she would have discovered it on her own, but I liked the anonymity. This adorable woman had no clue who I was, and for a while there last night, I was an ordinary guy on a regular date with a pretty woman.

After I let the truth slip, she gaped at me, wide-eyed and blinking rapidly. She didn't say a word for a solid minute. Then she spun around, unlocked her door, and slipped inside, the door slamming shut in my face. Okay, she didn't slam it, but it closed, hard. Probably the spring mechanism.

I've tried calling her room, but she hasn't answered. I unethically used my position to get her phone number off her reservation and sent her three texts, apologizing and telling her I wanted to spend the afternoon with her. I want to assume her silence is because she's out exploring the city on her own, but my gut tells me otherwise.

I sigh and push open the door to my suite, feeling defeated. What else can I do? She has a right to be mad. I made her out to be a fool. I should have known better and kept my identity to myself.

I flop down on the leather sofa and pull my laptop out of my bag, hoping to distract myself with some work. I don't get far, though.

I get up and rummage through my credenza drawers until I come across a folded brochure I picked up at the airport on one of my trips. I open it and flip through the pictures of all the things to do in New York City. Kaitlyn had said something about wanting to see a show.

Maybe that's what I should do. I can use my connections to get her into the best events. I scoop up my laptop and get to work, intent on finding Kaitlyn something I hope she'll like. I can't promise she'll forgive me, but I can at least give her a night to remember.

When I open my browser, my bookmarked list of clubs comes up, and I pause. What I wouldn't give to take Kaitlyn to a club. You can learn so much about somebody from how they respond to watching other people have sex. Would she be embarrassed or enraptured? Would she touch herself while she watched? Would she let me touch her? Considering we just met, I didn't even get to probe last night to see if she'd be open to the idea. But now I can't get it out of my head. I add visiting a club to my options.

I spend the next three hours planning for the afternoon and evening. I've purchased tickets to a few of the best shows in town throughout the week. When I'm done, I feel good, but now I have to see if Kaitlyn will give me a chance.

By noon, I haven't heard a word from her. With any other woman, I'd say fuck it and write her off. But this time, I can't. I am inexplicably drawn to Kaitlyn. I don't know what it is about her that keeps me entranced, that makes me want to make her happy. That makes me want to fix the hurt and betrayal I saw in her eyes when she turned away from me last night.

I pick up the hotel phone and redial her room. This time, it rings twice and then she picks up.

"Hello?" Her voice is soft and hesitant.

Relief washes over me. "Kaitlyn, it's Elliott. I'm sorry, I should have never kept who I was from you. I'd like to make it up to you if you'll let me."

I swallow and clear my throat, "I know I misled you about who I am and for that, I apologize. I had hoped last night would be...different. I had hoped to get to know you first before I told you." I must be honest with her. "To be honest, I just wanted to enjoy a night out with a beautiful woman."

She's still there. I can hear her breathing.

"Listen, I thought I could make it up to you. Take you out this afternoon to see a few of the sights. Please?"

"On one condition."

"Name it."

"You let me pay for this afternoon."

That I can do. The shows, and I hope the rest of my plans, will be on me, but I can let her buy me ice cream at Ellis Island. "I'll meet you in the lobby in an hour?"

"I can be ready in thirty minutes."

My smile is wide. It's going to be okay. I hope. "Thirty. Dress to walk, but pack a sexy dress for tonight."

"What's happening tonight?" Her suspicion is well founded, but I refuse to say a word. I can't fathom the thought of scaring her off.

"Tonight is on me. Just pack for the night and include a sexy dress and shoes. Trust me."

"Um, okay. So we're not coming back here?"

"Not until very late." Not until tomorrow, if I have my way.

"Okay."

We hang up, and I rush through changing my clothes and calling my driver and my pilot to confirm the arrangements.

Kaitlyn is standing in the lobby when I arrive, dressed in jeans and a t-shirt, but with a small tote bag hanging from her shoulder. She looks stunning. My heart thumps in my chest, and my cock stands up, taking notice.

"Ready for an adventure?" I ask her as I approach.

She nods, a bashful smile playing on her lips.

Whatever has been going through her mind since last night, she's giving me a chance. I'll take it.

I lead her out of the hotel and towards the car, ready to enjoy the day ahead and make it up to her.

"Where are we going?" She asks.

I love holder her hand, so I take one in mine and try to look reassuring. "I thought we would visit some of the places I love best in this city. We can start with the Statue of Liberty and then head over to Ellis Island."

She squeezes my fingers and follows me to the car waiting under the hotel entrance's canopy.

As we drive past some of the most iconic landmarks of New York City, I point out stories and interesting facts about each. She seems amazed by all of it, and I love experiencing it through her fresh eyes.

Once we reach Liberty Island, we step onto a boat that will take us closer to The Statue of Liberty. Kaitlyn is mesmerized by its size and detailing. I can't help but laugh in astonishment, watching her awe-struck face as she looks up at the towering monument before us. After exploring the area, we return to shore and then take a ferry over to Ellis Island, making sure to also stop at the gift shop, where she picks out a few souvenirs for her friends back home.

Our day ends with dinner at an Italian restaurant near Central Park, where we laugh and talk until it's almost time to head out on the next part of our evening. The part I'm paying for. The part I genuinely hope Kaitlyn is up for.

Our entire day together has been an incredible adventure of learning new things and, most important, getting to know one another. With no business distractions, I opened up more than I have with any other woman, even telling her about my family and the lack of emotional support I experienced. I mention my best friends and the Sutherland Group, though I don't go into details. They'll be time for that later, I hope. She tells me about her ex and her friend. How any guy could let her go, I'll never understand. I wouldn't let her out of sight if she were mine.

After dinner, we take a cab to the airfield, where I've chartered a plane to fly us to Atlantic City. Her eyes widen when she realizes an executive plane is waiting for us, one attendant standing at the bottom of the stairs, ready to take our bags.

"I'm confused. I assumed we were going dancing or something."

"We are."

"On a plane?"

"No, the plane is taking us to the club."

She stops in her tracks, jerking me back a step with her hand. "We're leaving New York?"

"We not going far. It's just faster to fly."

She glances at the aircraft, and for the first time since I've met her, I see fear in her eyes.

What an idiot I am.

I drop our bags to the pavement and take her hands in mine. "Kaitlyn, I promise you, this is nothing dangerous, nothing nefarious. I'm rich. I'm very rich. I travel by plane all the time. It's fast. I wanted to take you to a club tonight."

"I'm sure there are clubs right here in New York."

"There are, but I admit, I want to impress you. And I'd like to be somewhere that people won't necessarily recognize me."

"Oh." She swings her head toward the plane again. "You're not trying to kidnap me, so you can kill me and dump my body somewhere."

I cup her cheek. "No. I promise."

She studies me hard, her eyes darting back and forth across mine searching for the truth. "I shouldn't trust you. I hardly know you. But my spidy senses aren't tingling. That's good, right?"

"How about when we reach the stairs you give that man over there your name, phone number, and tell him where you live? I'll have him send it to somebody, anybody he knows, for safe keeping."

She looks at me like I'm crazy but slowly nods her head.

I kiss her quickly, eager for more, but we need to board.

On the jet, after a stop to hand over her personal information to the flight attendant, who seemed very perplexed by my request, I can't help but smile at her cautious enthusiasm as she stares out the window, admiring the scenery below. She turns with a questioning look.

Keeping my voice low out of respect for the pilot and for her. "I told you—tonight is on me. All will be revealed soon enough. Once we're in the air, why don't you change in the bedroom?"

"There's a bedroom?" She's like a baby owl, eyes big and slowly blinking as she swivels to look behind her.

An hour later, we're taxying to the terminal. Kaitlyn looks good enough to eat in a short, sequined turquoise dress that hugs every curve. She's piled her hair on top of her head, leaving a few tendrils to hang loose around her face, and her make-up is smoking hot. Those pink-tipped toes are teasing me from a pair of silver four-inch high chunky heels.

While she dressed in private, I quickly changed and cleaned up in the main cabin.

I arranged for a car to meet us. The driver quickly escorts us to the back seat and then whisks us away to our destination.

We haven't spoken much, but that's okay. I want her relaxed. I want her to enjoy what she's about to experience. My cock is already hard, eager and ready to please if she gives the signal.

When we arrive at the Velvet Room, we're greeted by bright lights at the entrance and surrounding buildings. Kaitlyn is speechless as we stroll through the venue, checking out all the rooms, bars, and dance floors. Her eyes are huge with wonder, and her mouth is gaping in amazement.

This place is like something out of a sultry fantasy. Guests enter an exclusive lounge with velvet curtains, exquisite music, and plenty of seating options. A large dance floor is the main focus on the first level of the club, with a DJ playing a mix of music genres to get the crowd going.

There's an array of private alcoves for couples interested in more intimate experiences. Upstairs there's a VIP area that offers more exclusive access to the club's more discrete amenities, with a complimentary bar and more private rooms.

This club has themed nights, from exotic adult shows to body painting and more. With its seductive atmosphere, this place is perfect for adults to explore their deepest desires.

And I want to explore a couple of mine tonight with Kaitlyn.

"Have you been here before?" She raises her voice enough to be heard.

"A few times." I've been tempted to purchase the place. Maybe build another in New York.

"I've never been to a place like this."
"Do you want to leave?"
She shakes her head.
My relief is profound.
"Are you ready for this?" I ask, tugging on her fingers.
She smiles, though it's a little shaky. "I think I am."

Chapter Five

Kaitlyn

My heart pounds as Elliott leads me deeper into the Velvet Room. The air thick is with the smell of burning candles and the scent of arousal. I feel a rush of both excitement and a little trepidation as my eyes adjust to the dim lighting.

I can feel the intensity of Elliott's gaze, making my stomach flip. I squeeze his hand, not sure if I'm reassuring him or myself.

The décor is exquisite. Everywhere I look, the velvet curtains, intricate wood paneling, and the staining of the modified streetlamps give the room an air of opulence and sophistication, as though I've walked into a secret gentlemen's club.

With a hand to my lower back, Elliott steers me towards a private seating area where we can talk undisturbed. I can't help but admire the way he touches me with such confidence. Brandon never touched me like that. We settle into the comfortable chairs, and my nerves slowly ebb away.

Elliott studies me intently, his gaze burning into me as he murmurs softly. "I enjoyed our afternoon together," he says, his voice low and intimate.

I blush, feeling a warmth spreading throughout my chest. "I had a great time, too." I reply softly.

A young woman in a black skirt, white blouse, and black vest, carrying a wine bottle wrapped in stark white linen, stops at our table. She has dark hair, delicate features, and small red-painted lips. "Would you like to taste the wine, Sir?"

"Yes, please. We'll take a small taste now, but would prefer to indulge in a private room, please."

"Of course." She hails down another waitress, snags a couple of glasses from her tray, and pours us each a glass of the plum colored alcohol. "I'll have a room arranged and waiting for you."

"Thank you."

I look at Elliott. "I feel like I just missed something."

"I told her I wanted a private viewing room."

"What will we be viewing?"

"You'll see."

I sip my wine slowly. I can feel my cheeks flush, and notice my breathing has gone shallow. It's because he's watching me. I can't believe I'm sitting at a table in a sexy dance club. I'm don't think Margo's suggestion I let loose and have an adventure included this.

The sensual lighting instantly establishes an erotic mood. The music is a sultry blend of modern and classic beats, making it hard to resist the temptation of the dance floor. And watching them move—it's like a symphony of couples embracing and grinding to the rhythm of the music. They don't seem to care they are amongst strangers; by the looks of it, they are lost in their own world, but emboldened by what's happening around them—like I am.

Elliott touches me lightly, his fingertips tracing circles on the back of my hand. I'm mesmerized by the intensity of his gaze, the warmth of his touch. Something powerful is building inside me. Something I can't describe.

The atmosphere is charged with a sensuality that I've never experienced before. For the first time in a long time, I let go of my inhibitions. Surrounded by so many beautiful bodies and an ambiance of untamed sexuality, I can't help but surrender to the beat. With every passing moment, I feel my reservations fading, my heart beating faster and faster. I feel so alive.

The music swells and Elliott stands, taking my hand. "Shall we dance?"

I nod, my heart pounding. I follow him onto the dance floor. As we sway together, I feel a sensation of freedom and wildness course through my veins.

I allow myself to be swept away by the moment, by Elliott's masculine strength and the melody speaks directly to my soul.

The song draws to a close, but my heart still races. I look into Elliott's eyes, feeling the energy sizzle between us.

"Our room will be ready," he says, his voice smoky, alluring.

He leads me through a door at the back of the dance floor where we ascend a flight of stairs. When we reach the landing, I'm struck with the smell of leather and candle wax. I can hear moans, cries. Pleading.

My breath catches as he takes me to a surprisingly sparsely decorated viewing room. I notice a bed and a couple of chairs, but it's the large window that draws my attention. I can see people through the glass in various stages of undress, practicing rope bondage. There are three couples, each doing their own thing, oblivious to the others in the room.

"It's a one-way mirror." He flicks a switch, and different sounds seep into the room. Heavy instrumental music. Soft, quietly spoken words I can't make out. Groans. Gasps. "We can see them. They can't see or hear us."

My whole body tenses as I watch, my eyes darting from one

pair to the next. I'm captivated. My heart is pounding, my breathing harsh. They are uninhibited and lost in their pleasure

"Go ahead, Kaitlyn," Elliott whispers into my ear from behind me. "Let yourself enjoy this."

I feel myself nodding slightly as I inhale deeply. I approach the mirror and place my palms against the cool glass, my nose almost touching it.

Elliott wraps an arm around me, his warmth reassuring.

My senses are tuned in to what's playing out in front of us—the moans and sighs, the movements of bodies intertwined, as though they are dancing to an extremely erotic tune.

I realize that I'm no longer just an observer—I'm aroused in a way I've never felt before. Elliott must be aware of my reaction because he tightens his grip around my waist and hauls be back against him. I can feel his prominent erection.

He turns me to face him, his eyes burning with desire as his lips find mine. We kiss hungrily. Our breathing is heavy and urgent.

Elliott's explores my body, gently moving his hands under my dress as he slides his fingertips gently along my sides. I can't help but moan with delight into his mouth.

The couples in the other room are a backdrop to what we're doing and it only serves to heighten everything tenfold.

He smiles against my lips, taking control of the kiss as he deepens it, searching every inch of me with his tongue. We stay locked in an embrace for an eternity before reluctantly breaking apart, breathless. I'm stunned by the power of every new sensation barreling through me and cling to Elliott as if he's the only thing keeping me from falling apart.

Elliott steps back, still holding onto me as he looks into my eyes. I can see a raw desire that makes me tremble in anticipation.

He spins me around, so I'm looking through the two-way

mirror again, watching the couples on the other side. He slides his hands down my body, resting them above my hips as his lips press against my nape. The warmth of his breath on my skin sends shivers along my skin and I brace for what's to come. I know it. I can't believe I'm going to do it, but I don't want this to stop.

Elliott's cock presses into the crack of my ass. The tension in the room is thick and naughty. A soft moan escapes my lips as my body responds to his touch. Heat unfurls in my belly, and arousal pools between my legs.

He slips one hand into the front of my dress to cup my breast, rolling my nipple between his thumb and pointer finger while gliding his other under the hem of my dress, dancing his fingers along my inner thigh.

I spread my legs.

He's like a missile skillfully aimed at its target. Without line of sight, he homes in on my clit, pulling my panties aside so he can touch my bare flesh.

"Oh fuck, you're so wet." He rubs that sensitive nub until I grind my ass into his crotch.

My body tingles as Elliott's lips brush against the column of my neck. He uses his tongue to trace patterns against my skin, creating sensual sensations I've never experienced.

He moves his hand lower, sneaking a finger inside my slick entrance, but I'm too turned on to be ashamed. His touch is tender yet firm as he flicks and teases until I'm panting. Then he adds his thumb, circling around the tightness outside, increasing pressure little by little until it blends seamlessly into a single point of pleasure that radiates throughout me when he finally fucks me with his finger.

I cry out into the quiet room. "Oh, God, yes!"

He adds another digit, plunging both deeper until I'm

begging for relief. I'm ready to come, but he pulls out, teasing me until I'm nearly delirious.

When I think I can't take it anymore, he slides both fingers back in tunnels them in and out in short thrusts. I'm beyond conscious thought now, my body aching for more.

Elliott withdraws again, and I can't stop the whimper that leaves my lips. He tugs on my hips, encouraging me to step back, and then presses a hand in the middle of my back, urging me to bend at the waist.

I hear a zipper and foil being ripped.

He flips my dress up over my backside.

Then his cock is nudging my entrance, looking for admission, sending electricity through me right before he slams into me.

I gasp and moan in pleasure spiraling into a state of pure bliss.

He grips my hips tightly, pulling me in to meet each hard thrust as he pumps in and out. Every stroke is deeper than the last, forcing my orgasm closer and closer until I'm wavering on the brim, ready to topple over.

His movements become faster, more urgent. He reaches down and finds my clit again, circling it with the pad of his finger until I'm trembling.

In one swift move, he slams into me one last time, pushing us both over the edge in a mutual explosion of pleasure.

Our bodies quiver together for what feels like an eternity before we finally collapse in a heap on the floor, our breaths coming in ragged pants.

As we lay there in each other's arms, I can't help but feel this was one of the most electrifying experiences of my life.

Elliott props himself up on one arm and looks at me with a satisfied expression. He brushes my hair away from my face, and I feel myself melting into his touch. He moves in, brushing his lips against mine. This kiss is slow and gentle but still leaves me breathless.

When he finally pulls away, he smiles. "Are you okay?"

I jerk my head because I can't form words as I take in his handsome features — those eyes that seem to peer right into my soul, that strong jawline that makes me want to run my fingers along it, and the softness of his lips that make me want to stay right here, on the floor, half dressed, kissing him forever.

I let out a long sigh of contentment as he pulls me closer. We're not in the most comfortable spot or position, entwined on the floor under the glass viewing window. All the tension building inside me throughout the evening has now washed away, leaving only limp.

Elliott finally breaks the silence. "That was...incredible," he whispers into my ear, sending tingles down my spine.

I came to New York for an adventure. I never, in my wildest dreams would have envisioned what happened here tonight.

"We should get cleaned up before we head back to the plane."

Oh, Lord. I forgot about the plane.

He stands and holds out a hand to help me. Over in the far corner of the room is a credenza I hadn't noticed before with a basket of hand towels. There's also a box of tissues and what looks like sanitizer.

"There's a bathroom just behind that door."

I thank him, locate my purse I'd dropped earlier, and excuse myself. Behind the locked door, I use the toilet and splash cold water on my face before touching up my make-up. There's a rosy glow to my skin. My eyes are large and sparkling. I gaze at my reflection, wondering how I went from a small-town girl dumped by her boyfriend for her best friend to have a fling with a billionaire who's chartered a plane to fly her to a sex club and having sex in that sex club.

I'm not sure, but I can't help but like this version I see in the mirror.

I giggle and slap a hand over my mouth.

Margo will never believe me.

Chapter Six

Elliott

"Hey man, how's it going?"

One of my best friends, Coby Weston, called before I texted Kaitlyn to see how she was doing today. Our flight back was non-eventful as she'd fallen asleep as soon as we took off, her head resting against my shoulder, her hands clasped in her lap. She wore the sweetest expression on her face. I hardly took my eyes off her the entire flight. She didn't wake when I lifted her in my arms, tucked her against my chest like precious cargo, and exited the plane. She only stirred when I buckled her into the car.

When we reached the hotel, I guided her back to her room, kissed her goodnight, and waited until I heard the deadbolt lock into place before I took the elevator to my penthouse suite.

I kicked myself for not simply bringing her to my room. I could have spent the night with her in my arms. But I didn't want to push. I didn't want to do anything that would drive her away any sooner than necessary. She's only in the city for a few more days. I can't afford to screw this up.

"Hey, Coby. How's the team doing?" Coby owns a professional baseball team. I think he did it to piss off his father, who'd had a shot at the pros but fucked himself out of a spot by getting addicted to drugs and alcohol. It only made him a miserable son of a bitch, and he took his failings out on his boys.

They both got even by getting out of dodge and making something of themselves. After Coby sold the gaming app he built, making him a billionaire a few times over, he had more than enough money to do what he wanted. And if pissing off his old man made him happy, then more power to him.

"They're doing okay. Sitting in third place in our division right now. We're playing in New York next month. Want tickets? I can meet you there."

"Absolutely. So what's up? You could have just emailed me the tickets."

"Have you heard from Teddy?"

"Not recently, why?" Teddy is another member of the Sutherland Group, the band of kids I hung out with throughout grade school and high school. Some of us went to different colleges after that, but we stayed closer than most brothers. Always ready to drop everything and be there for one another when necessary.

"I've heard a rumor that Pat wants to sell the bar."

I straighten in my desk chair. "What? Why?"

"I don't know. That's why I'm trying to connect with Teddy."

We grew up in the back of that bar. Pat Sutherland provided a bunch of trouble-making gangly kids a safe place to hang out, shoot pool, play arcade games, listen to music, and talk. That was after we cleaned up the graffiti on his building. The markings we'd put there. The other business owners we harassed weren't as accommodating or forgiving. Our parents never paid attention often enough to give a shit. Pat was the only one who did.

In that back room behind the bar, we did our homework, hung out, and had "I wish" conversations. We dreamed of one day becoming powerful, wealthy men with enough money to do whatever the fuck we wanted, when we wanted. We referred to ourselves as The Sutherland Group.

It was fantasy talk for everyone but me and Teddy. We came from money. I had a trust fund I tapped into at twenty-one. Money that helped me make loads more flipping real estate until I had enough to buy the hotel chain I renamed Fairchild.

"We can't let that happen, Coby." We all get together back in our hometown twice a year, and our first and last stop is always that bar. I can't imagine it without Pat.

"I agree. I'll keep trying Teddy and I'll let you know what I find out."

"Thanks."

"Listen, I've got to go, but I'll text you when the tickets are on their way."

"Sounds good. Thanks for calling."

The moment I hang up the phone my mind switches to Kaitlyn. Thinking her name sends a spark of hot desire through me. I urged her to shop or check out a museum to two today while I dealt with business, with a promise to spend the evening together. I plan to surprise her with theater tickets I purchased—a private box seat to one of the best shows in town after I take her to one of the most expensive restaurants in the city for dinner.

I grab my keys and wallet and head for the door. I have to meet my lawyer and accountant before we finalize the deal to purchase another hotel chain. But before I can open it, a thought occurs—maybe I should buy something nice for Kaitlyn and let her know I'm thinking of her. I consider the idea, debating it in my mind. I haven't gone shopping in

46

months, which would add a nice touch to the day. With that decided, I adjust my plans. My lawyer and accountant can wait.

My driver takes me to the nearest mall, where I wander aimlessly, unsure what I'm looking for, until I spot it—a small boutique tucked away in the corner. It's filled with romantic, sensual lingerie, and I immediately know this is what I'm looking for. The minute I step into the store, an attractive sales woman appears all bright eyed and eager to help, but I politely shoo her away. I want the thrill of choosing something for Kaitlyn myself.

I take my time, carefully browsing through the racks and selecting items I think she might like. I let my hands float across the satiny fabric. I admire the delicate lace and silky bows. Once I find the perfect pieces, I take them up to the counter. The clerk wraps the lingerie in pink tissue paper and tucks the package into an elegant black box, tying it with a delicate ribbon.

As I leave the store, I can't help but imagine what Kaitlyn will think when she opens this gift. Will it make her smile? Will she blush? The thought of her reaction has my lips stretching into a grin, and my cock stretching against my zipper.

The ride to the lawyer's office is uneventful, but when I happen to glance at the review mirror, even from the back seat, I see that my eyes have a spark of excitement, something I don't recall ever seeing before.

It's Kaitlyn. These last few days have changed something inside me; I feel energized and alive, ready to take on whatever comes my way.

I quickly call Celeste and asked her to have bouquets of fresh flowers delivered to Kaitlyn's room. When she returns from sightseeing, I want the room filled and fragrant. I want her to know she's been on my mind since she asked me to help her with her luggage.

Finally, my meeting is over. It took longer than I would have preferred, but at least the deal will close sooner rather than later. I plan to overhaul the small hotel chain I just purchased, making them a more affordable, family-friendly version of the Fairchild.

When we return to the hotel, I ask my driver to deliver the present to my suite and I head straight to Kaitlyn's room. She'd texted me to let me know she was heading back to shower and rest before our evening. I can't wait to see her.

Even I can't help but be amused by the spring in my step as I exit the elevator and stroll down the hall. Am I humming? I don't hum.

I knock on the door, and it's whipped open before I can pull back my hand. "Hi...hey, what's wrong?"

I push my way into the room before she even has a chance to explain. Her face is pale. She's trembling. There are tear tracks on her cheeks.

"What happened?" I ask, pulling her into my arms, ready to console or defend, whatever she needs from me. I look around the room but see nothing that might warrant this reaction. I also don't see a single bloom. Where the hell are the flowers I asked Celeste to get?

"Everything's gone."

"What do you mean, gone?"

She pushes out of my embrace. "I've been robbed. My clothes, my jewelry, computer, even my toiletries. Everything I brought with me is gone."

"How?"

"I don't know, you tell me. This is your hotel. When I left this morning, my bed was unmade, my clothes hanging in the closet and my toiletries spread out on the counter in the bathroom. Now, the room looks like housekeeping came in and emptied it out, cleaned it up and prepared it for the next guest. Except my key card still works, and the room is still assigned to me. I checked."

"That doesn't make sense. Housekeeping wouldn't take your things."

"Somebody did."

Anger rolls over me like a massive wave. I reach into my pocket for my phone and dial security. "Harry, it's Elliott Carrington. I need to you come up to room twelve fifteen right away, please."

While we wait, I reassure her that I'll figure this out. I promise to get her belongings back to her.

There's a knock on the door, and I let my head of security into the room. "Harry, this is Ms. Moore. She's been robbed."

"Sir?" His shock is evident as he swings his attention between us.

"Somebody came into this room and removed all of her belongings while she was out today."

"Um, unless you've checked out Ma'am, that would be very concerning."

"I didn't check out." She's sitting on the edge of the bed, stone-faced.

"What time did you leave your room today?" he asks.

"Just before noon, probably around eleven thirty."

"I'll head down to our security room and check the floor cameras. We'll know right away who took your things."

I pat him on the back. "Thanks, Harry. I'm going to take Ms. Moore up to my suite while we wait for your call."

"It shouldn't take too long, Sir. I'll just need about thirty minutes to go through the video for today."

When he leaves, I turn back to Kaitlyn. "I'm so sorry, Kaitlyn. We'll find out who did this. I will not tolerate this in my hotel."

With her shoulders slumped, we walk in silence to the elevator. I take her to my suite and pour her a glass of wine. Then, I sit down beside her and take her hands in mine, stroking my thumbs over her fingers. "I know this is a horrible thing to have happened to you. I'll do whatever I can to get your things back." I brush a loose strand of hair from her cheek and with a finger under her chin, nudge her head back until we are eye to eye. "I promise."

Relief floods her eyes. "Thank you, Elliott."

I get up to retrieve the present from the dining table where my driver left it and hold it out to her.

"What is this?" She asks, her sadness diminishing a little bit.

"Something I bought for you."

"You don't need to buy me things, Elliott."

"I wanted to, and after what's happened, I'm glad I did."

She unties the ribbon, lifts the lid off the box and pulls back the tissue paper to look inside. As she takes out each article of lingerie one by one, her cheeks flush a beautiful shade of pink. The room the other night was dark, but I imagine that's the color of her skin when she comes.

"Elliott, they're gorgeous." She inspects each teddy, one in black the other in a light blue and both with matching panties.

I can't not touch her. I gather her in my arms. "I wanted to get you something that would make you smile. And something that would make me smile when you model them for me later."

Her blush deepens, and I lean in to kiss her forehead.

We both laugh, and she puts her head on my shoulder. Her smell and warmth are like a drug, and I can feel my heart pounding in my chest, feeling more alive than I have ever felt before.

The phone rings, and we both jump. I let go of Kaitlyn and answer the call. After a few minutes of conversation, Harry tells me that they've identified the perpetrator and they're getting Kaitlyn's things back to her.

"Thank you. Please save that video footage. I'll take care of the individual myself." I didn't even ask who it was. I will deal with it later. I want nothing more to ruin tonight.

I hang up the phone and turn back to Kaitlyn. "Your things have been located and are being returned to your room."

Kaitlyn's body sags with relief. Then she wraps her arms around my waist, stretches up on her toes and presses her lips to mine. "Thank you for doing this for me, Elliott."

"It was nothing." I can feel the emotion draining away from her body as she relaxes against me. "Come on," I say after a few moments, "Let's grab dinner and forget about this for tonight."

We head out to the restaurant I had reserved earlier and enjoy a wonderful meal in each other's company before heading to the theater. We hold hands in our private box and make out between the acts. I've never enjoyed the theater more.

Despite the horrendous start to our night, it is one of the most memorable evenings of my life—one that makes me realize there is something very special brewing between us.

Something I don't want to lose at the end of Kaitlyn's week in New York.

Chapter Seven

Kaitlyn

I stand in the center of Elliott's suite, my hands laced behind my back as I survey my surroundings. Everywhere I look, I see evidence of his luxurious lifestyle. From the scent of his expensive cologne lingering in the air to a vast collection of books lining one shelf in a seemingly effortless fashion. Elegant pieces of furniture are arranged around the room in a way that creates an inviting atmosphere.

"The place is beautiful." It sure doesn't look like my hotel room.

I can't help but be impressed by the amount of money he must have spent to redo this suite to his liking. He mentioned he travels a lot, but I can tell he considers this place his home.

The plush carpets, the dark wooden floors, and the high ceilings create a sense of grandeur. The huge glass windows overlooking the city skyline.

"Can I entice you to stay the night?" Elliott is still standing in the doorway, his hands shoved deep into his pockets, a mischievous grin on his face. He is clearly enjoying my amazement.

I ignore his request for the moment. "Thank you for dinner and the show. I've never eaten in such a sophisticated place before. The food was unbelievable. And I don't know how you got tickets for that show. I searched online before I even flew here, but they were sold out." I can't help but feel overwhelmed.

He strolls across the room, stopping right in front of me. Our toes are almost touching. "Fancy restaurants, shows, all of this is nothing compared to spending time with you." He leans close and kisses me lightly on the lips. "How about that stay?" he whispers, his arms wrapping around me. "I can't wait to see you in my presents."

The heat of his breath on my skin sends a shiver up my spine, and I can't help but respond to his touch with a soft kiss of my own. We stand there for a moment, our lips fused together, using our hands to light each other up. I don't think either of us wants to be the first to break the connection.

Finally, I make the sacrifice. I drop my forehead to his chest, my hands fisted in his shirt, and take a moment to catch my breath before I raise my head. "May I use your bedroom to change?"

His eyes widen, and his nostrils flare. "Of course. It's upstairs, the only room up there."

Picking up my purse from where I'd dropped it on the sofa, the elegantly wrapped gift, and the tote bag I'd brought with my toiletries and make-up, I head for the stairs. I glance back briefly and catch Elliott watching my every step. My God, the man is gorgeous. And at least for the remainder of my time in New York, he's all mine.

The upstairs is just as stylish as the main level. Elliott's bedroom is decorated with stately furniture, luxurious fabrics, and artwork.

As I unpack my things, I can't help the nervous tension

building inside me. Since the beginning, this trip has not been at all what I envisioned when I spontaneously booked my flight. Although I normally would not have splurged on a place like this, I didn't give the cost of the Fairchild a second thought when they had a room available. My only thought had been escaping the big event. Once here to keep my mind off of what was happening back home, I planned to shop, take in a show, and visit the sights.

I've done all those things but never thought I'd do them with a man like Elliot Carrington as my escort. What do I have that a man as rich as him wants? I live paycheck to paycheck, working at a landscaping company. The very minute I walked into the lobby, I realized my travel attire made me look like an innocent country bumpkin. And then I mistook the owner of the hotel for a bellhop.

Margo will laugh about that for the next five years.

I spread the pieces of lace and silk lingerie out before me on Elliott's bed, unable to decide which one to put on first. They're all so delicate and beautiful. More expensive than anything I buy for myself.

Should I make him wait a little longer?

My thoughts swirl around in my head as I try to decide. Finally, as if in a trance, my hands reach for a black teddy set with intricate detailing and a plunging neckline that will just barely cover me.

Slowly, I unbutton the top of my dress and slide it off my shoulders, taking a deep breath to steady my nerves. I reach for the lingerie. I take a moment to examine it, marveling at how delicate and beautiful it is. I slip it on and look at myself in his standing mirror, admiring how it accentuates my curves.

Before I can finish and head back downstairs to where Elliott waits, there's a knock on the bedroom door.

"May I come in?" He doesn't wait for my response. The

doorknob turns, and the door swings open. As soon as he spots me, his eyes widen in appreciation.

Elliott stares at me in awe. I can see the appreciation in his eyes. I close the distance between us by a couple of feet, feeling emboldened by the situation and the sensations that come with it. But we're still so far apart. I'm worried we'll combust as soon as we touch.

His eyes move hungrily over me, his gaze like a physical touch, sending tingles up and down my spine.

The heat between us is palpable.

He prowls across the room until he's standing in my personal space, so close that the tips of my nipples scrape his chest when I inhale.

He strokes my cheek before leaning in to capture my lips in a gentle yet intense kiss that sets off a series of shockwaves of lust through my core.

"You look absolutely breathtaking."

Behind me, large windows look out over the city. Usually, I'd admire the view, enthralled by the stars twinkling in the night sky and the city lights dancing in the background.

But tonight, I only have eyes for this man. I wanted an adventure. I'm getting the best.

I push to my toes and press my lips to his, slipping my tongue inside his mouth. Sliding my hands up his chest, I shove his suit jacket back until it's falling from his body. Time to tackle his belt.

I want him naked.

I want him on his bed.

I want him, period.

He deepens our kiss and settles his hands on my waist, his thumbs moving in tiny circles over the lace. Then he lifts me onto the soft covers of his high bed, giving me a slight nudge so I tumble to my back. He crawls over me.

"Elliott, you're still dressed."

"You mesmerize me, Kaitlyn. I don't think I've ever encountered a woman who makes me want more."

"More what?"

"I don't know. Everything." He glides one hand underneath my teddy and cups my breast. I watch, transfixed, as he lowers his mouth to my nipple, sucking lace and all into his mouth.

The hard ridge of his cock throbs against my leg.

"I want to taste you." I never enjoyed oral sex with Brandon, but I'm desperate to discover Elliott's flavor.

"Oh, honey, I'd love to feel your warm lips around me, but I don't think I could last."

"Please." I reach down and grip him, squeezing in gentle pulses.

He lifts his head, closes his eyes, and groans. "God, that feels good."

I take advantage, fumbling to unzip his pants.

"Wait, let me." He backs off the bed and quickly strips out of his clothing. Then he's over me again, gloriously hard and naked, his body something an art student would drool over.

Not sure where the idea comes from, I encourage him to straddle my chest, urging him to scoot up until his thick dick is bobbing in my face.

"Are you sure about this?"

Oh, yes. I flick my tongue out, tapping it against the head of his cock, lapping up the drop of white pearled there. Opening my mouth, I bring him inside. He rocks forward, pushing past my teeth toward of back of my throat.

My God, he tastes good. Salty. Hot. Soft over hard. Silk over rock.

I adjust the angle of my head and neck giving him room to sink deeper into my mouth, while I lick along his shaft as he slides back out. Teasing swipes of my tongue send shivers through Elliott's body as he continues his gentle rocking motion.

Soon we're both moaning with pleasure. I'm drooling around his member. He's got his hands braced on the tall headboard over me, his hips pumping back and forth in a steady rhythm, his cock filling my mouth. In and out. In and out.

Elliott lets loose an animalistic growl that vibrates through every cell in my body, driving me even crazier for him than I already am.

My lips cling to him, never allowing complete separation as I use my hands to squeeze and stroke his shaft in time with each thrust of his hips.

He's close now. I can feel the tension radiating off him. I feel the quake of his thighs as he comes with deep, guttural grunts. Hot cum spills down my throat, and I swallow eagerly, before I take my time licking him clean. He slumps forward with a satisfied sigh before rolling us onto our sides, so we are spooning, still joined at the hip.

"That was amazing," Elliott whispers against my ear, sending shivers down my spine." His thumb grazes the tip of one nipple, and I jerk in response. He does it again.

He smooths a hand over my hip and down my thigh. "I knew this set would look stunning on you."

"Thank you."

"But it would be even more beautiful on the floor."

I giggle. "I beg your pardon?"

He shifts, and before I know it, he's removed my teddy and panties and he's got me on my back again.

He's reaches for his bedside table and retrieves a condom from the drawer.

I hold out my hand. "Let me."

He places the package in my palm.

I lift to a sitting position and rip open the small pouch. The rubbery material of the condom crinkles in my fingers. I roll it down his length and then lay back on the bed and spread my legs, just wide enough to give him a peek.

Elliott looks down at me, his mouth stretching in a slow, sexy grin. His eyes are dark with lust, his body trembling. Wrapping his fingers around each of my ankles he makes more room before settling between my thighs.

He nestles the tip of his cock against my entrance, glances up at me locking his gaze with mine and then pushes gently forward. I gasp in pleasure as he slides inside inch by tortuous inch until our pelvic bones meet and we become one. We move together in a slow dance—rocking, swaying and swiveling together—moves that swell to an such an intense level, we're sweating, panting, and clinging to one another.

My body is vibrating, on the brink of release.

He drops over me and braces and hand on either side of my head, driving into me faster. "You feel so fucking good, Kaitlyn. I've never felt this with anyone else."

My body feels tense, like a tightly wound coil ready to snap.

Suddenly, I explode. A whimper bursts free as absolute rapture sweeps over me, taking my breath away and setting off a fireworks display behind my closed eyes.

He grunts, thrusting harder.

I wrap my arms around Elliott's neck and hold tight as we ride our release together.

When it's over, he kisses me tenderly before collapsing beside me in a sweaty heap.

We lay there for a few minutes catching our breath before Elliott speaks up. "So now do you see why it was even better on the floor?" His lip twitches with amusement, and I laugh lightly before snuggling into him.

The night passes in a blur of passion and pleasure, whispered words, and soft caresses until exquisite exhaustion finally takes over. We fight sleep next to each other, holding tightly onto one another's fingers in the dark, our chests heaving on each inhale.

I'm astounded by the feelings I have for this man. Astonished that he's come to mean so much in such a short time. I've fallen hard for Elliott Carrington. A man I can't have.

A faint, pale gold illuminates the edges of the windows as the sun stars to rise. Elliott is snoring softly. I tuck myself against his warm body. My last thought before sleep pulls me under is how thankful I am for finding him and how fantastic the last few days have been.

I wanted an adventure. It can't get any better than this.

Unfortunately, all good things must end.

Chapter Eight

Elliott

Kaitlyn is leaving in the morning, early.

I've spent the last two days ditching work commitments to spend every minute I can with her. She's put up a few weak arguments about me spending money on her, but she's enjoyed the shows I've taken her to, the shopping we've done, and the food we've eaten. I think, I hope, she's as desperate to spend time with me, as I am her.

And I've been entertained by watching her. It's impossible not to smile when she's around. I'm sure my staff is confused, seeing this different, more light-hearted side of me.

I even convinced her to allow me to buy her a beautiful evening gown. She noticed it in the window of a shop we were walking past, almost yanking my arm out of the socket when she jerked to a stop, and I didn't. But, the longing in her eyes and the woeful sigh—I dragged her into the store to try it on. She looked exquisite. We argued for a few minutes, with her insisting she had nowhere to wear it and she couldn't spend money on something so frivolous. But I don't care if it hangs in her closet forever—every woman deserves a beautiful dress.

Especially after her experience at my hotel. When I watched the security video to discover who had taken her things, I was floored to see Celeste on the camera. When I confronted my Hotel Manager about her actions, she had the gall to insist I could do better. That *she* was a better woman for me. That *she* understood my needs.

The woman is old enough to be my mother.

I fired her on the spot.

Finally, after much prodding, Kaitlyn relented, thanking me profusely as we left the store with the silver garment bag draped over my arm. Maybe I can persuade her to wear it tonight, so I can at least see her twirl about the room in it once.

As the day wears on, it's like watching sand in an hourglass. The weight of it is suffocating, like a boulder on my chest. I don't want her to leave, but I can't bring myself to open my mouth and beg her to stay.

We spend day together talking, going from topic to topic, never running out of things to say. We talk about her family, her friends, about her job.

Kaitlyn opens up about her ex and how crushed she was when he left after she had paid his way through medical school. My fists clench as I think of what she went through and is still going through because of him. Seeing him or her friend everywhere in town. Their mutual friends and families consumed by wedding preparations.

She admits she escaped to New York to avoid the wedding. Only she heard from her friend Margo that the wedding had to be postponed because the bride fell ill.

I imagine many ways I could make her ex pay for his actions. A perk of being rich. I'd be happy to waste some cash hurting him like he hurt her.

What hurts my heart the most, however, is how she speaks with such sadness about losing her best friend, a girl she's known since grade school. They both betrayed her love and her trust. I hope they're both miserable now.

Every time the conversation turns to Kaitlyn leaving in the morning, silence falls between us. Neither of us wants to face the fact that this is the last time we will ever be together. Her family, her friends, and her job are back in her hometown. My hotels are everywhere *but* her hometown.

After dining on room service, opting to spend the night in, we've spent the evening wrapped in each other's arms in my bed. Our legs are tangled together as are the sheets around our bodies as they cool and the sweat from our lovemaking dries.

"I've done all the talking most of today. Tell me about your family."

I've let her do all the talking because of my desperation to learn everything I can about her. I'm taking inventory, keeping track of all the details so I can remember them in my dreams.

I join our hands together, stroke her fingers, and simply enjoy the warmth of her skin against mine. I can sense the minutes ticking away, and I'm already becoming sad and angry that we can't have more.

"Well, I grew up in small town like you. My family was one of the founders. We lived in a big house, with lots of staff."

"Seriously?" She tips her head back so she can look up at me. "I didn't realize you were that kind of rich."

"My parents come from money. My dad actually, but my mom really liked that he did. She's the one who hired all the staff. She never missed an opportunity to treat others like they were beneath her. Didn't make for a large friend circle."

"Where did you fit into all of that?"

"I didn't. I was a bit of a trouble maker."

"You?"

I tap the end of her nose. "Don't be sassy. They sent me to a private school for a while. I got expelled. They sent me to boarding school. I got expelled. They finally allowed me to go to the public school.

"Is that where your friends were?"

"I didn't have any friends. Not then anyway. Not until a group of us got caught marking up the schools and businesses in town."

"You didn't?" Her expression says she's not sure if she should believe me.

"We had to clean it all up. Took all summer long, six days a week, eight hours a day. Worst summer of my life. And then we spent the rest of the year providing free labor to the businesses we damaged."

"Is that where you connected with those guys you told me about the other day?"

I nod. "I don't know why any of them joined me. It's not like they knew me. They just started showing up on the nights I was out tagging and soon there was a group of us."

"The Sutherland Group? I think that's what you said. How did you come up with that name?"

"Pat Sutherland. He owns the bar we tagged. Unlike some of the others, he took pity on us, figured we needed a safe place to hang out so we wouldn't loiter around town. He gave us his back room. We started calling ourselves the Sutherland Group."

"They're good friends."

"The best."

The clock on my mantel strikes midnight, and the sound of it echoes through the room, bringing us back to reality.

It's almost time for her to go. She's got an early flight I tried to get her to change. I even offered to pay for a charter. But she refused.

I try to tell her how much I wish she wouldn't go, but the words stick in my throat. I can see the sadness in her eyes, and I want to take away the pain. I want to make her stay, but I don't know how.

So I hold her in my arms and kiss her with all the emotion I have in me.

I breathe in the smell of her hair and run my fingers down her back. I press against her, frantic to remember every inch of her against every inch of me. I need to burn the feeling into my memory.

When I pull back, her eyes are bright with tears.

I roll her to her back and lower my head, stopping when our lips are a breath apart. "I want to make love to you," I whisper.

I realize this is where I've been heading all along.

I love her.

She smiles, but her lower lip trembles. Her eyes dart back and forth over my face, as a tear escapes down her cheek, as though she's memorizing my features like I'm memorizing her touch.

I press tender kisses all over her shoulders, pushing the sheets away to expose more of her body.

I slide my hands over her. I want to feel every curve, every dip, and hollow. Everywhere my fingertips touch, my lips follow, savoring each part of her. I trace a path along her collarbone and down the delicate curve of her neck. I work down to her breasts, taking each sweet peak into my mouth and sucking gently.

I move down her stomach, dipping my tongue into her belly button.

She giggles and sucks in her breath.

I pick up her arm.

She gasps softly as my lips brush over the sensitive skin of her inner wrist.

I work my way up her arm and then back down. When I

reach the tips of her fingers, I kiss each one tenderly before letting go. I repeat it all over again with her other arm.

Feeling the smooth curve of her waist under each palm, I shift my body lower until I'm nestled between her legs. I press my face to her warm belly, just above her pubic bone, and inhale her scent, learning it, remembering it.

I glide my hands lower, running them along her thighs and then sliding them to the back and lift her legs to rest them over my shoulders.

Her skin is hot. She quivers. She responds to each singular touch with a sigh or a gasp.

I trail kisses down and up the inside of her thigh, savoring every moan that escapes from between her lips until finally reaching the apex where she is already so wet for me.

My tongue starts a gentle exploration, and she gulps in delight. Casting a glance up her body, I can't help but smile seeing how beautiful she looks in this moment. Her skin is flushed a rosy shade, her eyes are closed, her lashes fluttering on her cheeks, her expression one of pure bliss.

Desperate for a taste, I slide my tongue along her slit, dipping between her pussy lips to gather every ounce I can. Moving up to her clit, I circle it, press it between my lips and then apply gentle pressure. I slide two fingers into her, pumping them in and out while I suck that tiny nerve bundle. Her muscles clench around me.

Her hips buck, and she lets out a long, almost painful sounding moan.

Encouraged, I press my fingers deeper inside her and move them in and out in a quick rhythm. She responds instantly, the walls of her vagina gripping tightly around me as she grinds her pussy against my face.

The sound of her cries is intoxicating. I can feel her orgasm building as her body tenses and shudders.

I raise my head to look up at her as I continue to fuck her with my fingers. Kaitlyn's eyes are open now, but glazed over with passion as she teeters on the brink of paradise.

Reaching out with both hands, she grabs a fistful of my hair and tugs it hard as she screams out my name. Her body shakes beneath me as wave after wave washes over her.

Lifting myself, I kiss up along her belly, pressing soft pecks to her stomach and breasts as I use my knee to nudge her legs apart. I grab a condom and quickly cover myself. My heart is pounding in my chest as I enter her, the sensation of her slick warmth around me so intense it almost takes my breath away.

My arms shake. I thrust into her, faster and harder, as I feel my own orgasm building much too fast. I don't want this to end too soon, but I can't slow it down either.

Kaitlyn clings to me, her cries growing in intensity as she digs her nails into my arms. Her eyes drift shut as her body moves with mine. She wraps her legs around my waist, pulling me deeper inside her.

Oh, fuck.

She arches against me, her body shuddering as I continue to drive us both higher until she comes undone for a second time.

My balls tighten. Every nerve ending is ablaze, growing more extreme until it's almost unbearable. I drive into her, feeling her tight walls clutching at me as I reach the climax.

I cry out as my orgasm rips through me, shaking me to the core while holding tight to her as I fall over the edge.

Finally, we pull apart just enough to look into each other's eyes and exchange a long, tender kiss before collapsing back onto the bed in exhaustion.

We lay in each other's arms for what seems like an eternity while our breathing returns to normal. An eternity that ends way before I'm ready.

I wrap my arms around her and hold her close against me, shifting until we are face-to-face.

We stare into each other's eyes.

I kiss her deeply—tasting her sweetness, the salt of her tears, feeling everything that has passed between us over the last few days.

She nuzzles into my chest before drifting off to sleep as I lay awake, filled with a powerful emotion that nearly overwhelms me.

In that moment, I know that I am completely and utterly in love with Kaitlyn Moore.

Chapter Nine

Kaitlyn

"You need to go after her, man."

Coby arrived in New York after I ignored his texts for five days. He found me in the hotel bar chugging a bottle of my best whiskey.

I still think one of my staff tattled on me.

But after crying in my beer, spilling my sad sob story of the girl who left me, he dragged me up to my penthouse and tossed me in a cold shower.

Then while he made the coffee, I told him everything. We spent much of the night discussing my seven days of bliss with a woman who stole my heart. How she made me smile. How she made me laugh. How the hotel staff seemed to like her, or they liked the influence she had on me.

The sun hasn't even risen yet when he makes his statement.

"What's the point?" I ask him now. Nobody sticks around for the long term. What made me think Kaitlyn would be different?

"The point is from everything you're telling me, she's the one person who makes you happy."

"You make me happy, Coby. You and the guys. And my money. My money makes me happy." Neither my best friends nor my bank account will leave me.

He flips me the bird. "You know what I mean."

I scrub a hand down my face. I'm so tired. I haven't slept in days. Not since the last time I heard from Kaitlyn. I know she got home safely. She told me she missed me. And not a word since. At the time, I didn't think my looks bothered her. I didn't think she cared about the gifts or the fancy restaurants and sold out shows.

That was over a month ago. Five long weeks.

I should be pulling my hair out in worry, fearful that something terrible has happened to her.

But I know she's okay.

I have money. Which means I have resources.

And my resources have told me she's back at work at the landscaping company that employs her.

Maybe I should just count my blessings that I don't have to spend any more time and money on a woman who had no true interest in *me*. Maybe it was just a week long adventure for her. Nothing more.

Coby walks over to me and puts a hand on my shoulder. "Look, man, you can do this. You have the resources to find her if you really want too."

I can't look him in the eye, so I mutter instead. "I already did."

The asshole has hearing like a bat. "Then what the fuck are you still here for?"

"Because…"

"What if…"

I can't seem to finish either sentence. In every other aspect of my life, from when I was a troubling making rich kid to the moment before Kaitlyn mistook me for a bellhop, my confidence wasn't the problem. At least not for making decisions.

Leave my family home as a young adult? One of the easiest decisions of my life.

Use my trust fund to buy a hotel chain? Sure, why not.

But another hotel chain? Absolutely.

Make the hard business decisions? Without blinking an eye.

Charter a plane to find the woman I love and confess said love, hoping I mean as much to her and she'll drop everything and marry me? I'm a quivering mass of blue Jell-O.

Coby gives me a look of encouragement, one that says he believes in me even when I don't believe in myself. "I have to say, I can't wait to meet her."

An hour later, I've paid through the nose for a chartered flight to Idaho because I wasn't willing to wait two days for my regular crew. The cab ride to the airport is a blur; my mind is racing faster than the car on the highway.

I check in at the counter, get my ticket and go through security. The process takes forever, and I almost want to turn around several times. What if she won't see me? What if I'm too late? What if she doesn't feel as I do? My palms are sweating, and my stomach is in knots.

Finally, I make it to the gate and sit in one chair. The sun is setting, and I watch as the shadows lengthen across the tarmac. Lost in thought while my flight is delayed, I ignore the other passengers around me.

I have no idea what awaits me. All I know is this moment will determine how I will spend the rest of my life: in blissful joy with Kaitlyn at my side, or just more lonely nights on my own.

Finally, it's time to board the plane. As soon as I'm seated in first class, all thoughts vanish from my head, and all that remains is a single purpose: find Kaitlyn and tell her how much she means to me before it's too late.

My stomach sinks as the plane takes off. I close my eyes and try to remember Kaitlyn's flawless face, her voice, and bright laugh—all things I love about her. It feels like a lifetime ago since I touched her and kissed her.

I take a deep breath and keep my thoughts from wandering too far. I'm going to find her. I'll make her see how much I care about her. I'll make her understand that she belongs with me.

When the plane lands with a thud against solid ground, I'm out of my seat with my bag in hand, pacing until the pilot opens the door. Then, I race down the stairs and into the terminal. I hurry to the rental area steeling myself for what lies ahead.

On the drive to Hailey, the small town where Kaitlyn lives, I plan to practice what I want to say. I can't believe I'm so fucking nervous. I've never been this anxious.

But as I leave the airport, I'm met with a stunning landscape of rolling hills, lush green forests, and crystal blue rivers. The abject beauty works its magic, instilling a sense of peace into my soul for the first time since Kaitlyn left my suite.

The sun is shining, and the sky is a deep blue, with fluffy white clouds dotting the horizon. I can see majestic mountains in the distance and can picture them dotted with wildflowers and alive with wildlife. She never mentioned how magnificent the area is.

Thirty minutes later, I pull into Hailey. Now what?

Will she be at work or at home? I check the time. It's mid-afternoon, so she should be at work. From what she told me, I know there's just one landscaper in town, so the office shouldn't be too difficult to locate.

The town is charming, filled with vibrant colors and bustling activity. But more relaxed than in the city. The main street is lined with cafes, shops, and other businesses. Snow-capped mountains can be seen in the background. There are no towering skyscrapers or corporate chains. The air looks clean.

I drive aimlessly, searching for her place of work, feeling somewhat hopeless—like I'm searching for a needle in a mountainside.

Then, as if by divine intervention, I see her. She's right there, standing in the entranceway to a café, chatting with another woman.

I see a vacant parking spot on the opposite side of the street. Flicking on my signal, I whip into it and shut off the engine before climbing from the SUV.

The sweet smell of honeysuckle permeates the air, carried in on a soft breeze. In the city, the sounds and smells mingle, and I hardly notice them anymore. Here I can pick them out. It's not a constant buzz of noise. I'm instantly reminded of the small town I grew up in, and realize I miss it. I miss the easier more laid back atmosphere. I miss running into people I know. I miss hanging out in the back of Pat's bar.

I give my head a shake. Those are all thoughts for a different day. Right now, I look in both directions, and jog across the street and walk toward her, my heart pounding.

As I approach, she must either hear or see me or maybe even senses me because she looks up, her eyes connecting with mine, and the words she was about to say die on her lips.

For a moment, the world stops spinning. Time stands still as I take in her beauty, her brown hair cascading down her back, her eyes sparkling in the sun. Speech fails me as I realize that I'm still as infatuated with Kaitlyn now as I was when we first met. It feels like a lifetime ago. I want to run to her, take her in my arms and never let go.

I take a deep breath and smile weakly as I stop a couple of feet away from her.

"Kaitlyn," I say softly.

"Elliott? I can't believe you're here."

"I came to find you," My voice is shaky. "I had to see you. I had to tell you how much I've missed you."

A throat clears, and we both blink, remember where we are, and look at the blonde woman standing with her. The woman appears to be around the same age as Kaitlyn. She has a pretty features. Not as beautiful as my Kaitlyn though.

She holds out her hand. "Hi. I'm Margo."

I take it. "Margo. Nice to meet you. Kaitlyn's told me about you."

"Really? Huh. She hasn't mentioned you."

A blush stains Kaitlyn's cheeks. "I did, I just never said his name."

Margo looks back and forth between us, confusion marring her face. She glances at Kaitlyn, who is getting redder by the minute and avoiding my gaze. "Oh. Oh! You're Mr. New York."

"I guess that's me."

She turns her questioning look to Kaitlyn, but with a twinkle in her eye. "So...are you two together now?"

Kaitlyn's cheeks turn an even brighter shade of pink, and she stammers out an answer, her head shaking in denial.

"Yes, we are," I smile at Kaitlyn fondly before turning back to Margo with a wide grin. "She just hasn't realized it yet."

Kaitlyn looks back at me, her eyes glistening with tears. I think she will say something for a moment, but then she turns away.

I'm not sure if she's rejecting me, or implying she needs more time. But I'm determined to work with either.

Margo steps back, setting her hands on her hips. "Well, I'll leave you two to figure that out. I'm gonna go inside a get a latte. I'll see you later, Kaitlyn."

We watch her go before turning back to each other. I step

closer, lifting my hand to brush a strand of hair from her face. "I've missed you," I say, my voice barely a whisper.

She swallows, her gaze still locked on mine. Her mouth opens slightly, and she closes the distance between even more. "I've missed you too," she murmurs, her breath tickling my skin.

"I want you to know," I say, my voice thick with emotion. "You belong with me."

Kaitlyn looks up at me, her eyes wide, and slowly nods her head. "Yes, Elliott, I do."

Neither of us speaks as I make those last couple of inches of separation disappear. Not even a piece of paper could fit between our bodies.

The air around us is charged with emotion; it feels like we're in our own little world.

"Elliott," she says softly. "I'm sorry I stopped texting you. The longer I waited, the harder it got."

"It's okay," I say. "I understand."

"It had nothing to do with you. I was scared. We come from different worlds. How can I fit into yours?"

"You fit in just fine, Kaitlyn. But what's more important is that you fit me."

Kaitlyn stares up at me in awe, her eyes wide with wonder. "You really think so?"

I smile and give her hands a light squeeze. "Yes, Kaitlyn. I do. You fit me perfectly."

Oblivious to the people walking around us and the traffic on the street next to us, she slides her arms around my waist and hold on tight like she never wants to let go.

I wrap my arms around her shoulders and hold her just as tight, inhaling the sweet scent of her hair as we stand there in silence for I don't know how long.

I lean down slowly, afraid that if I rush, it will break the spell we're under. Our lips meet in a kiss that instantly deepens into something more passionate. The world melts away until all that matters is the two of us, together at last.

I feel like I'm home at last. "I love you, Kaitlyn."

Kaitlyn pulls back, looks up, and smiles, her eyes glistening with unshed tears. "I love you too, Elliott."

Chapter Ten

Kaitlyn

Thanks to the handsome man sitting next to me, his fingers entwined with mine, I can ignore the buzzing of gossip that followed us into the church. I barely take notice as the ceremony flies by.

When I first returned home, I never imagined that Brandon and Tiffany's wedding would have been postponed. My escape to New York was to avoid being in town for the wedding and all the rumors surrounding it. Although everyone else relished a front-seat view to my embarrassment, I had no desire to watch as my ex-boyfriend marry my ex-best friend. The hurt, the betrayal—it was all too much. Winning that money, though I needed to save it more than I needed to spend it, came at the best possible time.

As Brandon says his vows, my heart aches a little. Even though our relationship is over, deep down, I want the best for him and Tiffany. I can admit that now.

I glance over at Tiffany, somebody I played dolls with, had sleepovers with, and shared secrets about boys with—it seemed like such a long time ago that we were best friends. It feels like a lifetime ago since we exchanged Christmas gifts or stayed up late to watch scary movies on TV talking about our dreams until the early morning hours.

When I hear their promises to each other, I hope that one day she and I will find a way to be friends again. Despite everything, she still holds a special place in my heart.

But when I turn my head and look at Elliott, I feel an overwhelming sense of joy. His whole attention is on me, and only me. He lifts our joined hands and presses his lips to my knuckles. Then he winks, instantly erasing any discomfort I may have been holding onto.

I can't tear my gaze away as he looks into my eyes like he knows every thought running through my mind. He smiles softly and tucks a strand of hair behind my ear, sending a shiver down my spine.

Despite the performance unfolding before us, he brings a sense of calm that relaxes me in ways I didn't know were possible. With him by my side, I feel safe, secure, and cared for; the pain from the past fades away as if it never existed.

Over dinner and drinks, while the married couple shares stories I don't want to know about, Elliott sits beside me, his arm around the back of my chair, his fingers dancing along my neckline, teasing my hair. He leans in and whispers naughty words in my ears. We even sneak out to fool around in the coat room. I want to say it was all him, but I'm pretty sure I'm the one who put the idea in his head. All I can think about is how lucky I am to have found such a fantastic man who makes me feel appreciated.

After the ceremony, we walk arm in arm toward the limo, leaving all the gossip and drama behind. I can feel the other guests' eyes on us as we make our way to the car, thinking it must be for the newly married couple. I can't help but chuckle at their surprise when they discover otherwise. Elliott has gone out of his way to make *me* feel special today.

Since he appeared in town and confessed his feelings, we've been inseparable. Whether in Idaho or New York, we're never far apart. I'm finally using all that vacation I banked, which makes my boss and Margo happy. We haven't yet decided what our future looks like, but I'm spending all my free days in New York.

The benefits of dating a wealthy man are tempting: gorgeous hotels for getaways, delicious meals eaten at five-star restaurants, and tickets to plays and concerts. When Elliott asked me what kind of life I wanted to have with him, he said that money was no object, and if there was anything he could do to make me happy, I simply had to name it.

At first, it was a tad overwhelming; how often does someone offer you the world on a silver platter? But as time passed, I realized it's not about things or experiences. It's about enjoying each other's company and making memories.

My heart swells whenever he surprises me with something special or sends me flowers out of the blue. But nothing beats picking up the phone and hearing his voice or knowing that every day is a new adventure with him by my side.

"Have I told you yet today how stunning you look?"

I glance down at my dress. I'm a tad overdressed for this wedding, but I couldn't resist wearing it for Elliott. I remember when I first spotted this gown in the shop window in New York. The layers of tulle on the skirt, the elegant V-neck with spaghetti straps, and the slate blue color took my breath away. How it flows when I twirl makes me feel like a princess. And isn't that what every girl dreams of?

Before we get into the limo, Elliott reaches into his pocket and pulls out a small red box with a white bow.

"Kaitlyn," he begins, "I know today has been difficult for

you and I don't want to make it any harder, but I thought this might make it better."

I shake my head. "You being here has made today bearable. You didn't need to get me anything." I take the box from him and open it to find a gorgeous diamond necklace. The stones are perfectly matched and set in a delicate pattern.

"Elliott, it's beautiful."

"I wanted something special that you could treasure forever," he says, touching my cheek softly.

"Thank you so much." I throw my arms around him and plant a big wet kiss on his lips. I don't care who's looking. I don't care what they think. I don't care that they're probably focusing on me and my date and not the couple getting married today.

Elliott wipes tears from my cheeks—I cry so many happy tears with this man. "It's my pleasure. Just so it's clear, though, I plan to spoil you. It's something I can do and I like to do it. You'll just have to get used to it." He drops a quick kiss on the tip of my nose. "Now let's go. We have a plane to catch."

We make our way to the airport. I can hardly believe what Elliott has done for me. He has pulled out all the stops.

Once we are settled into the soft leather seats on the plane, I realize that what's happened in my past has led me here. Call it whatever you want, but things happened, and if they hadn't of the way they did, I wouldn't be sitting here today. I'd be heading to the community hall to celebrate my marriage to a man I can now admit I never loved. Not like I love the man sitting across from me.

I can't take my eyes off Elliott. He looks so handsome in his suit. The luxurious fabric is cut and tailored to fit his body perfectly, accentuating his broad shoulders and trim waist. The white shirt brightens his complexion. Even his shoes are polished to a glossy shine.

More than a few women in town gave him a second, third, and fourth look.

My heart flutters as I recall Margo's earlier words when she pulled me aside before we sat down to dinner.

"Honey, I have never seen you look happier. You are glowing like a star."

"I am, happy, that is. I didn't know that I could come here today. I didn't think I had the courage. But I didn't want everyone pitying me either. If I had stayed away, I would have been forced to deal with the looks and the whispers. Now, they can see that I'm okay. In fact, I'm more than okay."

"You deserve this, Kaitlyn. That man of yours is to die for. If he has a friend, I'm available." We laughed. "I'm going to miss you though," she'd said, a catch in her voice, a shine in her eyes.

"What do you mean? I'm not going anywhere."

"Oh, please, if I were you I'd pack all my belongings and catch the next chartered plan to New York."

We chuckled so hard; I snorted because that's precisely what I'm doing. Though I haven't made an official move yet. For now, we plan to go back and forth.

Eventually, the plane touches down in New York, and we disembark. Elliott takes my hand and leads me to where his car is waiting. I look up at the night sky and can't help but be filled with joy. I'm finally back in New York with the man I love.

We take the elevator up to the penthouse when we arrive at the hotel. The doors open, and Elliott takes my hand and leads me into the expansive penthouse.

I am speechless when I see it.

It is decorated with what looks like hundreds of flowers—roses, lilies, tulips—all in full bloom and arranged in the most beautiful patterns. The sweet scent of them fills the air. The curtains are pulled back on the huge window. All around us are twinkling skyline lights that give the room a magical glow.

Elliott takes my hand and leads me through the flowers to a table set for two next to the floor-to-ceiling windows overlooking Central Park. He pulls out my chair and helps me get comfortable before sitting across from me. I admire the view as Elliott lights the candles and pours us each a glass of champagne.

"How did you do this?" I can't help but feel like I'm in a dream world.

"I own the hotel. I can do anything." His eyes dance with mischief.

Far below, traffic is a sea of red and white lights. I can only imagine the bustle of activity, even at this hour.

But up here, it's just the two of us.

And a shit-load of flowers.

Elliott reaches across the table and takes my hand. "I know we haven't been together that long, but I feel like I've known you forever. I can't even remember a time before you came into my life. You are the one person who makes me feel most alive, and I want to spend every day with you for the rest of our lives."

He pulls a small velvet box from his pocket and places it on the table before getting down on one knee.

My heart races, and I instinctively clasp my hands over my chest.

"Kaitlyn, I love you," he says, his voice chokes with emotion. "Will you marry me?"

I stare into Elliott's eyes, unable to believe what I'm hearing. I can feel my heart racing and tears coming, once more, to my eyes. I nod my head. This is the happiest moment of my life.

"Yes, I will marry you."

He takes my hand and slides a ring onto my finger. It's a beautiful huge diamond solitaire that sparkles in the candlelight. He stands and pulls me into his arms, sealing our engagement with a passionate kiss that quickly lights me up like the Fourth the July, Christmas, and my birthday all rolled into one.

We spend the remainder of the night dreaming of our future together while feasting on New York pepperoni pizza and washing it down with only the best champagne.

Every moment I spend with this man fills my heart with more love. I can already tell this is it. We are meant to be together forever, and I wouldn't have it any other way.

I never would have thought a fifty/fifty draw would allow me to indulge in a spontaneous trip to the Big Apple, which would lead to a fling with a billionaire who would end up being the man I intend to spend the remainder of my days with.

But here I am. And I couldn't be happier.

About the Author

Anne Lange grew up with a love for reading. She reads many genres of romance, but prefers to write sexy stories, sometimes with a dash of humor, usually with a side of those sinful pleasures your mom never told you about.

Oh, and always a happily ever after.

Anne juggles a day job and a family while she looks forward to retirement and finally writing full time. She lives in Ontario, Canada with her wonderfully supportive husband, has three awesome kids and two fur babies.

Follow Anne on Facebook: https://www.facebook.com/Anne.Lange.Author

Or check out her Website: https://authorannelange.com/

Maybe even sign up for her newsletter, and get a bonus epilogue featuring more of Kaitlyn and Elliott: https://geni.us/FwaBBonusEpilogue

Bidding On The Billionaire

Darby Fox

Chapter One

Addison

"Listen, Adds, why are you so stressed about this?" My best friend, Julie, gestures with her wine glass. "There must be a hundred places that would love to take you on as an intern."

Julie is the assistant director of a nearby art gallery and I'm grateful she was able to meet me here for a last-minute lunch.

I place my empty glass on the table and level a stare at her. "I don't want to work anywhere else. The Cariston Group internship is the best opportunity for me." The Cariston Group owns the most prestigious hotels worldwide. An internship there is foundational to the future I've envisioned. "And before you say it, I don't want to ask my brother to call in any favors." My older brother, Jamison, has been best friends with Lachlan Cariston since they were roommates at university twelve years ago. I plan to get this internship on my own merits. "I just don't understand. I should have been the top candidate for the position."

I'd done my research; my graduate work project on the evolution of eco-tourism and the growth of local economies without damaging fragile ecosystems won me the medal for my program. The Cariston Group should have just waved me through the door.

Instead, I received a nicely worded letter expressing admiration for the project and stating that the internship wasn't being offered this year. I roll my eyes. All graduating students who participate in the Cariston internships go on to be incredibly successful in their own endeavors. Some stay with Cariston, of course, but many use that experience, and the connections, to launch their own empires.

I want my own empire.

"Maybe you were the top candidate. The letter said they aren't running that internship stream this year." Julie reaches over and pats my hand. "I'm sorry, hon. I know you're disappointed, but if you aren't going to call your brother, what are you going to do?"

"I'm going to reach out to last year's internship committee and try to change their minds."

Julie tilts her head. "Why don't you just call Lachlan yourself?"

"I don't want to use my family connections to get the position." I twirl my glass on the table, avoiding her knowing gaze. "Besides, Lachlan doesn't have anything to do with the internship program."

"Uh-huh. Is that the only reason?"

Lachlan Cariston is the bane of my existence. He might be my brother's best friend but to me he's just an arrogant jerk. Oh, he's gorgeous, but unfortunately that beautiful exterior disguises how emotionally stunted he is. My brother has told me how ruthless Lachlan can be, and not just in the boardroom. Jamieson doesn't talk about *that stuff*. At least not in front of his baby sister, but I've got ears and eyes and google. He's got a reputation as a playboy who'll never settle down and I think it's because he can't possibly love someone more than he loves winning in the business world.

Or maybe that's just what I tell myself.

I shrug. "It's not like Lachlan has anything to do with the main hotel side anyway. He's too busy with the construction and development portfolio, and his dating life."

"Well, what do you expect from a gorgeous billionaire? If he was holding a ball to find a princess, I'd throw my panties into the ring."

I shake my head. "I'm pretty sure that was a shoe. And you didn't grow up watching a parade of women line up just to talk to Lachlan as if he was some sort of god." Or have him ignore you because he thought of you as a baby.

"Oh, come on. You didn't ever have a tiny little crush on him?"

I ignore the flutter in my tummy at the memory of that one night and toss my hair over my shoulder. "I'm pretty sure everyone he's ever met has crushed on him, but it's pointless. First of all, he's the oldest Cariston brother, so he's eight years older. Jamison would have a heart attack if he knew his baby sister had a crush on anyone, let alone Lachlan." I close my eyes. *Go back to bed, little girl. You don't belong here.* "Second, he pays about as much attention to me as he does our family cat."

I turn on the bar stool and gaze across the street at the steel and glass tower owned by the Cariston Group. "George Mandrake was the head of the internship committee for the last three years." I check my watch. "I have an appointment with him at two thirty."

"You don't waste any time."

"I can't. I'm not a Cariston, so if I want an empire, I have to build it myself." I stand, brushing the wrinkles out of my skirt. "Thanks for lunch. Are we still on for this weekend?" Julie and I have a standing date the last Saturday of every month where we get together at one of our apartments and order pizza and watch a movie. Right now, we're working our way through nineties rom-coms, and I've got Pretty Woman in the queue for Saturday night.

Julie smacks her forehead. "I forgot to tell you." She winces. "I have to work Saturday night. The gallery is hosting some private event and our coordinator's assistant left on maternity leave three weeks earlier than planned. There's a company handling all the details, but I still have to be on hand for the gallery. I'm sorry."

I wave it off. "No issues. I'll put Richard Gere and Julia Roberts on hold until our next date night."

"Or, you could actually go on a real date." Julie stands, tucking her wallet back into her purse. "Remember those?"

"Ha, ha. Who am I going to date? I'm not interested in a close up of some guy's treasure trail over his heavily-filtered abs or worse, the dreaded dick pic. The last one I got, I responded with 'congratulations, you've sent the 500th dick pic' with a link to a confetti GIF and the guy had the nerve to ask if I'd ever seen a bigger one." I roll my eyes. "I'm done with apps."

"You could go out with someone we know. What about Bill? He's always flirting with you."

"Bill flirts with everyone." I reach over and hug her. "I don't need anyone but you." I push away the thought that I wouldn't turn Lachlan Cariston down, but that sounds like my teenage crush talking. It doesn't matter that I've compared every man I've ever met to the gorgeous jerk. To him, I'm Jamieson's baby sister and that's all I'll ever be. I sigh. Someday, somewhere, there has got to be a guy to makes me sit up and notice the way Lachlan always has.

Julie kisses me on the cheek. "Good luck with your ambush... I mean appointment."

"Mark my words, I'm getting that internship, no matter what I have to do."

Chapter Two

Lachlan

"Jesus Christ, Mother. You signed me up for what?" I stare down at the phone in my hand, dread forming a ball in my stomach.

"Don't swear at your mother, Lachlan. I raised you better than that. I told you all about this event months ago, but clearly, you weren't listening to me. And it's for charity." My mother's cool tone instantly makes my ears heat. I clear my throat, hating how her voice can reduce me to an awkward twelve-year-old boy in minutes.

"I have plans on Saturday night." I quickly look at my calendar, crossing my fingers. I always have plans so when I see the block in my schedule, I cast my eyes up in gratitude. "Sorry, Mother, my calendar is booked out for Saturday night. Why don't you ask King or Laird?" My brothers will want to kill me for suggesting it, but I'm pretty confident I can take them in a fight.

"Laird is on tour with that rock band of his and Kingsley is in Sweden. Also, your calendar is booked because I had your assistant schedule the event after I spoke to you about it."

I might not be able to see her over the phone, but I can picture the long-suffering look on her face. I rub the back of my neck. "A bachelor auction? Isn't that kind of tacky?"

Silence.

I refuse to back down. "Mother—"

"Lachlan Wilfred Cariston." I mouth *the third* wishing I could bang my head on my desk as my mother continues. "Do you honestly think I'd put my name on something *tacky*?" She says it like a mouthful of spoiled caviar. "A lot of research went into this. These events are quite popular and meant to be fun. I know our interpretations of fun may be quite different but honestly, how is this Saturday night going to be different for you than any other? You'll walk out of the event with some random woman, you may or may not know. From what I hear that's pretty much the norm for you these days, isn't it?"

Ouch. I don't owe her any explanations, however, and this time I let the silence draw out.

My mother sighs. "Paige says these types of auctions are very successful."

Ahh, now we get to it. Paige Arnoult is my ex-girlfriend who has let it be known that she wouldn't mind picking up where we left off a year ago after she broke up with me because she wanted to get my attention. I had been in the middle of finalizing a huge construction project after two years of delays and I couldn't drop everything to run to her. When I didn't run to her, she tried to make me jealous by crawling into Kingsley's limousine stark naked. King handed her his jacket and called me to let me know he was dropping her at home, much to her frustration. I wish I had been surprised, but that kind of drama is exactly what Paige brings to the table. I know exactly where this is going. "Mother, Paige and I are over."

"I never said anything, Lachlan. Maybe she won't even bid on you."

I grit my teeth. The last thing I want is to be cornered into a night with Paige. All she wants is the Cariston name, she doesn't particularly care who is attached to it. My mother is equally enamored of the Arnoult's global property holdings and reminds me that relationships often make good business deals. My mother loves me – loves all of us – but she doesn't understand that we don't exactly want a marriage like she and our father have. How do I get out of this thing?

"Don't even think about getting out of this, Lachlan. Like I said, it's for charity and as your mother, I'm asking you for a favor. It's one night. Well, I suppose two, because you have to take the winner on a special date."

I roll my eyes. "I have to go, Mother."

"See you on Saturday night, darling."

The line goes dead. I rake a hand through my hair, turning to look out the floor-to-ceiling window, noticing the sunshine for the first time since I walked into my office at seven this morning. A bachelor auction. As if I didn't have enough going on with this whole restructuring I'm dealing with. I stand, reach for my jacket and shrug it on, needing some fresh air.

My assistant looks up, startled, and starts to rise, but I wave her down. I just need two minutes to walk off this excess energy charging through my body. If I had more time, I'd change and go for a run, but a quick glance at my watch lets me know I have fifteen minutes tops before I have to head down to the eighth floor.

In the lobby, I take a minute to stop and talk to security. I like to know everyone who works for Cariston because, as this recent restructuring has shown me, you never know which portfolios might get moved around. Carl takes me behind the reception desk, to show me how the new security feed is working.

"Excuse me?" A woman's voice calls to us, and Carl turns

around. "I have an appointment on the eighth floor for two thirty."

"Yes, ma'am, who are you seeing?"

"George Mandrake."

I turn, because I'll be seeing George this afternoon myself, and surprise fills my chest. "Addy?" I step forward, scanning the short, curvy woman whose cheeks pinken when she sees me.

Addison North is my best friend's little sister. I can't quite remember how old she is now, I think she just graduated, but she's the baby of the North siblings. In fact, Jamie still refers to her as Baby Addy, the childhood nickname having stuck since he said it upon seeing her at the hospital when she was born. I haven't seen her in a couple of years, but there's nothing babyish about her today. She's in a pencil skirt that hugs her generous hips and thighs and a matching navy jacket tailored to perfection, open over a pale lilac silk blouse that drapes her serious curves. Surely this goddess isn't the same girl as Baby Addy.

"What are you doing here?" I ask, folding my arms.

She tosses her dark hair over her shoulder, shifting her laptop bag to that side. "I have a meeting."

"About what?" My curiosity is piqued. I nod at Carl. "I'll take her up, Carl."

Carl smiles and hands Addison a guest pass. "Just drop this back at the desk here when you're done."

Addy takes the pass and turns on her heel. "I'd rather not say."

I hold out my hand for her bag, but her grip tightens, and I shrug, leading the way to the elevators. "Does Jamieson know you're here today? He should have called me."

Her big brown eyes flash to mine. "I didn't realize I needed permission."

My head snaps back. "I'm just surprised to see you here."

She bites her lip, shaking her head. "Sorry," she mutters as we step into the elevator. Her perfume, a sweet scent that reminds me of summer strawberries, drifts around me. What is wrong with me? I shouldn't be noticing Baby Addy's curves or the way she smells.

"Please don't tell Jamieson you saw me," Addy says.

I turn to her, frowning. "Why not?" I let my eyes travel down her outfit. What could she be here for? There are no openings in George's area at the moment that I'm aware of.

The elevator stops and I step out behind her.

"What are you doing?" she asks.

"Are you on some kind of secret mission, Addy?" I ask, bemused by her sassy tone.

"It's Addison. And it's none of your business, Lachlan. Just pretend you didn't see me."

She struts away from me in nude-colored stilettos that intrigue me, her world-class ass distracting me from the fact that I shouldn't have even noticed her fuck-me shoes or the way her curves move under that skirt. I quicken my stride, catching up to her easily. "That's where you're wrong, Addy." I stretch out the nickname, just to see her bratty mouth tighten in displeasure. "It actually is my business. This whole building is my business."

She stops, turning to me. "You are in construction and development. Last I heard, the hotel side isn't actually your business."

I fold my arms. "I'm a Cariston. C&D might be my portfolio but let me assure you that we know exactly what is happening under our umbrella."

Her brown eyes flash again, and I ignore the spark of desire in my chest and elsewhere.

"You may as well tell me what's going on. I have a meeting

with George myself, this afternoon, and I can just ask him then."

"I'm applying for the hotel operation internship," she says with a frustrated sigh.

"We aren't running that internship this year."

"So, I heard." She sets off down the hallway again. "I'm meeting with George to discuss it."

We arrive at another reception desk, and the man behind the desk looks up, his eyes widening when he sees me. "Mr. Cariston, you're early." His gaze darts to Addison.

I nod at her. "Ms. North has an appointment with Mr. Mandrake, I'm just escorting her."

Her lips twitch at that and I smile, noticing the way Jonathon's gaze bounces between us, lingering on *Addison's* chest. Her outfit is completely professional, but her curves are definitely giving off naughty librarian vibes, and I catch Jonathon's eye, quirking a brow to let him know I caught him. He straightens his shoulders with a jerk and nods. "Right this way, Ms. North."

"It's fine, Jonathon, I'll show her where the office is," I say.

Addison hesitates as I fall into step beside her. "Do you mind?"

"Mind what?"

"Shouldn't you be busy with world domination or something?"

"I'm glad my reputation proceeds me."

She offers a delicate snort.

"What was that for?" This is the most fun I've had all day, all week and possibly longer if I'm being truthful. Jamieson's sister doesn't care who I am and from what I can tell doesn't have a simpering bone in her body. When did the girl I remember turn into this woman I can't take my eyes off?

"You have a reputation all right."

"For world domination?" I can't resist teasing her. I'm trying to keep my eyes off her sinful figure but watching her plush mouth twitch as she tries not to smile gives me a jolt more potent than the espresso I was planning to order before she walked into my building.

We stop in front of George's office, and she gives me a pointed look. I knock, but George doesn't respond. He doesn't even turn from his monitor. He must have been expecting her, as Jonathon would have let him know she had arrived.

Addison steps forward. "Mr. Mandrake?"

He waves a hand over his shoulder. "Have a seat, Ms. North, but I don't have much time, you already know we're not offering the internship this year."

His impatient tone doesn't sit well with me. The least he can do is greet her cordially. "Doesn't she have an appointment?" I inquire mildly, noticing how he jumps when he hears my voice.

"Mr. Cariston—" He spins in his chair so fast, I fear him flying out of his seat.

I hold up a hand. "Ms. North is here to discuss something with you, is she not?"

He gives a jerky nod, offering a bewildered smile to Addison. "Of course, my apologies, Ms. North."

Addison takes another step. "None required, Mr. Mandrake. I understand you are a busy man." She places a hand on the door, and meets my gaze, before shutting it in my face.

Something shifts in my chest as I stare at the dark wood paneling. Baby Addy is all grown up. I don't know why, but this makes me smile.

I head back to my office, a noticeable jaunt in my step. Seeing Addy was a nice twist in my day. My brow wrinkles as I remember her asking me not to mention that I saw her here to

Jamieson. I don't like keeping secrets from my best friend. I may have a wide circle of acquaintances and people who like to drop my name during interviews when asked about their friends, but as a Cariston, the reality is that the only people I can really trust is my family and, over time, that extended to Jamieson. He's never wanted anything from me, going so far as to turn me down when I asked him to work for The Cariston Group after he graduated from law school.

As I walk into my outer office, Tricia rises, an apologetic look on her face. "Your mother called," she says.

"Again?"

Tricia nods. "She said to remind you that you'll need to have a tuxedo for Saturday night."

Small mercies I suppose. At least it's a tuxedo and not some cheesy costume, or worse, being expected to parade around half-naked. I have no qualms about showing off my body, but I'm not about to do it on demand, even if it is for charity. Still, I'm surprised if Paige is involved that there isn't a tiny bit of payback hidden somewhere, unless she really does have a plan to buy me for the evening. It's not Cariston money, but the Arnoult family has plenty of their own to indulge their only daughter's whims.

My phone buzzes and I check the screen. It's a text from Mother's assistant, with a link to the event on Saturday night. Frustration tightens my shoulders like a vice. My good mood evaporates as if it never happened.

Baby Addy.

Correction: Addison North, in her curve-hugging pencil skirt with her molten chocolate eyes and hair shining like silk.

And thinking of Addison gives me an idea.

Chapter Three

Addison

"Ms. North!"

I turn at the sound of my name. The security guy is waving at me, and I glance down at myself to see if I've forgotten anything. I slid my guest pass across the desk as I walked out, but maybe he didn't see it. I point at the counter. "I already gave it back."

He crooks his finger for me to come back, and I sigh, stifling a groan. George Mandrake was useless. He held the line that the internship wasn't available and didn't seem all that interested in discussing my project or the potential for future work with their hotel division. I plod back to the security desk. "Is there an issue?" I ask.

"Mr. Cariston would like to see you."

I frown. "Lachlan?" Why would he want to see me? All I want to do is leave. My tights are digging into my waist and I'm tired and frustrated. The last thing I want is a reminder of everything I can't have.

The guard nods, handing me another security pass. "Twenty-third floor."

I stifle a sigh. He *is* Jamieson's best friend. I turn and press the button for the elevator.

The doors open to a bright and airy area ringed with windows. A woman in her fifties looks up with a smile. "Ms. North? We're glad we caught you."

I shift my bag to my other shoulder, just as Lachlan comes to the door of his office. My heart slams in my chest and I'm so annoyed at myself for noticing the way his black hair is ruffled, like he's run his hands through it one too many times. I can't believe my bad luck in bumping into him. I hate how unbalanced he makes me feel, like I'm still a fifteen-year-old girl with a stupid crush. I used to get so tongue-tied around him and I swear, for a minute there today I felt my cheeks heat and my throat close over when he smiled and asked why I was here. I'm not normally so rude, but years of being around Lachlan, and the butterflies he drives wild in my belly, have taught me some self-preservation techniques. Plus, I really don't want Jamieson to know I was here.

My brother is amazing, but to him, I'm still a little girl, and he loves to help me. It's not that I'm not grateful because I am, it's just that sometimes his idea of helping can be overwhelming. Like the time I was having difficulty with my middle school science fair project, and he got his then-girlfriend, who happened to be a freelance science journalist, to reach out to an award-winning team of microbiologists to 'assist' me.

Or the time I needed a date for prom, and he talked Laird into taking me. Laird is far closer in age to me, I think just a year or two older, and he had my friends swooning with his charm and good looks. Which was fine but I spent the whole night imagining I was dancing with Lachlan.

Lachlan crooks a finger at me and the hair at the back of my neck stands up.

This happened to me once when I was at the zoo and one

of the big cats broke free from the trainers during a demonstration. As the animal prowled toward me, I was mesmerized, my feet rooted to the floor, even though every cell in my body was screaming for me to run. Luckily, the trainers regained control quickly, but I never forgot that prickly, hair-raising experience.

Right now, my survival instinct is telling me I'm in trouble, only instead of it being a big, beautiful jungle cat, I'm staring down a big, beautiful billionaire. Why does he have to be so impossibly gorgeous? Bright, blue eyes that stand out all the more because of his inky-dark hair and those sharp cheekbones and square jaw. I'd say he looks like a model, but his body doesn't bear any resemblance to the lean, wispy adolescent boy shapes that are currently stylish. Lachlan is tall, with broad shoulders and thick thighs and he looks like he could lift me against a wall and pin me there with only his hips.

Heat washes through me as he turns, and I follow him into his office.

Once there, he leans against his desk, crossing his arms, and I don't notice the way his lean, tanned forearms look so strong and masculine against the white of his shirt. I swallow. Nope. I don't notice it at all.

He nods for me to sit down but doing so will put me directly at the level of his crotch, and I certainly don't need another body part to not notice. I place my bag in the chair instead and lean a hip against the high back. "You wanted to see me?" I ask.

"How did your meeting with George go?"

I grit my teeth. "You probably already know how it went. There is no internship this year, at least for that department." I tip my chin up. "Why is that, anyway?"

Lachlan's gaze travels up my body, and I'd swear he was touching me with that intense gaze. I resist the urge to cross my arms as my nipples pucker, and I glance down to make sure my blouse isn't gaping where my large breasts are straining the middle button.

He catches me looking and his head snaps up as his arms fall before sliding his hands in his pockets. "That area is restructuring and we're reviewing the programs, including the internships."

His phone rings, but he ignores it. "I didn't know you were interested in the hotel business."

"The internship is an amazing program."

"You want to work for me?" His eyebrow quirks up.

"It wouldn't be for you. It's not your portfolio. And the Cariston Group is the best, so of course I want to work with the best."

His lips twitch. "We are the best. And you would actually be working for me. I'm looking at heading up hotel development now with the restructuring."

My eyes widen. This is industry news that has been kept quiet. He nods as if he can read my mind. "Right, and that's confidential at this time, okay, Addy?"

"It's Addison," I blurt, then bite back an exasperated sigh. He'll never see me as anything other than Baby Addy.

"Addison." He says my name like he's testing it on his tongue, and I hate the way my body responds to hearing it in his deep, smooth tones.

"As I'm now in charge of reviewing the area, I have a proposition for you."

I straighten. "Will you bring back the program? I can provide my application and transcripts—"

Lachlan holds up his hand. "Hang on, I won't bring back the full program, as it really does require a review, but I could extend an internship as part of the review process, focusing on a couple of key areas. I have a new resort I'm looking at, and I will be putting together a team, so an intern would be helpful."

I nod, my mind racing. An internship involving the launch of a new Cariston Group project? That would be a huge opportunity for me. "How long do you think the selection process will take?"

Lachlan smiles and I'm reminded of the jungle cat again. "It's yours, if you do one tiny favor for me first."

No application? "What kind of favor?"

Chapter Four

Lachlan

I glance down at my gold watch trying to quell the butterflies in my stomach. Actual fucking butterflies. It's Saturday night and I'm in a makeshift backstage area that looks like a cross between a fashion show and a high-end brothel. There are a few men I recognize, but for the most part, it looks like some of the younger sons of my mother's friends with a few 'occupation' themes thrown in. I catch the eye of a guy around my size, wearing the bottom half of a firefighter uniform while a makeup artist contours his already impressive ab display. I don't have anything to complain about, but this guy looks like he could have his own calendar.

At least I don't have to worry about body makeup. I wave off the guy who approaches me with a large brush and bronzer, ignoring his eye roll as I pull out my phone to see if Addy – *excuse me*, Addison – has texted me. We've been texting each other all week. First, just to set up the details for tonight, and then, somehow, it moved to something more. It didn't matter if I was in a meeting, I would send her a quick question about her favorite color. Or on my commute home, I'd ask what she did that day. I texted her ideas about the new project I'm thinking about, and her responses were clever and insightful. I even asked her for dinner ideas, just because I wanted to know what she was doing. The last couple of days, I've looked forward to her good-night message. The image of her curled up in her bed, of me being the last person on her mind before she falls asleep, makes me smile.

But now my phone is silent, the screen blank. I step up to the curtained area, trying to peer into the audience, but I can't really see anything.

Paige has been texting and calling me all week with instructions and reminders under the guise of it being for the event. She even expected me to take two hours yesterday to attend the rehearsal for this thing. As if I have two hours on a Friday afternoon to spare. I received an irate phone call from her when she discovered I sent one of my assistants to fill in, take notes, and let me know what I was supposed to do when I got here.

Other than wait to hear from Addison. Where is she, anyway? Along with the internship, I gave her access to bid on whatever she wanted at the auction, as long as it includes me. And she needs to ensure she's the successful bidder for the evening with me. I'll come out and do my part for charity, and wave and wink and flirt with the crowd like my mother expects. But I won't be easily manipulated into spending time with Paige, who has been dropping little hints all week about how we should get together and how we should put the past in the past.

I've had no problem ignoring Paige.

I'm looking forward to using the auction as an excuse to sweep Addison off her feet. When did my best friend's little sister grow up? I remember an awkward teenager in oversized sweatshirts and ponytails, not the bombshell in my office last week. And it's not just how she looks. Her texts are funny and sweet, and she has amazing ideas for this internship. I pulled her application and file. Her analysis and ability to narrow down a business issue, take it apart, and provide a valid direction for improvement made me really sit up and take notice. I shouldn't be surprised, Jamieson is one of the smartest guys I know, and it's clear his sibling also possesses the brainiac gene.

I shouldn't be thinking about her this much. And while Addy might look a lot different from how I remember her, she's still Jamieson's sister. Second, I don't chase. I don't need to. I prefer to be in control at all times. I only go after what I want once I've analyzed it from all angles.

My reaction to Addison makes me feel out of control. The morning after she was in my office, I woke from a dream about her dark brown hair in my fist, those chocolate eyes glazed with lust as I pulled the straining buttons loose from her blouse to reveal her generous tits, nipples hard and achy for my touch, my mouth. I took myself in hand, stroking my cock the way I want her to touch me, coming with such force, it made me think it's been far too long since I was with a woman.

But it's more than just wanting any woman. The woman I want is my best friend's little sister.

"Listen up, gentlemen!" A sharp double clap has me turning to see what's going on. A woman with a clipboard in a slinky blue dress continues. "We've got an eager audience tonight and we're going to let them have a little sneak peek by having you mingle with the guests during the cocktail hour, so finish up your hair and make-up and get out there." She titters and waves to one of the make-up artists who is assisting some guy in what looks like a cowboy costume. "Marco! Less glitter, more tan on that one," she directs. "Remember to let the event photographers pose you near the artwork for the gallery, as many of the exhibits are for sale this evening as well, with a portion of the profits going to our charity."

My mother is going to owe me big time for this. I could have just signed a massive cheque for the charity. In fact, next year I will ensure that the charity doesn't need an event like this because they will have suddenly found themselves in receipt of an extra-large donation.

The last thing I want is to go out there and mingle with the guests. Did Addison change her mind? I check my phone again, pushing down the disappointment I feel seeing the blank screen. Reluctantly, I shove it in my pocket and head to a table in the back where a station has been set up for champagne, snagging a glass and wishing it was my favorite bourbon instead.

"Well, there you are," a voice croons, as a proprietary hand slides across my back. "Why are you hiding back here?"

I turn, not surprised to see Paige standing far too close for comfort. Her blond hair is swept back, highlighting the angles of her face, and her black dress hugs her slim figure. She may have been my girlfriend once, her icy beauty drawing me in like a perfect diamond, but now she simply leaves me cold. I step back, giving her a nod as I place my flute on the table behind me. "I don't hide from anything," I say.

She pats me on the shoulder like I've just missed the joke, squeezing my arm. "Of course you don't. I have to say though, I wondered why you weren't mingling in the crowd." She leans in close, "I don't mind that the others don't get to see you. You really are quite devastatingly handsome in that suit."

I look over her shoulder, and I finally spot Addison. Something eases in my chest at the sight of her. Her long brown hair is styled in a cascade of small curls, held back from her face by two tiny combs at her temples. She rises from the table where she is sitting, and my mouth goes dry. She's wearing a dark red dress that emphasizes all the curves she was struggling to contain the other day. This dress doesn't hug or cling, but rather drapes itself like a loving caress over her body, revealing her shape like a goddess emerging from the sea.

Jesus Christ, now I'm waxing poetic over a dress. I can't help it though, as my cock hardens, and my pulse quickens just from catching a glimpse of her. While I'm watching, the firefighter from backstage approaches her, his abs gleaming. My entire body clenches as he lifts her hand and kisses it like he's in a bad version of *Romeo and Juliet*. Her free hand flutters up to the pale column of her neck, and the room fades around me as I think, '*Mine*'.

"Excuse me," I say, stepping around Paige and heading straight for Addison. Her lips are stained a deep berry color, like she painted them with cherry juice, and her beautiful face is lit up when she smiles at whatever that bastard is saying to her.

I want all her smiles directed at me. She's like a rose and I want to be the sunshine her petals bloom for, the raindrops she needs to survive, the soil she's rooted to. I shake my head at these nonsensical thoughts, feeling like I won't be able to breathe until I'm next to her.

"Addy," I say deliberately when I reach her, needing the reminder of who she is but unable to stop myself from sliding my arm around her hips. I bend to kiss her cheek, ignoring her look of irritation. "I'm so glad you made it."

I hold out my hand to Firefighter Ken. "Lachlan Cariston."

"Travis Goodman," he says, shaking my hand before turning back to Addison as if I weren't standing there with my hand inches from her round ass. "I'd be happy to show you that painting when we get a break from all this. And remember, I'm Bachelor Number Six." He flashes a smile and I wonder if he'd mind if I rendered him as anatomically bland as the Ken doll he resembles.

"I'll remember," Addison says, her voice squeaking when I

splay my fingers, pressing into her delectable curves. She clears her throat and lifts her glass to her lips, but I notice she doesn't pull away from me, instead she leans her hip in closer to my body.

Travis wanders off to another group of women who appear only too eager to talk to Bachelor Number Six.

I reluctantly drop my arm and step away from her. "What painting was he talking about?" I ask, still stinging from the way her lips curved as she smiled at another man.

"Oh, my friend works at this gallery." She looks around, her curls swaying prettily around her shoulders. "Actually, she's supposed to be here tonight, but I haven't seen her." Addison shrugs. "Anyway, I fell in love with a painting by a local artist, but it sold. The firefighter guy, Travis, he said he knew the artist and that they recently sent a new work to the gallery. I haven't seen it yet, but he was going to show it to me."

I bet he was. "Maybe I can help you find it."

Addison peers up at me from under her lashes. I have a sudden image of her on her knees, lips wrapped around my cock, while she looks up in the same way. I shift, trying to quell my rising desire. *Baby Addy*, I repeat to myself. But it does little to distract me when the full-grown woman is standing in front of me, the warm notes of her perfume, some citrusy scent that reminds me of mimosas and beaches, makes me want to drink her in like sunshine.

"I didn't know you were interested in art?"

I step closer, taking her hand in mine. "I'm always interested in beautiful things." I grin down at her, loving the flush of red that blooms on her cheeks. We make our way across the room just as someone steps to the stage with a microphone, announcing that the bachelors must return to the backstage area so they can start the auction.

Strangely disappointed to leave her side, I release her hand.

"I don't care how much money it takes, make sure you're the successful bidder when it's my turn."

"Am I only supposed to bid on you?" she asks.

"That's the plan." Jealously nips at me again. "Is there anyone else here you want to bid on?"

She bites her lip and I lean down brushing the shell of her ear with my lips. She shivers, and her slight tremble makes me smile. "You can bid on every single bachelor here tonight. But I'm the only one who can give you what you really want."

Her chest rises on a quick intake of breath. "What is that?" she murmurs.

I can't resist touching her one last time, and I reach out and tug on an errant curl. "An internship at The Cariston Group."

Chapter Five

Addison

"Adds? Is that you?"

I turn to see Julie hurrying toward me, dressed in a fitted, black cocktail dress, her tablet in hand. When she reaches me, she stands back and gives a whistle. "Wow. Where did you get that dress?"

I start to answer but she waves me down. "Wait, what are you doing here and was that Lachlan Cariston I saw licking your ear five seconds ago?"

A couple of women walking past us hear her and turn back to look at me. "Shhh, Jules, keep your voice down. I'm here for the auction."

She arches an eyebrow and takes me by the elbow. "This auction?" she says, steering me back towards the tables. "Which one are you sitting at?"

I point it out and we head over, weaving our way around the people still sipping champagne as they mill about the event room. "Why didn't you tell me you'd be here tonight?" she asks.

"I wasn't sure I was going to go through with it until the last minute." And it's true. I agreed to do this in Lachlan's office, but I struggled with the decision all week. His texts threw me. Fun, flirty, friendly, and definitely not sounding like a guy who spends all of his time focused on work. Between his project questions, to questions about my favorite coffee and the shows I watch, to his sweet check-ins at the end of the day, it was too easy to forget I'm doing this to get the internship I want.

After leaving his office, I kind of half thought Lachlan was kidding about having me do this until a man showed up at my apartment that evening and handed me an envelope with a black card inside. He told me he was to wait until I had activated it to ensure there were no issues. Accompanying the black card was a contract outlining the details of the internship, which made it very clear that my acceptance was contingent upon me satisfying my end of the bargain and ensuring Lachlan comes home with me tonight.

Metaphorically, of course. This is a business transaction. A service for consideration.

But the way he looked at me when he saw me talking to the firefighter didn't seem like business. The possessive way he touched me didn't feel like business.

I shake it off. Lachlan is a notorious flirt, but there's never anything behind it. It's just what he does to get what he wants. And what he wants tonight is to look like he's doing a good deed without actually having to do the deed. Although I guess he actually is doing something good, because it's his money going toward the charity, and he said I could bid on anything.

I wonder what he'd do if I actually did buy another bachelor? I probably should go out more, and Travis seems nice.

Who am I kidding? Being on the receiving end of Lachlan's attention is bringing my teenage fantasies to life. I can't help but remember that night, so long ago, when Lachlan invited our whole family to stay at one of their resorts. The place was amazing, with little luxury cottages overlooking a spectacular lake. I was fifteen and staying in one of the cottages with my parents, while Jamieson, Lachlan and their friends stayed in a cabin at the edge of the property. I woke up one night to twinkling lights and the faint sound of music drifting across the water. There was definitely a party happening somewhere. And I knew without a doubt it was my brother and his friends. I threw on a sundress and carefully closed the door behind me, thrilled by the adventure and the very secret part of myself that hoped I get to see Lachlan. Or rather, that he'd take one look at me in the dress that would give my mother a heart attack if she knew I'd snuck it into my bag, and really notice me. It was short, tight and made my boobs look amazing. As I approached the party, some girl wearing a dress even skimpier than mine threw her arms around me like I was her long-lost sister and dragged me up to the porch where two guys were engaged in a fierce beer pong match. I wandered around for a bit, trying to look like I belonged, while hoping I didn't run into my brother. I heard some girl shriek as I passed the pool area just in time to see one couple get taken down in what looked like a game of topless chicken. I remember it as though it were last night, the shock of seeing girls with their breasts bared, the smell of sunscreen, sand, beer, and the way the fairy lights twinkled around the pool. And presiding over it all, like a king on his throne, was Lachlan Cariston. He had not one, but two girls cuddled up to him on his lounger, and I felt something throb deep inside as I watched him idly playing with one girl's ponytail, lazily wrapping it around his hand before tipping her face up to his and taking her mouth in a kiss that left me heated and dizzy even as jealousy burned in my stomach.

 A hard shove to the middle of my back drove me out from my hiding spot into the glow of the lights. "Hey, if you want to be out here, it's skins only," the guy slurred as he hooked a finger into the fabric of my dress. "Let's see those pretty titties."

My face flamed as my gaze met Lachlan's. He lifted his head, eyes widening as recognition dawned. He jumped up from the lounger and my heart lifted. "Shit. Trey, get your hands off her." This was it. Lachlan didn't want this other guy touching me, he'd take me by the hand and lead me inside and tell me I was beautiful and special, and...

Suddenly, he was in front of me, frowning. "Does your brother know you're here, Baby Addy?"

I shook my head as the girl who followed him over titters at the nickname. I straightened my shoulders. "I'm not a baby, Lachlan."

"Hey man, I ain't never seen a body like hers on a baby. But if she needs a sitter, you can pass her to me."

"Shut the fuck up, Trey. She's Jamieson's little sister." His eyes darkened and he stepped between me and the drunk idiot. "Go home, Addy," he said, lifting his phone and typing out a message.

"What are you doing?" I shrieked. "You can't tell Jamieson I'm here."

"I'm not. I'm having one of the resort staff escort you back to your cottage." He put a hand on my arm and steered me away from the pool, around some ornamental potted trees and to a side gate. A few minutes later, a golf cart pulled up, the driver an older woman dressed in the resort's uniform. Lachlan waved me towards the cart with a flourish after giving the woman my cottage number with strict instructions that she was to see me inside.

"Go back to bed, little girl. You don't belong here," he said, patting me on the head like I was some sort of overgrown toddler.

"Earth to Addison." Julie snaps her fingers at me, bringing me back to the elegantly appointed gallery.

"Sorry," I mutter, shaking off the residual embarrassment. I get it now, of course and I'm grateful nothing worse happened that night besides my ego getting a little bruised. There were plenty of guys at that party who wouldn't have thought twice about my age, if they even thought to ask in the first place. I lived in fear the rest of the summer that Lachlan would tell Jamieson, but my brother never brought it up and he would have if he'd known.

"Are you going to tell me what you're doing here?" Julie frowns. "This doesn't really seem like your crowd."

Uh-oh. The terms of the non-disclosure document flit through my brain. I can't tell anyone Lachlan put me up to it. I hate lying to my best friend, but I think fast. "Jamieson put me up to it."

Her face lights up. "Oh, he wants you to get out more, too? I mean, this is a bit over the top, but I guess it works."

"It's more about the charity," I say taking a big gulp of champagne to help swallow down my discomfort.

The lights flash, indicating the show is about to start and Julie stands. "Well, that's my cue to head back to my office. I have several orders I need to go through already." She bends to give me a quick hug. "This crowd likes pretty things."

I settle back in my seat and reach for the paddle in front of me, snickering like a teenage boy when I see the number sixty-nine on the front. Two women are on stage, explaining the rules and introducing the director of the charity. Apparently, we can bid as many times as we like on as many bachelors as we can handle.

First up is a guy dressed similarly to Lachlan, in a fancy suit. While the bidding starts fast and furious, as each of the bachelors strut their stuff down the runway, I can't help but compare them to Lachlan. That guy doesn't walk with his easy confidence, like he owns every room he's in; this guy doesn't have perfectly-groomed hair that makes my fingers itch to rumple; that guy doesn't have a gaze that pins you to your spot and heats your body in all the tingling places.

I lift my paddle a few times for fun, but finally, it's time for the main event.

Lachlan's bio is read by the auctioneer, and the man adds the fact that his mother signed him up for this, which elicits a few awws and coos about what a good boy he is. I roll my eyes and tighten my grip on my paddle, heart racing for some inexplicable reason.

Lachlan strolls out, his killer smile in place, but I can see the tension in his shoulders, the chill in his eyes, even as he throws a wink, playing to the crowd.

One of the women who'd been on stage for the opening remarks starts the bidding and I tilt my head, wondering why she looks so familiar. Her silvery blonde hair is up in a high ponytail, and when she turns her head the light catches in diamond pins, making them sparkle. She whispers something to the person next to her, her pillowy lips a sharp contrast to the hollows in her cheeks. Recognition dawns when Lachlan's smile slips as she tops the last bid.

That's his ex-girlfriend.

I recall seeing pictures of them, and Jamieson talking about how awful she'd been to Lachlan. The bids fly back and forth between the ex and two other women, all of whom seem set on winning Lachlan for the evening.

On stage, Lachlan is playing to the crowd, opening his jacket, and executing a perfect runway turn as if the crowd needs more enticement. Suddenly, his gaze locks with mine, and he quirks his eyebrow in question. Slowly, I lift my paddle. I don't even remember what the last bid was.

"Five hundred thousand dollars," I shout.

Heads spin toward me, but the auctioneer doesn't even

miss a beat. "Number sixty-nine. Five hundred thousand dollars. Going once..."

I don't even hear the rest of the it, not until the auctioneer is asking everyone to join him in applause to acknowledge my generous bid.

Lachlan jumps off the stage and heads directly for me. My heart thumps in my ears. Is he going to kill me for spending that much of his money?

He stops in front of the table, sweeping a bow that triggers a longing sigh from the woman next to me. Biting my lip, I meet his blue-eyed stare, hoping he can read the apology I'm desperately trying to convey to him.

"Well, it looks like sixty-nine is my lucky number. I guess I owe you a hell of a date."

Phones are up and aimed in his direction, but he doesn't spare them a glance, instead he holds out his hand. My heart is beating a million miles a minute and flames heat my face when I feel the eyes of everyone in the room on me. Slowly, I lift my hand, not really trusting this moment, until I feel the warmth of his fingers close around mine. I rise to my feet and Lachlan smiles. It's a real smile, one that reaches his eyes, and my breath catches in my throat.

"Any special requests?

Is he kidding? What would he do if he knew how I really felt? How I've felt about him all these years? This playful side of Lachlan is beating down the defenses I thought I'd shored up against my hopeless crush.

I should play it cool, but I feel like that horse left the barn the second he asked me for this favor. Maybe it's not too late to brush it off, head home and pretend my whole body didn't light up like the Fourth of July when he put his arm around me earlier.

Chapter Six

Lachlan

Addison looks like she's seconds away from bolting. Her hand trembles slightly in mine as we make our way through the room. The event photographer motions for us to stop, and I paste on my cheesiest grin all while trying to figure out how much lead time I need to give my flight crew, because all can think about is getting her alone and dazzling her somehow.

When I heard Addison's voice ring out with that ridiculous amount of money, something snapped in my chest. The amount didn't bother me in the slightest, and as my mother relentlessly reminded me, it's going to a good cause. No, it was the way she claimed me. My whole life, I've always been the one to stake a claim first. I know it's just a charity event and in the grand scheme of things, having dinner with a woman for the sake of charity isn't a big deal, as long as it's not Paige. I wouldn't be able to sit across the table from her for fifteen minutes.

And the sad part is, crawling naked into my brother's limousine wasn't the worst thing she did. It was the manipulation, the way she crafted a life with me that didn't really include me at all, as long as she had access to the Cariston name and money. I almost fell for it.

But I never once looked across the room at Paige and felt what I did tonight when I saw Addison's smile.

"Do we have to do anything before we leave?" I ask.

"Leave?" She glances up. "We can just leave?"

"You just spent half a million dollars. I'm pretty sure you can do whatever you want."

We move into the gallery hall, away from the noise of the auction. The hall is softly lit, save for the spotlighting on the five or six sculptures on display. "I just spent half a million dollars of *your* money," she says, closing her eyes. "I'm so sorry. I don't know what happened."

"I don't care about the money."

She rubs her arms and I notice the hall is quite cool compared to the main event room. I take off my jacket and tuck it around her, ignoring her protest. It's long on her petite frame and I can't help but think she looks like a little girl in her daddy's coat.

"Thank you," she says softly. "I just need to call an uber."

"What are you talking about?" I ask.

"You want to leave. I'm going home." She frowns. "I kept up my side of the bargain and that means I'm starting my internship next week."

"I owe you a date."

Her lips part slightly. "You really don't."

"You don't want to go out with me?"

She looks away. "This deal was so you didn't have to follow through with the date, wasn't it?" She shrugs. "It's cool. We don't have to go out."

I turn her so she's facing me. And laying my hands on her

was a bad idea because I'm not sure I'm going to be able to walk away. "Are you turning me down, Baby Addy?"

Her eyes spark, burning me with their intensity. "I'm not a baby anymore." She lifts her chin, and my gaze drops to her delectable mouth.

"You're not, are you?" I move my head toward her, just an inch, giving her ample room to stop me. Instead, her hand comes out and grasps the front of my shirt, her fingers curling into my chest. "When did you grow up, Addison?"

"A while ago. You just never noticed." She licks her lips, and before I can stop myself, I close the remaining space between us, touching my mouth to hers and everything – the gallery, the auctioneer's voice from the event space, the reasons why I shouldn't be kissing her – it all fades away.

When I lift my head again, her eyes flutter open. "What was that?" she asks, a flush staining her cheeks.

"That was me telling you I've noticed." I brush my hand over her hair, threading my fingers into her curls and tip her head back up. "What do you want to do? Do you want to run home and pretend this never happened? Or do you want me to prove I'm worth the half a million dollars you bid?"

Those chocolate eyes blink up at me. "That was your money—"

My hand slides around her neck and up to grip her chin, holding her still. "I never told you how much I was worth. It was your bid. So, what do you want, Addison?"

She fists her hand tighter in my shirt, pulling me even closer. "Show me what you've got," she says, leaning up on her tiptoes, pressing her lips against mine.

I wrap my arms around her, loving the way her body melts into me and the kiss goes on and on until she breaks free with a soft moan. I tap the screen on my phone to have my car brought around and issue instructions for my crew to ready the jet.

Gripping Addison's hand tightly in mine, I tug her down the hall to the gallery entrance and we step out into the night.

The limousine is waiting, and my driver opens the door for Addison to slide inside. As she does, my coat gapes open revealing a tantalizing glimpse of her full breasts encased in red silk. I sit next to her, raising the panel between us and the driver. My hand is on her thigh and the rapid rise and fall of her chest is doing interesting things to her cleavage. I lean in and nip her bottom lip, and sanity overtakes me for a second.

My cock is aching for Jamieson's little sister.

He'll fucking kill me if I hurt her.

She's mine. I would rather die than hurt her. And with that thought, I know. I'll never hurt her. I'll spend the rest of my life treating her like a queen. My queen.

"Do you want me, Addison?"

Her eyes connect with mine and I realize I'm holding my breath. I've never asked anyone that question before. I've never had to. That's not bragging, it's reality. I'm not a troll in the looks department and I'm a Cariston, which means money, privilege and power. Usually, I'm asking myself if this is what *I* what, or if I should wait five minutes until another opportunity arises.

The second I recognized Addison in my office, her sassy attitude smacked me right in the face, and I know what I want.

I want to kiss her. I need to kiss her.

But first, I need to know she really wants this too. That she really wants me.

She nods.

"I need the words, Addison."

Her eyes widen and she leans over, the perfume from her hair making my chest tight. My coat drops from her shoulders as she shifts closer, sliding her dress up to lift her leg over my lap, straddling me. She takes my face in her hands, her thumbs gliding over my jaw. "I want you." She kisses my temple. "I want this."

My hands skate up her back, pressing her to me, as I feather kisses along her collarbone. I'm hard as a rock and her soft curves are driving me crazy. I pull the straps of her dress down, letting my mouth drift across the warm satin of her skin. She sighs as I plump her tits together, lifting them out of the confines of her dress, drawing the tight bud of one nipple into my mouth, her throaty moan nearly causing the zipper on my pants to bust. I lick and suck her nipple while she writhes on my lap and she drags my other hand up to her other breast where I pinch it gently, loving the way she shivers.

"That feels so—" she gasps as I gently scrape my teeth across the tip and grinds down on my cock. "So amazing."

We definitely have too many clothes on. I check my watch, noting that I don't have nearly enough time to savor Addison the way I want. But, I plan on making the most of the minutes I have. I ease out from underneath her and spin her so she's sitting on the seat. Then I slide down to the floor in front of her, spreading her legs and lifting them to rest on either side of my shoulders.

"What are you doing?"

"Shh." I bite the inside of her thigh, just hard enough that she squeaks in surprise. "I'm going to bury my face in your pussy. I'm going to lick it and suck your sweet pink flesh and fucking feast until I'm sated, and you can barely remember your name." I lower her legs and reach under her dress, swiping my finger up her slit, which is hot and wet and feels as perfect as I'd imagined. She quivers as I hook the sides of her panties and slide them off. I lean back just enough so she can see me as I hold them to my face and inhale her scent, watching her eyes darken in desire, before crumpling them in my fist and putting them in my pocket. They're mine now, just like her sweet pussy is about to be.

I nudge her legs open farther, licking the silky softness of her thigh and spreading her apart with my thumbs. Her hips tilt toward me and I slide my tongue through her wetness, loving the way she threads her fingers in my hair, holding me where she wants me. I tease her, licking and sucking and swirling my tongue around her clit while she moans and whimpers above me.

Her thighs clamp around my head and her nails scrape my scalp when I insert a finger into her slick channel. Tension tightens her hips and I slow the flicks of my tongue, circling her swollen flesh until I feel the first ripples cascade through her body, her pussy clenching on my finger as she comes all over face. I want her pussy choking my cock with her pulsations as she screams in my ear, but as she goes limp above me. A fierce surge of protectiveness overwhelms me. I breathe her in one last time, pressing soft kisses to her hip bones before I smooth her dress down over her legs. Her bottom lip is red and pouty from where her teeth abused it as she came apart, and the high flush of color on her cheeks make her eyes sparkle in the low light as we race toward the airport. I ease back slowly, and lift a latch on one of the seats, exposing a small storage area. I pull out a soft blanket to drape over her. She cuddles in close to me, pulling the warm cover over us both.

My cock is harder than it's ever been. I ache for her, but when she drops her hand to my lap to undo my zipper, I place my hand over hers.

"What's wrong?" she asks.

"Nothing." I drop a kiss to her head, this fragile tenderness weaving through me a completely foreign concept. "Are you satisfied?"

Her hand caresses me through my pants and I squeeze her

fingers. At this rate, I'll come in my pants like an eager boy if she keeps going.

"Well, obviously. You might have a bald spot on your head now, I'm that satisfied." She shifts against me. "But you're not. This has to be uncomfortable."

She doesn't know the half of it, but when I finally thrust balls deep into her sweet, hot pussy, I don't want to rush it. "Baby..." I bite my lip as she tenses under my arm. "That's a term of endearment."

"So is 'Daddy'," she mutters.

My cock hardens even more despite the fact that I've never thought of that particular word as sexy before. "Say that again."

She sits up, biting her lip. "You're not that old," she says smiling.

The car slows, turning into a large gated area, and I realize we're at the hangar where my plane is stored.

I check my phone, where I see a text letting me know we're about twenty minutes from boarding. The crew deserves a bonus for how fast they've readied the jet.

"This is an airport." Addison's voice sounds uncertain. "We're flying somewhere?"

"I promised you a hell of a date, remember?"

"I don't have my passport."

I frown. "I know Jamieson created a secure digital file where he scanned the important documents for your entire family. I know because he ensured all of us Caristons do the same." A small pang of guilt spears me at the thought of her brother. Jamieson will have to understand. I didn't really *see* her until now.

And now that I have, I won't look anywhere else again.

"We can just stay here for our date."

"At the airfield?"

She slides the straps of her dress up her shoulders, attempting to put herself back together. "No, here in the city."

Suddenly, I notice the way she clutches the edging of the blanket she's wrapped around herself, her knuckles white. The flush that stained her cheeks a few moments ago is gone and she's pale.

Is she having second thoughts?

Chapter Seven

Addison

I glance out the window at what I'm certain is a very luxurious private jet. I should be happy, ecstatic even, after the incredible orgasm Lachlan just gave me. His broad shoulders block the bright lights of the hangar, but behind him I see all the flight preparation activity.

This is what Lachlan does. Exactly what he wants, anytime a whim takes him. I swallow hard. It's not like I grew up poor, but the Caristons are out of everyone's league. They're like royalty and I'm second-guessing what the hell I'm doing here. Half the women in that room tonight probably could have bid on Lachlan with their pocket change. They would be used to this kind of treatment. They probably jet off on shopping trips every weekend.

I squeeze my fingers tightly, wrapping the ends of the blanket in my fists.

They probably don't need an entire pharmacy just to step onto an airplane.

I know I want to build an empire, in the hotel industry, and that means travelling. A lot. I do travel, and I manage just fine, but I am usually able to plan for it. I speak with my therapist, I do a lot of meditation, and I have an entire ritual that includes prescription drugs and a weighted vest I can zip myself into for the flight. I glance down at my flimsy dress. I'm not even wearing underwear for crying out loud. A tremor vibrates through me, sweat prickling the back of my neck. Tears blur my vision and I blink, trying to maintain control of the situation.

I want to do this. "How long before we leave?" I whisper, keeping my gaze fixed on the twists I've made in the blanket.

Lachlan places his large hand on my thigh. "Addison, what's wrong?"

I press my tongue to the roof of my mouth, hard. I'm certain most women would be giddy with excitement at the thought of being whisked away on a private jet with Lachlan Cariston. "Nothing is wrong." *Think fast.* "I'm just worried about... my plants." I swallow.

"Your plants." He says it slowly, like he's trying to figure out if I'm serious.

I lift my head. "Yes, they need water, sunshine and love, you know," I snap. God, I'm a moron. I should just walk toward the plane so the probable heart attack will kill me and put me out of my misery.

He holds up his phone. "I can take care of that. Just tell me the details for access to your place." He peers over at me. "And just in case you think I'm a weird stalker, you can use the credit card I gave you to hire a company to come in and re-set your codes when you get back."

I can take care of that. Of course he can. I sigh.

"Is there something else, Addison? If you're uncomfortable, we don't have to go anywhere."

I hate that I have this panicky feeling. People get in airplanes all day, every day. I can accomplish anything I put my mind to, but I can't get over this fear. I shake my head. "No, it's fine. I'm fine. My plants will be fine. It's all fine." There's a knock at the window and a whimper escapes me. I smile tightly at Lachlan. "Sorry, that startled me."

The door opens and I suck in a deep breath of the cool night air. Lachlan steps out of the car and holds out his hand. I force myself to let go of the blanket and grab his fingers, inching forward like he's encouraging me to jump out of the airplane.

I squeeze my eyes shut as a wave of nausea washes over me. *Don't think about jumping out of airplanes.*

I'm shaking like a leaf when I step out of the car and Lachlan's eyebrows draw together as he reaches behind me and grabs his jacket, wrapping it around me. "Addison, sweetheart, what's wrong?"

The tenderness in his voice bolsters me. I can do this. "Nothing. Let's go." I walk toward the plane, trying to count to ten and realize ten thousand might be a better objective. I must have a death grip on his fingers as we climb the stairs and I'm pretty sure I scared the attendant with a smile I'm certain was more of a grimace.

I'm momentarily stunned when I step into the interior of the plane, which looks more like high-end boutique hotel. There's art on the walls and a tray of succulents sits on a mahogany console table. A small bar area is set up near a bank of leather seats that look more comfortable than my living room furniture. Lachlan places his hand on the small of my back and gently nudges me forward to one of the plush leather seats.

The attendant follows with a bottle of champagne and my mouth sours. On stiff legs, I lower myself into the seat farthest away from the window, waving away the glass. I pull Lachlan's jacket tighter around me, the chill of the air conditioning welcome on my sweaty face, but uncomfortable on my bare arms.

Lachlan speaks briefly with the attendant who hurries to

the sliding door at the back of the plane, disappearing into what I think is a bedroom from the glimpse I saw, and returns with the plushest bathrobe I've ever seen. She hands it to me with a smile.

"Would you like to change out of your dress?" Lachlan asks.

I nod, then shake my head. I'm afraid to move. This might be the most beautiful airplane I've ever been on, but it's still an airplane, and panic is clawing its way up my throat while a thousand birds beat their wings inside my chest.

Oh god. Didn't I read an article about a plane that hit a bird mid-flight and crashed? Don't think about birds. Don't think about *anything*.

My breathing is shallow and little sparkles of light appear around the edge of my vision. I grip the arms of the seat, my fingers sinking into the cushy softness. Lachlan gets out of his seat, crouching in front of me, his hands gripping my knees. His concerned gaze warms me from the inside.

"Addison. Tell. Me. What. Is. Wrong." His voice is stern.

I shake my head.

"I can see something is wrong. We can get off this plane if you need to. Have I done something to make you uncomfortable? You don't have to do this."

"No. You haven't done anything." My whole body is screaming for me to take him up on his offer and get off this luxury deathtrap. I take a deep breath. "I'm a little bit scared of flying."

"A little bit? You're shaking like a leaf." His big hands squeeze my legs. "What do you need?"

A watery chuckle escapes me. "A lot." I lift my hand, counting on my fingers. "A pep talk from my therapist, a weighted vest, prescription drugs and to close my eyes and wake up wherever we're going."

"We don't have to go."

I clench my jaw. Smash my lips tight together. And close my eyes. I'm a grown woman. I can do this. I open my eyes and forcibly direct my body to lean forward so I can place my hands over his. "This is silly. I want to be in the hotel business. I *can* fly, it's just hard for me sometimes."

Lachlan holds my gaze. "Okay, you really want to do this?"

I nod. "I need to try and do this." My chest feels like it's being crushed as I breathe shallowly through my nausea.

"What kind of prescription drugs do you need?" Lachlan leans over me, pressing a button I didn't notice previously. The attendant appears beside us.

"Yes, Mr. Cariston? We're about ready for take-off, and we do need you in your seat for that."

He stands. "We need about ten more minutes."

A soft moan escapes me, and he turns, his eyes full of concern. I swallow down the nausea. "I don't want to cause a delay, please. I just want to move."

He steps away to speak with the attendant, who returns immediately with a small box and hands it to Lachlan. When he opens it, there is a selection of small pill bottles. "My mother generally keeps a working pharmacy on board. Please look and see if anything matches what you need."

I swallow. "Is there anything in there for anti-nausea?"

He smiles. "Absolutely." He nods to the attendant who gets me a glass of water while he passes me two small pills. Once that's dealt with, he settles into the seat next to me and we buckle in. "Do you think you can handle taking off, or do you want to give the pills a chance to work?"

"Aren't you afraid I'll throw up on your shoes?"

He shrugs. "I have other shoes." He reaches over, prying my hand off the arm rest and lifting the barriers to pull me toward him. "Just hold on to me and I'll get you through this.

But if you need the plane to land at any point, tell me, and I'll have the pilot get us down. You only have to say the word."

The thought that I have some control in the situation provides a measure of relief. I hang on to him for dear life as I'm pushed back in my seat by the force of the acceleration, shutting my eyes tightly as Lachlan repeatedly tells me to imagine that I'm on a beach, warm sand under my feet and to focus on the steady rush of the waves against the shore. His voice is deep and soothing. He gathers me closer, and I press my ear against his chest, letting the rumble of his words flow into me.

"Are we going to a beach?" I ask.

"We are, but my yoga instructor does this guided meditation, and it was all I could think of."

"Are you my therapist now?"

"I'm whatever you need me to be." He rests his chin on my head.

My chest tightens, but not from fear. A rush of tears at the tenderness in his voice prickles behind my eyes. The attendant steps through the arch and I feel Lachlan shift. "We can move around freely now." His lips brush the top of my head. "Do you want to change out of your dress?"

I've still got that shivery feeling and my arms feel like they're locked in place, but I nod. At least I don't feel like I'm going to throw up anymore. Maybe the robe will help warm me up. Lachlan eases me off him and stands, drawing me up next to him, while he gathers the robe I tossed aside. I lean into his solid strength and pretend I'm in a fancy hotel somewhere. It's easy to pretend when he steps aside for me to go into the bedroom area I noticed earlier. If I didn't feel the smooth vibration under my feet, reminding me that we're hurtling forward, suspended in a metal cylinder, I wouldn't know. Everything is cream and navy blue. The bed is piled high with soft looking pillows, a thick duvet and a cashmere blanket is folded at the foot.

Lachlan places the robe on the bed. "Everything is clean, I promise."

I reach around to undo the zipper of my dress, but Lachlan's hands are already there. "Let me." His voice is low, and he's standing so close I can feel the heat of his body down the length of mine.

I sweep my hair over my shoulder, and he leans in, blowing softly on the back of my neck. "Your hair looks so beautiful tonight," he says, as he pulls the zipper down, slowly, his fingers a caress on my newly bared skin.

My body reacts like it did in the car, instantaneously, nipples tightening as the material loosens, and my dress pools around my ankles. Lachlan groans behind me, his hands skimming over my curves. Stepping around me, he snatches the robe off the bed and looks over my shoulder as he tucks me into it, tying the belt with a firm knot.

"Why don't you lie down and try to sleep," he says, bending to pick up my dress.

"Where are you going?" What happened? One minute I thought he was going to bend me over the bed and the next he's folding back the covers like he's going to tuck me in.

Hands fisted at his side, he stands by the door, looking like he's going to bolt at any moment. "I'm just going to head back out front and get some work done."

Work? Right now?

I definitely did something wrong. Did something happen when he took my dress off? Maybe once he saw my hips and ass under the light, he realized I look nothing like his model-slim ex-girlfriend, and it turned him off.

He may be looking everywhere but at me, but I can see the bulge in his pants from here. He's clearly not turned off.

I'm not going to lie quietly wondering whether he wants me. I got on this rocket coffin to prove to myself I can do hard things. What's the worst thing that can happen?

Well, that I'll be humiliated, brokenhearted, and pretty much naked in this high-end deathtrap, I guess. But at least I'll know once and for all that I can close the door on my Lachlan Cariston fantasy.

"Do you really need to work, or do you just want to put some distance between us?" I can't believe my voice is steady as I ask this. I don't even hear a hint of the insecure teenager who is slowly dying of humiliation inside my chest.

Lachlan blinks, straightening shoulders. "I'm trying to be a nice guy here. You're not feeling well and you're my best friend's little sister."

"Were you thinking of Jamieson when you took my panties off in the limo?"

He flinches like I've actually struck him, but I need to know. I can't keep pining for a guy who isn't in my reach. Especially after the taste he gave me earlier tonight.

"Addy..."

I hold up my hand. "It's Addison. And it's fine, Lachlan. Heat of the moment and all. Go do your work." I wave him away and turn toward the bed. Maybe the comforter is heavy enough, if I wrap myself tightly, I can hide my tears and I'll be able to fall asleep. Maybe when I wake up, I'll realize this whole thing has been some sort of anxiety dream brought on by my panic about the internship.

Shit. The internship. I'll be working with Lachlan too.

Hands grasp my shoulders, spinning me around, and then Lachlan's mouth is on mine, hard, and his tongue is in my mouth, deep.

My hands are in his hair, and I moan, as he hoists me with a single arm and lays me back on the bed.

"I don't want to work," he mutters as he breaks the kiss.

"Are you thinking about my brother now?" I ask.

"Christ, Addison. Since you walked into my office, all I can think about is you. But I'm not an asshole." He strokes my hair away from my face. "You're sick and scared, and if I'm within touching distance of you, I want to have my hands on you. I want to have my mouth on you."

I'm definitely not feeling cold at the moment. "I'm feeling better right now."

He shifts and my robe parts enough for me to open my legs, and I gasp as his hips settle against mine. "You're better than a weighted vest."

"What is a weighted vest?"

"It's like a thunder coat for humans." He frowns in confusion. "Have you heard of weighted blankets?"

He nods slowly. "Yes, I just read an update on them, as we've added them as room options in the hotels."

"Right, so it's the same thing, only a vest I can wear for flying. It helps with anxiety."

"Well, I can lie here the entire flight and be your blanket if you need me to."

I shift and he groans slightly, lifting himself off me. "I'm sorry," he says.

"Why are you apologizing?"

"Because I meant what I said earlier. I don't know what it is. I don't know why you were a little girl to me one minute and last week... it's like I noticed you for the first time. And I didn't just notice you. I had a visceral reaction to you."

"I haven't been a little girl for some time."

"I get that. I do. I guess in my mind, you belonged in a category of girls that were just off-limits." He bends and kisses me softly on the lips. "If I was just fucking around, you'd still be off-limits."

"You're not just fucking around?" My heart slams in my chest.

"No, I'm not. This feels different. When you screamed out that number, you sealed the deal, baby. Like it or not, you bought me, lumps and all."

I smirk at the thought of him being some kind of disappointing grab bag. "Like you have any lumps."

He rolls his hips, pressing his cock against my cleft, the material of his pants abrading my heated flesh. "I might have one or two." He dips his head again, drinking me in like he has all the time in the world.

The plane drops slightly, and we experience a few bumps that make me gasp, but Lachlan simply wraps his arms around me, licking a path from the column of my neck, down to my breasts, leaving my skin electrified. He kneels up, quickly removing his shirt and flinging it on the floor before undoing his pants and shoving them off. His body is big and thick, and my mouth waters as my gaze drifts down from his broad shoulders to his muscular chest, to tapered hips, and my lungs stutter out a breath when I see his cock. He is big and thick *everywhere*.

I don't have a moment to think before he's back, his weight heavy and reassuring over me. I arch as much as I can, my breasts brushing against the edges of the soft robe.

"Tell me what you need, Addison," his voice is a low growl in my ear.

"I need you, Lachlan."

"You need me to touch you?" His hips press forward again as he leans up, parting the robe so it frames my breasts, revealing and restraining them at the same time. My nipples hard and aching in the cool air between our bodies, but all I can do is nod.

"Like this?" He rubs just the tip of his thumb over the aching peak, the feather-light touch sending lightening arcs through my body. His eyes are on mine as he does it again, watching my body shiver. "You like this."

His light, teasing touches intensify and he pinches one aching nub, making me groan. His hand skims down my body, sliding over my hip and between my legs. "You really like this." He circles my clit, with the same light caress. "You're so wet."

He rubs his cock along the seam of my pussy, watching my reaction. "I want to know everything you like. Everything that turns you on. I want the sound of my voice to make your body ache and the sight of my hands to cause you to soak your panties because you know what I can do to you." He slips inside, notching himself against me. "So hot and wet for me, aren't you?"

I nod, lifting my legs to dig my heels into the backs of his thighs. I want him closer. The empty ache inside me builds and I cry out as his warm mouth closes around a nipple, alternating between hard pulls of his lips and gentle strokes of his tongue.

I can't take it any longer. My body feels like it's on fire. "Lachlan, please."

Chapter Eight

Lachlan

Her eyes drift shut as her plea stutters out brokenly. My dick is hard as steel, her slickness is coating me, those hard, pink nipples are like candy under my tongue. I quickly rearrange her robe, not wanting her to be cold, but needing to see those luscious globes, heavy and perfect, jiggling with every shiver she makes. I lift her tits, tightening the robe around them so they're plumped up for my mouth. I suck on each one, loving Addison's breathy little moans, the way her legs widen, her little heels digging into my thighs, urging me on.

I don't want this to be fast. As much as I want to fuck her, I want to savor it. Having a taste of her in the car didn't satisfy me in the least. I want to have her under my tongue again, writhing and crying and spilling her sweet cream all over my face. I grip my cock, hard, trying to keep myself in check as I slide it through the wetness between her legs. As I gentle my mouth, back to the teasing, light touches that seem to drive her wild, I wonder at the exquisiteness laid out before me. She's so perfect, so responsive, and I want to keep going just to see if I can make her come just like this.

Her sweet begging intensifies, and I can't hold back any longer. With a final pinch to her nipple, her broken cry echoing in my ear, I lift myself up, loving the way she reaches for me, her eyes wild.

"I'm just getting a condom, love." But I can't stand to be separated from her for even a few seconds, so I grip the front of her robe, hauling her into my arms and tuck her against my chest. I reach back, yank the drawer next to the bed open, and feel around until I find the box I know is there. I grab it, fumbling with the plastic with my free hand.

Addison pulls me back down on top of her, legs spread wide as she wiggles under me. "Hurry," she says her hands sliding over her body, down to my cock. When I feel her small hand wrap around me, I nearly come then and there.

I grip her wrist. "Naughty girl."

She pouts. "It's taking too long." She eyes the box. "I want to feel you inside me. Raw." She whispers the last part, and something breaks in my chest. "I'm on the pill and I haven't been with anyone in a long time." She looks away.

"I haven't been with anyone either."

Her eyes fly to mine. "But, Addison, I want to do this right. I meant what I said, I'll never hurt you. It's my job to protect you."

"I trust you."

Her words fill me up and I drop the box. "Are you sure?"

She nods and reaches for me again. "Please, Lachlan."

I shift again, rubbing the tip around her opening. "You beg so prettily, love." I push in slowly, her pussy spreading around my cock. It's snug but she's so wet, I slip in easily and I love knowing I made her this hot, this eager.

I lean over her, caging her between my arms, as I surge in, that first thrust like heaven, feeling her pussy grip my cock and ripple as I dip my head, swiping my tongue over one of her nipples. She's like honey, the way the sweetness hits my tongue and slowly intensifies, the soft, thick luxurious feel of it in my mouth. I sink into her welcoming body, feeling her tense under me as I lazily circle her taut peak and draw back, her pussy grasping at my cock. "Tell me how it feels, sweetness."

"It feels good," she groans the last word as I slowly push forward again, watching her eyes flutter close. "I want..," her head rolls back and forth. "I want—"

I press again, rolling my hips, stretching her open beneath me, feeling her slickness on my balls. "What do you want?"

She stutters out a breath, lifting her hips, as I slow even more, dragging myself back while she whines, trying to press me deeper with her heels against my thighs.

I still inside her, dropping a hand between us and find her clit with my thumb, loving the way her legs clench around me. "Tell me, sweetness." I keep my touch light, not moving, even though the way she's pushing herself onto my cock makes me want to pound into her softness.

Her fingernails rake down my sides. "I want it hard."

Her words electrify me, lightning streaking down my spine. I thrust in, to the hilt, watching her beautiful mouth open on a gasp. Her neck arches and her nails curl into my muscles, leaving little crescents. I want to tattoo her marks on me so I can remember this moment exactly. The moment she claimed me.

I pull out, her strangled cry echoing in my ears, and I lean down to capture her mouth with mine, plunging my tongue inside as my hips surge back against hers. "No more teasing, sweetness, I promise."

I slam back inside, pushing her up the bed. The wild tangle of dark hair against her white robe, her lips red from my kiss, her plum-colored nipples moving with the force of my thrusts, is an image I never want to leave my brain.

Chapter Nine

Addison

I feel like I'm flying. Even better, there's no fear, just this spiraling pleasure he's wringing from my body as he pounds me into the cloud-like mattress. His hand slides under my back and he lifts me slightly to suckle one of my nipples and pleasure streaks through me. His weight presses me down as I feel his other hand slide between us and he stretches me open with his fingers so every hard thrust hits my clit, jolting little shocks of sensation that push me closer and closer to the edge.

"I feel you, Addison," he grunts. "I feel your greedy, little pussy tightening on my cock. You're going to come all over it, aren't you? You're going to drench my dick with your sweet honey."

"Yes," I cry as he slaps against my sensitive flesh, his dirty words making me as hot as his hands and tongue.

"But you like my mouth on these pretty tits, don't you?" He captured a nipple between his teeth and bites gently and my entire body clenches, the orgasm ripping through my muscles as he leans over me, pumping into me harder and harder as he chases my pleasure, spilling himself into my melting body with a hard groan.

His thrusts slow and he circles his hips as he withdraws, growling again when my pussy contracts around him. He kisses my forehead, gathers the sides of my robe closed and cuddles me next to him. "Fuck, sweetness. I don't even have words for that." Smoothing my hair back, he tips my chin up so I can see his face. His beautiful cheekbones are ruddy, and his hair is loose, hanging over his eyes, which are concerned as he searches mine. "Are you okay? I didn't mean to go so hard."

"I wanted it exactly like that." Happiness steals through me and I swallow it down. What we shared was amazing, but this is Lachlan Cariston. I'm sure every woman he's ever been with has felt amazing afterwards.

He frowns. "Hey. Your words don't match the look in your eyes. Are you still scared? I will hold you tight in my arms until we get there. I'll be your weighted blanket."

His words warm me, but I feel shy, uncertain and all to aware of the mess I'm probably making on this gorgeous comforter. "I should go clean up," I say slipping out from under his arm. I head to the washroom and close the door behind me. The inside looks nothing like an airplane washroom. It's small, but beautiful, with a marble counter and brushed gold accents and there's even a shower. I grip the counter, my knuckles whitening around the edge.

What just happened? And should I trust it?

Tears flood my eyes and I wipe them away impatiently. I'm not some silly teenager anymore with stars in her eyes whenever her brother's best friend pays the slightest bit of attention to her.

Although the tenderness between my legs and my overly sensitive breasts reminds me that Lachlan's attention wasn't exactly slight. What do I do now?

A soft knock at the door makes me jump.

"Addison, are you alright?" Lachlan's concern is a balm to my doubts, but I still don't know. Did I lose everything by leaving with him tonight?

"I'm fine." I look in the mirror at my tangled hair and red-rimmed eyes. I just had my world rocked like never before. I should be an adult and take it for what it is. But my poor heart is already aching.

My gaze snaps to the door as I hear the handle turn. Lachlan steps into the small space, looking uncertain, as he rakes his hair back.

"I don't want to invade your privacy, but you don't sound fine." His gaze drops to the death-grip I have on the counter. "Tell me what you need."

"Why?"

He's taken aback by my question. "What do you mean, why?"

"You don't have to worry about this." My gaze skitters away, and I see a stack of white fluffy facecloths in a basket next to the sink. I snatch one up and turn the water on, wetting it in the warm stream before pressing it to my burning eyes. I can only assume this overwhelming emotion must be the result of the adrenaline crash from my earlier fear.

Lachlan takes the cloth from my hand. "What is it you think I'm worrying about?" His eyes meet mine in the mirror.

"That I'm going to tell my brother about this." I shrug. "That I'm going to become obsessed with you and follow you around the office, embarrassing you and reminding you about the time you slipped up with the intern." My voice fades at the end. God, maybe he won't even follow through with the internship. I swallow hard.

He sighs, placing the cloth on the sink and wraps his arms around me from behind. He looks like a prince from a fairy tale with his rumpled, dark hair that somehow still looks as styled as when he walked down the runway, and his bright, blue eyes framed with inky lashes. In comparison, I look like a bedraggled peasant from one of those movies where all the villagers are in burlap sacks. My hair is a tangled mess and mascara is smudged around my eyes.

"First of all, our messaging back and forth made one thing clear – you're going to be an amazing intern for The Cariston Group. And not because of whatever is between us. In fact, if you are concerned, I'll ensure you report to someone other than me for the project." He nods. "As for the rest of it, do you think I'm worried about any of that?" He shakes his head. "I know this happened fast, but I don't regret anything about us." He drops a kiss on top of my head. "Well, I regret that you are questioning it."

"How could I not question it? You've been around forever, and you've never noticed me the way that I…" I trail off, but I see his eyebrows narrow at my words.

"The way that you what, sweetness?" His fingers skim up my arm sending a riot of shivers through me.

"Oh, come on, Lachlan. You never noticed me mooning after you whenever you were around?"

He shakes his head. "I'm sorry. You were closer in age to Laird and Kingsley and I… well, I guess I never noticed you as anything other than Jamieson's sister. You were Baby Addy."

"But not anymore." He turns me in his arms. "When I saw you in my office, it was like someone had opened the blinds and let the sun shine in. It was instant attraction for me. And then all week, texting with you, your funny little quips and ideas. I looked forward to hearing from you, learning what you liked, having you share your day with me. I was so worried you weren't going to show up to the auction."

"You just wanted to get back at your mother."

"No. At first, I wanted to control the auction and the bidding for me. I didn't want to end up on a date with—"

"Your ex?" I ask, drily, glancing up at him.

"You know about that?"

"Lachlan, everybody knows about that. You guys were like a soap opera couple or something."

"A soap opera is a good description. There was a lot of drama. Too much drama."

I bite my lip. "Did she break your heart? Is that why you didn't want to end up with her?"

He tilts my chin up. "At the time, I was embarrassed. I... I don't know that I would say I was hurt, even though that's what she was going for. She accused me of having no feelings, of being in love with my work, my image. She said if I wasn't a Cariston, she would never have wasted her time with me."

I gasp. "That's terrible." My eyes narrow. "What a bi—"

He strokes his thumb across my lip. "So fierce on my behalf." He shrugs. "My whole life, everyone expected me to take care of things, including myself, and I'm good at it. I'm good at taking care of things. And maybe I was cold and unfeeling and married to my work, or maybe I just hadn't found the right person. So back to your earlier point. I don't care if you tell your brother about this. In fact, I'm going to be the one to tell him about us, because there isn't anything for him to worry about. This isn't a fling to me." He lowers his voice. "I hope it isn't one for you."

A tremor runs through me. Fairytales aren't real. Falling for someone in a week isn't real. Although, the tightness in my chest reminds me that something has happened here, between us. The way he took care of me. He really is good at it. Something blossoms in my chest, a little sprout of hope that I want to nurture.

I don't want to lose this feeling. "It isn't a fling for me either."

"I know you're scared, but you were scared to get on this plane, and you did it anyway." He raises his hand, cupping my cheek. "Every time you feel a shred of doubt, I want you to remember I'm by your side." He grins, leaning in to bump his nose with mine. "Not just by your side, but around you, behind you, on top of you. I'll be your weighted blanket whenever you need one. Every single night, for as long as you want."

I sigh, tipping my face up and brush my lips against his. I know I don't just want him for a night, I want him for a lifetime. "How many nights does five hundred thousand dollars buy me?"

"How about we start the bidding at forever?"

I smile as he wraps his arms around me. "Bidding on a billionaire was a pretty good deal."

"I promise you'll never regret it."

He nudges me out of the washroom and back into the bedroom, where he tips us both onto the bed. I snuggle into his arms and press my ear to his chest, letting the steady sound of his heartbeat lull me to sleep.

Who would have thought facing my fears would bring me my fairytale ending.

About the Author

Darby Fox writes deliciously naughty contemporary romance that she hopes tempts her readers to stay in bed all day with a good book. Her stories feature rockstars, billionaires and other swoon-worthy heroes who usually fall first and fall hard making for an extremely satisfying happily-ever-after. She is living her own happily-ever-after with her own real-life hero, a tween princess determined to steal her shoes and a prince charming-in-training.

Follow Darby here: https://www.facebook.com/darbyfoxauthor

https://www.bookbub.com/authors/darby-fox

https://amzn.to/3vN1oxU

Or join her newsletter to get exclusive news, freebies and more! http://bit.ly/3m8e9z7

Inn Love or Money

Ida Duque

Blurb

About *Inn Love or Money*

Don't miss Inn Love or Money, Ida Duque's addition to Romancing the Billionaire collection.

Alma and her friends have finally opened the bed-and-breakfast they've worked so hard for. Alma is positive, driven, and completely focused on the success of their new business. She's also hilariously obsessed with zombies.

When both a hurricane and a mysterious stranger show up on opening week, Alma might lose not only her business but worse than that, her heart. Will Alma figure out how to save both in time?

Chapter One

Alma

We actually did it! *Oh. My god. It's opening week.*

A few years ago, me and my best friends from college, Leyla, Julie, Christy and Maria decided it would be a great, – no– an *amazing* idea to open up a hotel in South Florida. Fast forward to three hundred years of paperwork and an extensive renovation later and here we are. Not with a hotel but with a small bed and breakfast.

It is a twelve-room, Mediterranean-inspired, bed and breakfast in the city of Coral Gables and after extensive renovations, she is gorgeous. *Yes, I am aware that I am referring to the house as female.* Also, just to clarify, I meant three years of paperwork and renovations. You do realize, it would be impossible for me to be three hundred and thirty-five years old, unless I was in fact a vampire. As much as I love vampire and zombie movies, I'm definitely not one. I'm your average run of the mill Cuban-American girl living in Miami.

Me, non-zombie, non-vampire, is only a regular hospitality industry professional, stressing out about a brand-new venture and hoping it all goes according to plan. It's our first week in business and it's been busy. We've been booked back-to-back and I couldn't be happier for us.

Once upon a time, I was a semi-influencer. I use that term lightly as I don't consider myself one and for me, it was a means to an end. I traveled the world on a cruise and documented the whole thing on social media. In the beginning, it was mostly because I was bored, then because I was broke and towards the end, because it was cool to share my experiences with people who have no idea what it was like to actually live on a cruise ship.

Thanks to sponsored posts, some affiliate posts and advertising revenue and the time I did it, I made a nice chunk of money. I saved most of it, and thanks to that, I was able to invest in this venture. Originally, we were looking at places in North Florida. I was not happy about the Miami location. I'll be honest and say I was looking for a fresh start somewhere else, but still, I guess it all worked out in the end.

After my cruising adventure ended and we started this project, I quickly pivoted. I started sharing the whole experience of remodeling an old Spanish house and turning it into a bed and breakfast near Miami.

I was lucky that my high school circle of friends were well-off and many of them went on to become models, influencers or yachters. In all honesty, I had to call in every favor owed to every nepo baby in South Florida. Kind of. Sort of. I mean they were my friends at some point; some were just friendly, but still.

In case you're wondering, a nepo baby is the offspring of a famous person, who follows their parents into their career. *Nepotism.* And no, my parents are not celebrities. What they are is very wealthy and annoying. My Cuban American parents are waiting for me to come home, marry well and make *more* Cuban Americans. Which, truth be told, I have no intention of doing.

On the other hand, I'm happy to report that our plan worked. I spent months sharing updates on social media, making videos, creating perfectly timed posts, crafting the perfect fliers and sharing as much as I could through social influencers. In the end, we created a huge buzz around opening week and managed to book the whole month solid. It seems that everybody wants to be here and be the first. Including some very respectable clientele.

My goal? Five-star designation. Even better, if we can break a record on how fast we do it. *Let's go!*

Since I love cooking, I've spent this week making breakfast and yummy treats for our guests. I'm also making afternoon cookies and brownies and fresh tea and coffee. I'm still considering if we'll host an evening wine reception with light bites or keep it simple with evening wine and a cheese, fruit and crackers charcuterie set-up.

Typically, after breakfast and daily checkouts, the craziness tends to die down. After I clean the kitchen, I head over to our registration desk. Julie and her brother Ben intercept me. "Hey, can you come with me?" she asks. "Ben man the desk so that we can have a quick team meeting."

"Oh, sure." I look at her cute brother and give his sculpted body a quick rundown. He winks at me.

Julie wiggles a finger at me. "Hey, stop it. No flirting with the brother."

"He's the one flirting with me."

"You're hot," said brother smirks and I laugh out loud. We're both laughing now, and he kisses the side of my head as I walk past him. I have no interest in the guy. He's like a brother to me and it's all in good fun. Not too long ago Ben's best friend, Alex, fell in love with Julie. Ben didn't agree but eventually, they worked it out. These days Ben loves to tease her about it. I guess he's trying to give her a taste of her own medicine. *She is not amused.*

I walk with Julie to the little house. It's located on the back of the property, and originally, it was a guest house. Now it's our base of operations. When I walk in, I see everybody gathered in front of the flatscreen TV attached to the wall, facing our huge conference table. *Okay.* "Did I miss something? Is the zombie apocalypse finally starting? Did South Beach finally go underwater?" I ask nobody in particular as I get close to the group. When I look at the TV, I see it.

It's the middle of July and there's a huge hurricane forecast cone on screen. The next picture has the spaghetti model that makes no sense to anybody and is the summer joke of all South Floridians. Except this one has Miami smack in the middle of several of the lines that go across the state. *That's not good.*

Obviously, we knew it was coming. But it takes days for hurricanes to reach North America, and I've been too busy this week to watch TV and keep up with the news.

I stand nearby, frozen, and join my friends as we all stare mindlessly at the screen. We wait for the weatherman to say something about the path of this storm. The truth is, I don't even have to wait for him to say. I already know what he's going to say. I suspect all of my friends do too, but still, we wait.

Finally, he confirms it. As it stands now, the storm, currently a Category Two, will probably be a direct hit over Miami as a Category Two or a Three. *Oh my god.*

Chapter Two

Alma

Less than five minutes later, the mayor is on TV. He immediately institutes a shelter-in-place and evacuation for coastal areas.

We all look at each other. I almost wait for all of us to run around like cartoon characters. But thankfully, we don't. Instead, we're all frozen in place. "Guys... Guys!" I finally hear Alex, our architect, and Julie's boyfriend. We all turn our attention to him.

He stands up, his hands on the table. "You guys have to cancel everybody right now. Get on the phone. Get everybody out of here," he says calmly.

"No, no, no. We can't. We just opened. It's our first week. We cannot *afford* to cancel everybody." Julie's saying from her chair. She's right. We've invested a lot of money and if we do as he asks, we'll have zero income.

"Julie, you can and you will. You have to. We cannot guarantee the safety of all of these people. We need to cancel everybody. Then we need to secure the big house and our own houses." He pauses and looks at Julie, then at the rest of us.

"Guys, it's going to be fine." *Is it, though?* I mean, it's a hurricane. There's no way to stop this thing. It's a huge natural phenomenon, and it's coming straight for us. "I need to make some calls. I have a few projects that need to be secured against hurricane-force winds." Before anyone can say anything, he turns and grabs his cell.

"Wait. Wait one second," Maria says wide-eyed. "Will the house blow away?"

That's an excellent question. I glance at her. We're all holding our breaths and waiting for Alex to answer.

"Unless it's a direct hit by a Category Four, no, it shouldn't. I promise the house will be fine." He looks around the room as he says it. "Ladies, the house will be fine. I'll make sure of it," he repeats in a softer voice. I look at my partners, and we all exhale. *Okay, that's good.* As long as the house doesn't blow away, we're good. *Right?*

Alex is cool and collected when he says, "I'll come back later in the day, or I'll send a crew to board and secure the big house. Maybe we'll get extra wood and Jason, Ben, and I can board this one up too." He pauses and takes a breath. "It's going to be fine. In the meantime, Jason and Cristina can work on the accounting. See how much money we need to refund. Leyla, find out who needs a flight before the airport shuts down. Get them out of here. Maria, do your thing." Finally, looking at me, he says, "Go and man the desk. You're the reason many of them are here, go and reassure them that everything is fine." I nod.

Obviously, the five of us have spent years working in hospitality but out of everybody here, he's the only person with small business experience. His family has been in business successfully for years. It's reassuring to know they have our backs.

We spend the day doing exactly that. We help people get home, make calls to everyone we can think of, we call even more favors to people that we went to university with and that work in hotels in the area and outside of the area.

Finally, it's nighttime. Thankfully, the big house is secure. We were able to get all of our guests out safely, and the guys are currently outside boarding up the little house. All things considered, we're okay.

My partners and I are all in the living room. Maria works on risk assessments. We're throwing numbers, adjusting numbers, and working on a new opening plan for November. Unfortunately, we're set to lose half of the bookings for the month. *Our opening month.* It's disheartening. At the same time, it's better to be safe than sorry. We'll deal with the rest later.

I'm about to start a list of things for our new opening in November when I hear a noise coming from the stairs. It sounds like someone is talking and coming *down*. We all freeze. "Dude, if it's a ghost, I'm out of here. A haunted house is a no-no for me. I don't do ghosts, absolutely not," Maria whispers, shaking her head.

"Did we forget anyone?" I look at my friends. They all nod or shrug. Maria has a mild panicked face. I guess she doesn't deal well with ghosts. To be honest, me neither. I love zombie and vampire movies, but if a ghost or a vampire shows up, I'm out of here. And for the record, I do realize how ridiculous this whole thing sounds.

A second later, a tall guy appears. He puts his phone in his back pocket and looks up. He most definitely does not look like a ghost. *A vampire? Maybe?*

We all look at each other in a mild panic. *Oh shit. It's a guest.*

Chapter Three

Alma

At that moment, Alex, Ben, and Jason are all walking through the door, having boarded up the little house. As promised, earlier Alex sent a crew of his people to take care of the big house. The three of them stop talking, almost crashing against each other. My friends and I are speechless.

"*Buenas noches*," the stranger says with a sexy Spanish accent. He looks around at us. We're in front of him, and the boys are not too far off his side. "*Todo bien?*" He wants to know if everything is okay. Everything is *not* okay, this is like a grownup version of *Home Alone*. We almost left *him* home alone. *Literally.* I almost want to slap my forehead. Actually, I'm thinking slapping both my hands on my face while I scream, like the titular child, might be more fitting. *Or not.*

He's glancing back and forth between the two groups and looks adorably confused. Because the house has been boarded up, it's darker than usual here. He's around six feet tall, with piercing blue eyes, and a chiseled jaw. Actually, he's the most beautiful man I've ever seen.

Christy, who is next to me, pushes my mouth closed with

her index finger. I look at her. "Close it," she whispers with a crooked eyebrow. I do as she says, then turn back to the guy. *Holy shit.* Where did *he* come from?

His eyes land on me but he's serious and he's not saying anything.

"*Buenas noches,*" Alex says in perfect Spanish. "*Estamos cerrados.*" *We're closed*, he informs the stranger. "*Viene un huracán hacia Miami.*" For a few hours, I forgot that a hurricane was actually coming to Miami. Hearing Alex tell the stranger, reminds me.

"*Cuando?*" the stranger asks, brows furrowed. He wants to know *when*.

"*Mañana,*" Alex replies. "*Desafortunadamente, tienes que irte.*" *Unfortunately, you have to go*, Alex is saying. "We have a shelter-in-place order for the next three days. I mean– *Tenemos–*"

"I understand," the stranger replies. "I speak English. I attended university here in Miami for hospitality." There's a few nods and a little murmur of people talking. He runs a hand through his hair and looks at us. "I'm sorry, I'm jet-lagged. I flew in this morning, and I've been sleeping all day. Where is everybody? The other guests?"

The good news is he's a guest and not a ghost. Bad news, what the heck do we do with him now?

Julie replies, "Gone. We helped everybody find bigger hotels, rent cars or fly home before they close the airport tomorrow morning. We're a small operation, and we're brand new, we wanted people to be safe. What's your name?"

"Lucas. *Me llamo Lucas. Con permiso,*" he walks through the living room. He just excused himself and walked to a far corner of the room. He pulls out a cell phone from his pocket and starts making calls.

The guys are now next to us. "Should one of us call an

airline? See if we can get him out of here?" Julie asks. I raise my hand and tell her I'll do it. "Can somebody else call hotels and car rentals?" Two of my friends raise their hands.

"Okay, we came to get a few things, we'll finish securing the little house and we'll be back soon." Alex glances at the guy. I have a feeling he doesn't want to leave us alone with him but there's a hurricane coming. *Priorities.* Not to mention, it's five against one. I'm sure we'll be fine.

The five of us huddle together. I glance at the stranger pacing at the far end of the living room. He's on the phone, I'm assuming trying to get out of the city but based on this face, it's not going well. Can't say it's going better for us.

"You guys, he looks familiar, but I can't remember where I've seen him," Julie says, peering at the guy.

"He said he came here for university *and* hospitality. He looks around our age, maybe we saw him around campus, but we just never talked to him," Leyla says. Makes perfect sense to me.

In the blink of an eye, an hour goes by. All of us are on our phones or laptops when the guys return a short while later. Ben comes my way and sits next to me, an arm behind my back, probably to tease Leyla, who immediately notices and shakes her head. I try not to laugh.

"What's the story?" Alex asks as the boys sit in between us, pulling chairs as needed.

I take a deep breath. "Nothing. We can't get him a flight anywhere in time. There are no cars, and the hotels are completely full or evacuated." I pause. "In other words, he's stuck here." I look at my friends.

Alex rubs his face with his hands, then drags them down his face with a sigh. "Lucas!"

When Alex calls him, he walks in our direction, pulls a chair, and sits across from me.

Lucas glances at everybody as he talks. We learn that he's in town for business. He's attending a conference next week and would rather stay around town, but unfortunately, there's nowhere for him to go. "I called a few hotels too, friends that work in hotels and nothing," he's lamenting.

"I have an idea. Can Carlos take him to the dorms?" I ask, looking at Leyla.

"That's not going to happen. Carlos is on campus trying to get students home, and those that can't leave, like international students, will go into local shelters with a few staff." Carlos, her boyfriend, is the student dean at the local university.

Glancing at the stranger, Julie says, "I think Alma or Maria should take him." She glances at the both of us. "You're single," she mouths, looking at me. Yes, Maria and I are single, but what does that have to do with anything? I raise an eyebrow.

Maria is shaking her head and pointing at her laptop with her hand. "Yeah, I don't think so. Has anybody noticed that he didn't give us his personal information? No offense." She glances at him. "All we have is the name and address of a company... in Spain. We're not taking a complete stranger to our homes. I'd like to *not* get murdered, thank you very much."

"You're so dramatic. His company is paying a shit ton of money for him to be here for a week. He's a businessman, here on business. Why would he come to Miami to murder people when he could easily do that in Spain?" Julie asks.

When Maria replies, "A businessman who comes to Miami to murder people. It's the perfect alibi!" we all groan. Yep, she's the dramatic one in our group. "I'm just saying, you never know, and I'd rather be safe than sorry." She glances at him again. She's completely unapologetic for her behavior. I can't tell if she's scared shitless, clueless or just doesn't care that he might kill our reputation. One bad review on Yelp. That's all it takes.

Lucas raises a hand and waves. For a full minute, I forgot he was here. "You guys know that I can hear you, right?"

"So, what do we do with him?" Maria asks, looking around the group again.

"I have another idea," Julie says. This time, I'm afraid to hear it. "Instead of taking him home, maybe one of us– one of you, can stay here with him." Her hand pointed at me and Maria as she said it.

Maria is shaking her head. *No!* She mouths.

"You guys, I'm still here," Lucas says. "Maybe I'll just leave so you guys can close up and go home. I'll figure it out."

"Wait. Wait. We're not going to leave you in the city in the middle of the hurricane. We're usually nice people. I mean–"

"Alma," Alex says. I look at him. He's sitting down with one arm across the arm of the chair and the other behind Julie. He's micro-nodding at me but I have a gut feeling so I go with it.

Go big or go home... or something.

I wait a beat. "Okay. I will... stay here with him. I don't have any family, kids or boyfriends– I mean boy-friend, one is more than enough," I correct quickly. "If you think about it, besides getting murdered, I'll be safe here; we own the place. What could possibly go wrong?"

"Is this a rhetorical question?" Maria asks. "I worked in risk management. I can think of ten things that could go wrong, starting with the hurricane coming our way, destroying the house, with you in it, all the way up to you getting chopped into tiny little pieces." She touches her thumb and index finger as she says it. *Ouch. That's a grim picture.*

When I glance at him, he's looking straight at me. This murdering thing... maybe I should think this through.

Before I can say anything, Julie jumps in. Followed by everyone. Because that's what you do when there's a hurricane coming. You find a handsome stranger in your hotel and you have less than twelve hours to figure something out, so you descend into chaos, like *Lord of the Flies*, and lose all ability to govern yourselves. For a second, I picture the five of us and the four boys on an inhabitable island.

Thankfully, no chaos is necessary and after a little back and forth discussion, Alex and Maria finally agree, as do the rest of my friends, that I should stay with him.

Jason takes Christy home around the same time Carlos arrives to pick up Leyla. Alex and Ben take Julie home, and I tell Maria to go with them.

Thankfully, my roommate Christy and her boyfriend Jason return less than an hour later with a bag full of clothes and makeup. *Yes!*

After they're gone, I take the room next to Lucas, and settle in. All things considered, I can think of worse places to be during a hurricane than a brand-new bed-and-breakfast in a recently remodeled charming old house. She is beautiful. *Yes, I mean the house.*

A couple of hours later, I go down to the kitchen for dinner. It's not long before he shows up, no doubt hungry. I honestly don't think he's eaten much today. "Hey," he says, approaching me slowly.

"Hi. Hungry?" He nods. I make turkey, cheese and egg sandwiches on buttered croissants. Mangoes are in season, and I cut one. This was supposed to be tomorrow's breakfast, so I have everything I need on hand.

For now, I've taken over the brand-new kitchen. I love to cook. The truth is, during college and for the few years I lived alone afterward, the kitchen became my place of refuge. One might say, it's because it's the only place I felt in control and to an extent, I do recognize that's true. At the same time, not only is cooking a great way to relieve stress, but home—cooked meals made from scratch are cheaper, they taste better, they're usually healthier, and since you made them, you always know what's in them.

These days, I enjoy making our guests happy with my cooking. I'm fulfilling the *breakfast* part in our bed and breakfast. I'm re-discovering joy and satisfaction. Not to mention, amazing conversations come up over food. As a social person, I love meeting people and making new friends.

Lucas is sitting across the counter from me, and I serve him. I plate mine, but before I eat it, I take a picture of it. Occasionally, I glance at him as he eats. He is very quiet, throwing glances at me from time to time but not making conversation. He's not rude per se, but I get the impression he doesn't want to be my BFF. Much less take pictures of food or commiserate about our social media pages. After we eat, he says thank you and leaves.

Since we were busy helping guests get home, most of the rooms were left in disarray. With nothing else to do, I go around the house cleaning and restocking toiletries. If anything, this will keep me busy for a few hours. It also means we'll be ahead when we open in a few days. *Win-win.*

After I clean up and go to bed, I notice that the weather is changing. The wind and the rain are picking up in intensity. I know that Alex said the house is safe, and it's completely boarded up, but in the back of my mind, I still worry. We've invested a lot of time and money into this venture. We'll be closed for at least four days, and we've lost over half of the reservations for the upcoming weeks. This and similar thoughts keep me up. *It's going to be a long night.*

Chapter Four

Lucas

Shit. I'm stuck here. I'm stuck in a brand-new hotel with clueless owners. *Outstanding.* I spent an hour calling anybody I can think of in South Florida, and abroad, and so far, nothing. No room, no flights, not even a car to drive away. I call my best friend in town and he's stuck *outside* of Miami.

After an hour, I look up at the five girls huddling together. They keep glancing my way, no doubt trying to decide what to do with me.

This is South Florida. Don't they have a plan for this sort of thing? Amateurs.

Fortunately, or unfortunately, after a little back and forth, they agreed to let me stay. Which, honestly, I am grateful for. Spending the night in a hard seat at the packed airport or outside, in the middle of a tropical storm, is not appealing to me.

There's five of them but only one volunteered to stay. Of course, it had to be her. I noticed her when I checked in, but she barely glanced at me this morning, and I don't think she remembers checking me in.

On the other hand, I noticed her immediately. She has light brown hair, hazel eyes and is taller than the other girls by a couple of inches. She must be around five foot nine or ten. *She is stunning.*

Finally, they all leave, and the girl, whose name I learn is Alma, settles in the room next to mine. Fun fact, Alma means soul in Spanish. I wonder if she knows that. Although, since this is Miami and they all look Latinas, I have a feeling that she does.

Once in my room, I grab my phone and search for her online. As it turns out, she's spent the last few years working on cruise ships. How do I know that? Because she's been posting about it on social media. *Ugh.* Yes, she's one of those. *An influencer.* Somebody that has little or no talent outside of social media. A little harsh? *Maybe,* but I've worked hard all of my life for what I have. Even coming from a privileged position, my parents instilled in me the work ethics and drive necessary to be successful at anything.

If you think about it, how much effort does it really take to make a video go viral? The right images and key words, and you're it. Although, in her defense, apparently, she's one of the owners, so maybe she had something meaningful to contribute to this partnership besides her social media skills.

Since I flew in from Spain and spent all day sleeping, now I can't sleep. By two AM, I'm restless. I get dressed and go downstairs.

I reach the stairs landing when I see her. *Filming.* Of course, she is. She walks around the living room, describing some things about the house, like the architecture or some cool old books they found and have on display. I have to admit, even I'm hooked and now *I* want to know more about the house. Despite my opinions on social media, I do have to admit, she's good at this.

When Alma sees me, she glances my way and seems taken aback but recovers quickly. After a few more minutes, she ends the transmission.

"Hi," I say as I saunter in her direction, my hands in my pockets. She's wearing jeans, a t-shirt, and very little makeup. Her hair is all up in a bun. I can't help but glance at her neck. Her neck is shapely and elegant. I stop a couple of feet from her. I'm close. Maybe too close. I can smell her perfume, lavender, and it's a complete turn-on.

"Hi," she replies. "Can't sleep either?" I nod.

I focus on her fingers as she gently touches her neck dimple, that hollow area between her collarbone and the breastbone. She's sexy as hell.

"I made some tea. Do you want some?" she asks.

"Sure. That would be very nice." I follow her to the kitchen. We sit next to each other on high stoools next to a kitchen island, as we drink our tea in silence. "If you don't mind me asking, why are you filming?"

Alma clears her throat. "Well, I figured if I'm stuck here, I might as well have some fun with it and share my experience. Not only am I trying to keep the buzz about this place going, but I'm pretty sure there are a ton of people out there, in other parts of the world, that have never been through a hurricane. I'm documenting as much for them as for me. You never know, this house could blow away, and this could be my last video."

Okay. "I've never been through a hurricane before. I mean, I came to university here but always went home for summers." I glance at her. "What are the chances of the house blowing away? You're kidding, right?" This causes her to grin, and her eyes light up. I can't help but grin back.

"Oh my gosh. You're actually smiling. I need to take a picture of this. Don't worry. It's only a Category Two. We're probably going to be fine." She aims her cell phone at me, and I block my face and her cell with my hand, just as I hear a click.

"Hey, no posting," I warn her.

"Oh my god. Your face on social media. ¿Como? ¡Qué escándalo!" She mocks me. I almost want to roll my eyes. Almost. She has no idea how much of a *scandal* it would be if I let her post a picture of me. "Come on, help me. Make yourself useful," he says as she hops off the stool. I instinctively follow her as she starts walking around the house and enters a room.

"What are we doing? I'm a guest, remember" I tease as I enter behind her.

"You still are. Kind of."

I can't help noticing that the room is nice. It's beautifully decorated and smells amazing. "This is nice," I say as I look around. "Why didn't I get this room?" I ask, kind of in jest.

Alma beams. "Thanks for noticing! I cleaned all the rooms last night and left behind scented candles." She gives me her cell phone with a stand, and I wait. "I'll go around the room, try to follow. Okay?" I nod.

Without a word, she releases her hair from the bun, and for the next hour, I film her going through different rooms in the house. She describes cool things about the room or the idea behind a particular theme or decoration in others. I make comments and I can't help noticing that she laughs easily and often. I can see why she has a following.

After an hour, we walk together to our rooms. "Thank you. That was *interesting*," I observe as we go up the stairs.

She narrows her eyes. "I can't tell if you're being sarcastic or if you really mean it."

I give her a lopsided grin. "I'm not trying to be rude. It *was* interesting."

Alma pauses in the middle of the hallway outside of our rooms and looks at me. "At the risk of sounding like a lunatic, I was wondering, can you pick a lock?" She looks down, then back at me.

I pause. This is an interesting question. "Ummm. Why are you asking?"

"We need to break into the little house."

"*We?* Do you mean that in a figurative way or in the literal sense?"

She shakes her head sideways. Her hair moves and I almost want to touch it. "Literally. Have you ever committed a crime before?"

Oh fuck.

Chapter Five

Lucas

Annnd we're done. No matter how pretty she is, I'm not breaking the law for her. "*No.* Have you?"

"Nope, but there's a first time for everything." She winks at me and I shake my head.

"Seriously?" I ask after a second. She nods. "Technical question, what's the little house?"

"Oh, it's a smaller house next to this one. It was either a guest house or an in-law's house back in the day. Now it's our private space and base of operations."

"Got it. Before we break any laws, can you at least tell me why we're resorting to breaking and entering?"

"My camera and my purse are there. Also, there's alcohol there, and I don't want to go alone."

I rest on a wall and look at her as she ties her hair in a messy bun. "Of course, there is. *Booze.* The perfect excuse for breaking into a house. You realize that we're not in college, and this isn't a frat house?"

She stands in front of me, hands in her back pocket, glancing at me as she speaks. I glance at her mouth. After a second, she moves and also, rests on the wall. We're almost shoulder to shoulder. "Technically, it's my house, or a fifth of it is. It's not breaking and entering if you own it."

"The police *might* disagree with you on that." I glance at her again.

"There's a hurricane going through the state. I think the police have better things to worry about." She pauses. "You know what, we're wasting daylight... or night-light. Let's just go for it. Do it for the booze. Come on."

Do I have a choice? I honestly don't know. She's so... *endearing.* I follow as she quickly goes down the stairs like an excited teenager. "Booze? For the record, that's the worst excuse I've ever heard to commit a burglary. My parents are going to kill me when they find out about this."

"My parents... will probably call me to complain about the fact that I ruined their reputation." Once at the door, she turns and from a little closet, she pulls a pair of umbrellas and glances at me. "Maybe we don't tell them?"

"We'll need somebody to post bail for us when the police catch us," I deadpan.

"What are business partners for, if not for aiding and abetting?" she winks. *All righty then.* I can't tell if she's kidding or not, but she must have the best partners in the world.

Since the house has been wrapped in plywood, we have to go out the front door. We step out in the rain, and within seconds we're soaked. I follow her around the house, to the back of the property. I can't help noticing the pool and a small house across from it.

When we reach the little house, she kneels. I notice that she has a bobby pin and inserts it into the lock. She's really thought about this. I don't know whether to be scared or impressed. After she tries for a few minutes, I realize, this is not like in the movies. This isn't going to work.

This goes on for a few more minutes until we're drenched. It's raining and the wind is howling. "Hey, I don't think this is working," I'm almost screaming. She stands up. "What about a key? Don't you have one?" I ask.

"The key? Oh my god. The key! Wait here!" She disappears and reappears a few minutes later with a set of keys and opens the door quickly.

"Where did you find those?" I ask as we step inside, and she turns a few lights on. Compared with the wind and rain outside, it's quiet here.

"I was checking people in this morning and it was so busy, I put them in a drawer. I meant to put them in my purse, but I forgot about them until now. Come on."

I follow her into the kitchen, she passes me some beers and wine, and I put them on the counter. She also grabs some chips and other snack items. After she's done opening cabinets at random, she tells me she'll be right back. A few seconds later, she reappears with a purse and a camera. "I take it, those are yours?" She nods.

Disappearing again, she returns with a duffel bag and we pack everything inside. The camera, her purse, snacks, the beers, wine and another bottle that looks like either rum or whiskey.

"Alright. Ready to get out of here?" she asks. I motion with my hand and when she hands me the duffle, I lead her out, and we run in the rain. A couple of minutes later, we're back in the big house.

We're at the door, shaking off the excess water, and I look at her. "You're insane. If I die from pneumonia, I'm coming back as a ghost to haunt you," I complain.

When she looks up, she's smiling from ear to ear. "Come on, that was fun!" It kind of was, but I'm not admitting that. I can't remember the last time I went running in the rain, much less with a woman. Usually, I'm stuck in an office making deals.

Without intending to, I look at her chest. The wet t-shirt is leaving little to the imagination. All the blood in my brain flows south. "It wasn't that much fun," I say as I start going up the stairs. "We could have gotten in trouble."

She stops climbing and I turn back. She looks up at me. "What are the chances of the police being outside *this* house at four AM? In the middle of a hurricane?" I open and close my mouth. She's got me there.

I start going up the stairs again. "Well, I'm going to take another shower, change clothes and go to bed. I'm afraid of what other ideas you'll come up with."

She laughs out loud. "Give me an hour. I can come up with ten ideas." She makes a ten with her hands, and I shake my head. "Tell you what, if you get pneumonia and turn into a zombie, I promise to kill you fast," she says.

"Why would I turn into a zombie?" I ask, glancing back at her again. "That's so random."

"The *chupacabra* would be random. Zombies are not that random."

"The *chupa-what*?" I look at her.

"The *chupacabra*? The legend from Puerto Rico? Don't you watch TV or surf the web?" I raise an eyebrow. "Never mind. The zombie pandemic will start with a virus, somebody getting sick or an animal germ jumping species. Just watch," she says casually, using her fingers to make a point. Finally, we're outside the rooms.

When she stops outside her room, I take a few more steps, and hand over the duffle bag then turn back to my own door. "Maybe you need to stop watching zombie movies? Good night, stranger." I say as I insert the smooth plastic card into the slot and yank it out, then open my door.

She's beaming when she answers, "Well, thank you for coming out with me and getting wet. I appreciate it." A few seconds later, she says good night. I watch as she goes into her room and closes the door.

It occurs to me, I don't think a girl has ever invited me to commit a crime before or offered to kill me if I turn into a zombie. *Out of all things to say.*

She is one of the most beautiful, random and unexpected people I've met in a long time. *I'm so screwed.*

Chapter Six

Alma

The next day I wake up later than usual. I guess being stuck here in the middle of a hurricane has been a blessing in disguise. For one, I'm stuck with a handsome man, but also for the ability to sleep and actually rest after a few long weeks of nonstop activity.

I go down and open the main door. For a few minutes, I record the falling rain, then make a few comments about the weather. When I close the door and turn, he's standing there with clear blue eyes aimed in my direction. I rest on the door for a few seconds.

"Buenos días."

"Buenos días," I reply as I walk towards the kitchen, with him not far behind. "I'm starving. Are you hungry?" I ask. He nods. I cook eggs and pancakes and serve them with a healthy portion of butter and syrup.

"Of course, you're hungry. All that breaking and entering? Running in the rain?" he jokes as I serve him. I try not to laugh. "If you don't mind me asking, where did you learn to cook?"

"During high school. My maid taught me." He pauses

chewing mid-bite. "It's okay. It was a long time ago. My parents were busy building an empire, and once I was in high school, they figured I could take care of myself. Which I did, to a point."

"I'm... sorry to hear that?"

"Don't be. It is what it is. I consider myself lucky that I had someone watching out for me. She taught me how to cook, took care of me, and also taught me how to take care of myself. She made sure I got good grades and stayed out of trouble." I pause. Was that too much info? *Maybe?* "Sorry. Talk about a side of drama with breakfast."

"It's fine. What's her name?"

"Her name is Marina. She's retired now. We still talk from time to time. She's probably the reason I'm not an entitled arrogant bitch who wants to marry a trust fund baby or something. I guess she wasn't afraid of me or my parents and as I got older, she made me clean and cook for her, but then she also cheered me on when I accomplished something, so–." I shrug. "What about your parents?"

"They're great people and wonderful parents. They let me work at their hotel every summer. The first time, I hated it. They set me up to start with the housekeeping team and the supervisor was somebody that had been there from the beginning and was friends with my parents. He didn't actually give a shit if I was happy or not." Lucas glances at me and shakes his head at a memory. "He had me wash floors, change dirty bed sheets, and clean toilets. After a week or two, he told my dad that I sucked at it and that he was done with me but I didn't want to be fired. I was embarrassed so I asked for a second chance. He kicked my ass for the rest of the summer, but he also kept an eye on me and gave me advice. I learned a lot from him about working hard and valuing our employees."

"Did you go back after that?"

"Every summer. I loved it."

"What about your parents?"

"My parents encouraged us to follow our passions and be happy–" He stops. "Now I feel bad telling you this."

"Don't be. It's all in the past. In my case, it gave me the freedom to do my own thing." I take a sip of my orange juice.

"Like work in the cruise industry?"

I pause with my fork mid-air. After a second, I take the bite and point the fork in his direction. "I don't remember telling *you* that. Have you been spying on me?" I give him an exaggerated gasp.

"Not at all." He pauses. "Okay, fine. Yes. Maybe a little. Last night, you surprised me with your delinquent ways. I wanted to make sure you weren't going to murder me in my sleep." He eats some eggs and chews. "It's interesting because your friend thought I was the murdering type. Does she know about *your* nighttime activities?" He gives me a lopsided grin.

I try not to laugh. "I'm so sorry about that whole conversation. Maria tends to be a little dramatic. If it's any consolation, I knew you weren't going to murder us."

"Did you? Are you sure about that?" When he grins, his dimples are on full display. *He's so beautiful.*

He has a killer smile, and he seems self-assured. The mysterious guy vibes he's giving off are all part of the package. *I'm digging it.* I give him my best smile in return. "Actually, now that you're saying that, I think I might sleep with my bat tonight, just in case," only half-joking. This causes him to laugh.

He holds my eyes. "I promise, *if* I go into your room, it won't be to murder you." Then he turns back to his plate.

Wait, what? Oh my god. I clear my throat. "I will keep that in mind," I murmur, then focus on my own food. The rest of the meal passes by in similar fashion: eating, talking, and flirting.

After breakfast, we watch TV and catch up on hurricane news. So far, the hurricane is veering north of us. With a little bit of luck, it'll keep that path and miss us completely. Besides the excessive amounts of rain, and the danger of flooding in low-level areas, I'm honestly relieved. Our house, our business, should be okay.

After lunch Lucas goes to his room, and I don't see him again for a few hours.

When I go down for dinner, he reappears. I'm filming myself cooking and he waits. He's standing off to the side, behind the camera, arms crossed leaning on a wall. He's wearing jeans and a long-sleeved white shirt. The sleeves are rolled up and he looks sexy as hell watching me.

When I make jokes, he smiles. Sometimes, he makes little comments. To be honest, it's hard to keep my eyes on the camera. Usually, I have an idea of what my followers will like. I try to record videos in batches, edit them and post them, but any reaction I get (or the video gets) happens after the fact. In this case, I'm posting some videos as quickly as I can before the storm, and the novelty of it passes. It's interesting to see somebody, (other than my partners,) react in real-life to something I'm filming.

After I've finished cooking, I stop the recording and invite him to have dinner with me. "Maybe I'll hire you to do our social media," he says as we eat.

"Hire me for what?" I ask before my next bite.

"I'm sorry, I thought I mentioned that I work for a hotel."

I make a mental note to ask him more about his hotel at some point. "You kind of did... but I already have a job. Business owner, remember?" When I wink at him, he grins.

"Here's an honest question, does having that phone in your hand all the time make you feel better?" he asks.

"Does having a bad attitude all the time make *you* feel better?" I ask. He tilts his head and I wait.

Ignoring me, he stands up, grabs the bottle of wine and starts serving us. I glance at him as he sits down again. "You realize that I'm European. We're not rude per se, we just have a different culture. We're not extremely friendly with random strangers as Latinos are." When he raises his wine glass, I do the same and we click our glasses. "*Salud*," he says.

"I've been to Europe and I think, this is a *you* thing, not a European thing. If you keep it up, you're going to die alone and wrinkly, and you're going to rot in your hotel. Like a zombie."

He's cutting a piece of his meat and pauses. "First of all, you seem to be obsessed with zombies. You should do something about that. A therapist might help. Second, that's a disturbing mental picture... Now I'll spend the next few nights thinking about rotting in my hotel. *Not*."

"Sure, you will. With the little I know about you, I'm guessing you'll probably be thinking about the millions the hotel is making you."

"Actually, both. I'll be rotting in my hotel... while we make millions."

I shake my head and try not to laugh. "Let's face it, you'll probably look like a zombie, old and decrepit."

"Well, if being handsome, smart, and rich is wrong, I think I'm in great shape. Not to mention, do you know how many women are attracted to rich old men? They're attracted to the maturity, the wisdom, and the financial stability old men can provide."

I can't tell if he's serious or if he's kidding. "Okay. I agree some might be attracted to that. Let's say five percent?" I raise an eyebrow.

"Come on, it has to be higher than five percent."

"Ten?" I pause. "For the other ninety percent, there's actually a term for that –gold-diggers. Do you seriously want to spend the rest of your days with somebody that's only interested in you for your money? That's a depressing thought."

"I feel called out." When he says this, we burst into laughter. He's quiet for a few seconds. "Actually, all kidding aside, no. I want a kind person. Somebody level-headed with good listening skills that likes my friends and finds me funny. Somebody confident. Confidence is hot."

When I say, "I don't think you're funny," he smirks. I take a bite of my food. "Please, continue."

"More? Umm... somebody that has a career of their own and friends. You can learn a lot about people from their friends. Also, smart and that smells nice. How's that for a list? Too much?"

"Nope, not at all. That sounds perfect actually."

We look at each other for a few seconds then break eye contact. I can feel a shift. In my first impression of him, he seemed conceited, snooty, cocky, uptight and maybe a little full of himself. Now, I wonder if it's all a front. If this is the case, I might be in serious, serious trouble.

Chapter Seven

Alma

After we eat, he follows me as I open a closet and pull out some board games. While he settles down in the living room, I go to the kitchen for two glasses and the wine. I sit on the sofa and he sits across from me.

Again, he grabs the wine and serves it. During the next few hours as we play, we talk a lot. As expected, he's snooty not only about social media but about a lot of things. "See, I knew the booze would come in handy," I say. "You're so snooty."

"I'm not. I have standards. There's a difference."

"Sure. Keep telling yourself that."

He takes a sip of his drink. "Do you talk with your family?" he asks suddenly.

"Not that much. No."

"If you don't mind me asking, why?"

"I'm going to need a drink. Hold that thought." I stand and get two shot glasses, then sit again. Quietly, I grab the whisky and fill the two tiny cups.

"Ready?" he asks. When I nod, we both take the shots at the same time. He scrunches his face. My mouth tingles and a second later, my throat burns and my eyes water. I wait a few seconds for the feeling to pass. "You alright there?" he asks. I nod.

I tuck my legs under me. "I'm ready. My parents paid my way through college, which I'm grateful for because unlike many of my friends, I don't have any student loans. They paid for everything. Room and board, tuition, food. Then after college, they wanted me to come home and get married."

His eyebrows go up in surprise. "An arranged marriage?"

I take a deep breath. How do I explain it without making my parents sound like medieval people? "Not exactly, more like a *recommendation* based on what was best for the family at the time."

"I hope you said no," he frowns.

"You would be correct. I actually got lucky. My brother married well, and they left me alone. Then I started my career in the hospitality industry. Still, they paid for my apartment, car and everything. About two years in, they asked me to come home. I could either get married or join the family business. Neither option appealed to me, but being the dutiful daughter that I am, or was at the time, I came home.

I moved into the fancy family home until I found my own place, I attended fancy events and tried to help the fifty fancy charity galas they're involved in. I mean, don't get me wrong, helping charities felt very nice, but the nine-to-five job in a lonely office as a sales manager for airplane parts was soul-sucking. Not to mention, what's the point of being a manager, just for show? None of my ideas were taken seriously. I was withering away in the wasteland of despair."

"Airplane parts? That's the family business?"

Out of everything I said, is that the only thing he heard? I nod. "Yep. While your family business is hotels, mine is airplane parts to North America and Latin America. My parents got lucky early on. The company is one of the more than three thousand NASA contractors."

"Wow. I can see how going from working at a hotel to a boring office would be soul-sucking. Then what happened?"

"Again, they suggested, it was time to get married. But then I thought, why should I tie myself up to keep this vicious cycle of appearances they have going on? Why should I be miserable? Around the time they threatened to cut me off, for the second or third time, I saw an ad for a cruise job. I had a hospitality degree and experience, and I decided that was it. I cut myself off. Best decision ever." I fill out my shot glass and take another shot. "Your turn."

He raises an eyebrow. "Can I just say I'm very impressed by your determination and your confident personality?" He pauses. "My family is great. They're great people and encourage me to find my passion. They owned hotels and I knew early on that I wanted to take over and continue the legacy for them. They made it clear I didn't have to but I wanted to... The people there are family. You know?" He pauses. "Do you have brothers? Sisters?"

"Yes. I have an older brother. You?" I ask.

"I have two brothers."

"Oh my God. I feel so bad for your parents. Three like you?" This makes him grin.

"I'm the middle one, but they're not like me as much as you might think. We have very different personalities. Enough of our parents and siblings, tell me something nobody knows about you."

"Like a secret?" I ask. He shrugs. "Ha! You're insane and besides, why would I tell you a secret?"

"If you think about it, we're never going to see each other again. Think about me as your bartender or hairdresser," he says. Umm he brings up a good point but at the same time, I

185

don't think he's met a Hispanic hairdresser. They're the gossip queens of the neighborhood. They know everything.

When I say, "I'm going to need another drink for this," he makes two shots and lines one up in front of me. I'm feeling myself walking towards the *"this is a very bad idea,"* part of the evening but fuck it. He's right, after this we're never going to see each other again.

"Ready?" he asks. I grab the tiny glass. and on the count of three, we both take the shots at the same time. Again, my throat burns. "*Coño*. That burned." I wait a few seconds for the feeling to pass.

His face is scrunching and he shakes his head before turning his attention to me. "You okay?" he asks.

"Okay. I got it. Here's one I've never told anybody, I hate G-strings. They're so damn uncomfortable. Like who the hell came up with that or thought it was a great idea?"

"I will not comment on that particular subject because I'm a guy, and from where I'm standing, they're okay. Not to mention, that's not one I will ever wear."

"No Speedos for you?" I joke, and he shakes his head. "Let's see, oh, I've got one another one. I hate Bloody Mary's. They taste horrible. How do you even think that mixing tomatoes, spice, and salt would be a good idea or appetizing in the slightest?"

"I agree. I hate kombucha." We grin at each other. He grabs the bottle and serves us a third shot. After we drink it, I feel myself relax and my body feels warmer. A few seconds later he says, "Maybe we should switch to water now," and I nod.

He brings two water bottles, and we start drinking. "Do you ever feel pressure to be perfect? This idea that we have to be the best at everything, to live up to our parents' expectations every single hour of every single day... It's exhausting. Don't get me wrong, my parents are awesome and I love them, but this expectation to be better than they were—to achieve or surpass what they achieved—"

"I agree. It's tiring. I'm tired just hearing you. At the same time, that's one of the reasons I disconnected from my family."

"Was it worth it?"

"I don't know if it was worth it. I mean, I have very little contact with them except for the occasional phone call but I'm at peace." At least I found my family with my friends. It could be worse. When he drinks water, he keeps his eyes on me. His eyes are intense and I feel self-conscious. I take a deep breath and wait. "Do you have any tattoos?" I ask as a way of changing the conversation.

"Nope. You?" I nod. "Show me."

I shake my head a little. *Should I?* I guess I'm never going to see him again, so... I get up and pull my t-shirt up. His eyes are huge. "Relax," I say. I lower my pants and underwear a little but don't take them off completely. On my hip bone, there's a small tattoo of a ship.

He's glancing back and forth between the tattoo and my face. "Oh, my god. Is that... a cruise ship? Seriously? Where you drunk?" I can tell he's trying not to laugh.

"I wasn't. I spent several years working in the industry. A few of my friends and coworkers suggested it one day, and after a bunch of people agreed, we did it. It was more like a bonding experience," I say as I flop on the chair again.

We spend more time talking and share more random secrets. An hour later, I'm sitting on the floor, my back on the furniture and my legs stretched in front of me. I find myself enjoying the conversation and the way we're trying to outdo each other. After he shares an embarrassing story about crashing his dad's car at sixteen, I feel bad, but my competitive spirit comes out.

When I confess, "I lost my virginity during my first year of college. He lasted a minute," Lucas sputters his water to the side, and I laugh.

"I don't even know—" He's shaking his head. "Let's take a break. I think that's enough sharing," he says. Immediately after, he jogs to the kitchen and when he starts cleaning the mess, I stand and go to the bathroom. When I return, he's standing there in the middle of the living room.

"We should dance. Come on." He lifts a hand.

"Dance? There's no music," I get closer, slowly, and take the hands he offers.

"I can fix that." He grabs a little box from his pocket. From there he pulls out a pair of earbuds. He gives me one and keeps one. He's glancing at me as he presses the screen on his cellphone.

"Can I pick the music?" I ask.

"Nope. I'm the guest. I'm picking the music." I try not to laugh. He finds a nice Spanish ballad, then grabs my hand and holds on to my waist. My body is hot and tingling. This is not how I expected my day to end. Dancing in an empty hotel, with a handsome stranger in the middle of a hurricane. "You're not a bad dancer," he says after a few quiet minutes.

I can't help teasing him. "For a European, you're not too bad yourself."

"Well, I'm trying to impress you. Is it working?"

When I say, "Maybe a little," the back of his fingers gently caresses my cheek.

"Now?"

"Getting closer." I glance at his mouth, and he glances at mine, then turns his head slightly and tentatively brushes his lips against mine. We kiss slowly at first, and I find myself savoring it. He's a great kisser and it's been so long since I kissed someone. Obviously, there are no feelings involved but there's a lot of physical attraction and an undercurrent of desire, mixed with compatibility and hormones.

Yep, I'm doing this. I'm going to have hot sex with a handsome mysterious stranger with a killer smile, in the middle of a hurricane and it's going to be epic. *I'm seizing the day or in this case, the hot guy.*

Within a few minutes, the kisses turn more frantic. When clothes start coming off, we stop and look at each other. Unexpectedly, he takes a step back and offers a hand. I glance at it. We're both breathing hard. Without thinking about it, I take it. Before I know it, we're running up the stairs to the bedrooms, laughing like two crazy people... *yep... this is happening.*

Chapter Eight

Alma

I open my eyes. Since the windows are boarded up, it's dark. I close them again. A finger runs the length of my arm. It trails from my shoulder all the way down to the center of my wrist and back up. My skin lines up with goosebumps. "Ummm." I open my eyes and look up at him. He's laying sideways, his head propped on his hand.

"Hi," he whispers, then kisses my shoulder.

"Hi," I look at him again. His bed hair makes me smile. His hair is sticking up in all places and his blue eyes sparkle. It's a contrast to his (sometimes) uptight personality.

"Did you sleep okay?" he asks with a lazy smile.

Ummm. Are we talking about sleeping or *sleeping*? I clear my throat. "I slept great. Thanks for asking. You?"

When he says, "Better than I had in years, like a zombie," I grin. A slow smile appears on his lips. That smile and those sexy dimples are going to get me in trouble. Lucas bends down and kisses me. A slow toe-curling kiss. The previous night comes to mind. Like a movie of highlights, or a preview of the best scenes playing and damn, we had an amazing time.

When he looks at me and gives me a sexy grin, it occurs to me that round two is about to be even better.

Around midday finally I leave his room. As I take a shower, I think, *we had a one-night stand.* Actually, it was more than once... the point is, it's no strings attached. We're both consenting adults having fun... and what fun it was. Doesn't mean anything. *Right?*

We're in the kitchen making lunch. *We're starving.* Surprisingly, this time he offered to help. While I cook the meat, he chops vegetables, and while I finish, he sets the table.

"What's something you're looking forward to?" he asks when we sit and start eating.

"Are we sharing random secrets again?" I ask.

"Nah, just a question."

"Okay, fine, I'll play. I'm looking forward to this business succeeding and being a mom one day."

"That's a great answer."

"You?"

"I'm looking forward to my business succeeding and getting married one day." He takes a bite. "What would you be doing if you weren't here?" he asks.

"I think I would probably still be working in the cruise industry. My plan was, at some point, when I got too old to walk up and down the ship, to settle down somewhere warm."

"That sounds nice. I love the beach. Do you like the beach?" I nod. "How did you meet your friends?"

"I met them during college. We hit it off right away. Did you meet anybody you keep in contact with?" I ask before I take a sip of my Sprite.

"I do. My friend Marcos. He's a local. We got paired up at

random during freshman year, and we hit it off. We were roommates for the whole four years. I have other friends that I keep in contact with. Some live in Miami, and others just came to study and then they went back home, like me."

"I can relate. We also made a lot of local friends at the university. A bunch of them helped us get some of our guests to safety and spread the word on their own social media channels when we opened. We both got lucky. It's a great program."

After a few seconds of silence, he asks, "What's the most romantic thing someone has ever done for you?"

I know I'm probably never going to see him again when this is over, but do I really want to answer *this* question? *Oh boy. Here we go.* "Yeah, I haven't been as lucky in that department. Career, yes. Friendships, one hundred percent. Love, not so much. I haven't had anybody want to sweep me off my feet yet," I answer truthfully.

"That's a shame. If I lived in Miami, I might take a shot at it."

His comment makes me pause. *How do I even reply to that?* "Yeah, I don't know. You seem too—"

"What?"

"Do you really want to know what I think?"

"Yes. Tell me, what was your first impression of me when we met?"

"Are you sure?" I ask again and bite my lips. "Okay. Here we go, but you asked for it. I thought you seemed uptight, a little cocky, and maybe a little full of yourself."

"*Ouch.* Don't hold back."

I try not to smile. "I'm sorry, but you asked." I pause. "What did you think about me?"

He clears his throat and has trouble keeping eye contact.

"What? Come on. I told you. You have to tell me."

"Okay, fine. I was waiting in the living room to be checked

in— it was full of people. Somebody told you a joke and when you laughed, I thought you were the most beautiful woman I had seen in a long time."

I can feel my cheeks warm. *Damn.* "Wow. I don't know what to say. I don't remember."

"No worries."

We go back to eating. I take a deep breath. The air is charged with something. *Attraction? Hormones? Stale air?* Something's definitely in the air because as soon as we finish eating, he invites me up to his room to nap. In Spain, it's customary to nap after lunch. Can I say, I don't remember the last time I napped? Much less, with a hot guy next to me.

This is turning out to be a very unexpected but surprising time. After a nice nap, we do it again.

The rest of the day unfolds similarly, more eating, talking and flirting and another awesome night in bed, this time with candles as there's no electricity for a few hours. To be honest, I'm not complaining, it's romantic and sexy as fuck.

It's the middle of the day on day three. We're in the kitchen hydrating when I hear the front door opening. Within seconds, the kitchen is invaded by my loud friends. It takes a minute, but they all come towards me, hug me, and kiss me. They're all happy to see me. It occurs to me these are my friends *and* family. They chose me.

I glance at Lucas smiling at me as my friends envelop me in a group hug. After a few minutes, he excused himself and leaves.

My friends and I huddle in the living room and catch up. We're talking about the weather. When we're sufficiently satisfied that he's probably up in his room, they throw twenty questions at me. "Oh my god! *Calma mi gente.* Guys, one at a time." I tell them to *calm down.*

"First question: Did you sleep with him?" Julie asks.

When I say, "What do you think?" there is collective screaming and laughter.

"I knew it! He likes you!"

"That doesn't mean anything," I warn right before I take a sip of my energy drink. The electrolytes or whatever is in these, it's awesome.

She pins me with a look. "Doesn't it? You must be blind. I can feel the attraction and the chemistry from a mile away."

"*Que exagerada.*" It's not like that at all. She's definitely *exaggerating.*

"Does anyone else agree with me?" she asks no one in particular and when they all raise their hands, I laugh.

I shake my head. "You guys, of course, we like each other. He's actually nice. A little conceited, but nice. But there's no way. He doesn't even live here and I'm not moving to Europe. I just came home. This isn't going anywhere… so let's not get too excited."

"What are you talking about? It could go *a lot* of places," Julie exclaims. The way she says this, suggestively makes me and the other girls laugh. She's clearly in love with Alex and is seeing things where there aren't any.

"You are awesome and you deserve to be happy and in love. You never know. He's already lived in Miami. He could do it again," Christy says.

For a second, I consider this. I won't be the one asking, but she's right, he could. If he wanted to. Right now, I have too much on my plate to add relationship drama to the list. If he suggests it or offers it, I might be willing to entertain the idea. Until then, there's no point in worrying about something that might or might never happen.

Maria clears her throat. "I hate to be the dramatic one," she begins and we turn to her. I raise my eyebrow, "You know what? Fuck it I already am. I hate to burst your bubble and everything but did you find out who he is what he does? Did you at least Google him?"

"I was too busy cleaning, cooking, and filming to go into spy mode, but we talked... a lot... I mean, he said he's a businessman. He works for his family in their hotel. He's one of three. His parents sound like great people—"

"In other words, you know nothing?"

"Ummm, I can't think of anything right now. I guess I was too busy slee—flirting to interrogate the guy." When I say this, there are a few more laughs.

"Did you at least get his number?"

"So far we haven't shared digits, but we'll see." The truth is, I'm waiting to see how the next couple of days pan out. His conference is not for a few more days, and I refuse to take his personal information from his reservation. I have ethics but more than that, I won't be calling a company number in a foreign country and talking to a random secretary to ask for him... when he could have easily shared his information, if he wanted to.

"Okay. Okay, enough of the hot guy. Let's talk business. The architects will be here soon and we need to get moving. Have you seen our social media pages?" Leyla asks. I nod. I have been posting some videos as I make them but I haven't gone back in as much as I typically do and checking stats. "We have news. Exciting news! That's the reason why we came, one of them at least. It turns out that some of your videos of the storm are going viral."

"Okay."

"People are commenting on the whole hurricane experience. Sharing their own experiences... and others some are commenting about his voice and asking questions... Everybody wants a picture."

"A picture of what? Of Lucas?" I pause. "How?"

"You can hear him talking in the background, in some of the videos, women are going crazy. They want to see him."

"Oh my God. No way. He doesn't want his picture out there. He hates social media. Besides, I don't actually have a picture of him. I only have is a picture of his hand, with a blurry face in between some of his fingers, that I took to tease him. I'm not sharing that."

"Then what do we do?"

"I'll talk to him about it, but in the meantime, it'll be good for our social media. Maybe some of those people might want to come out to stay here. We'll leave it alone. People will forget about the videos eventually."

When Alex arrives with Mikaela, his assistant, we follow them as they inspect the house. Thankfully, the house is intact. Unfortunately, the garden might need some love. Since some of the plants and flowers were recently planted, they hadn't taken hold yet and were uprooted or damaged with the wind and rain. At the same time, if the only thing we have to do is replant a few things, I think we're in great shape.

Chapter Nine

Lucas

It's the middle of the day when her friends and partners show up. The shelter-in-place order was lifted, and they made their way to the house. I take advantage of this and arrange my own get-together. I call Marcos, my former college roommate and my best friend in Miami. He was on a business trip and was stuck out of town.

Since I didn't have a chance to rent a car, he agrees to pick me up for dinner. When he texts me, I finish getting ready, and meet him downstairs. When we see each other, man-hugs are exchanged. "You look great man," Marco says, taking a step back but holding onto my shoulder.

"Thanks, man. You don't look too bad yourself. Come on, let me introduce you to some people before we go." We walk to the kitchen, where the girls are gathered, and I make introductions.

Without thinking much about it, I stand close to her. The smell of lavender hits me, and I get a few flashes of her in bed. Alma glances at me a few times. When she smiles, it's hard to take my eyes off her. After a few minutes of pleasant conversation, we leave.

We head to a fancy restaurant in downtown Miami. To be honest, this is one of my favorite places to visit when I'm in town. As the sun is setting, the views of the bay are amazing.

"What's with the house and all of those hot girls? Who are they?" Marcos asks as soon as the waiter takes our order.

"Those five women are the owners of the bed and breakfast where I'm staying."

"*They're* the owners? I've seen some of the buzz on social media. But didn't they just recently open? How did you find them? More importantly, how did you even get a room?" he asks.

"I didn't. My secretary did. She thought it would be good to stay in a brand-new bed and breakfast for a change. Since we're looking at the expansion."

"I see. How's that going?"

"I came to look at properties but ran into a hurricane. I would say, right now, it's not going anywhere."

A different waiter approaches us and fills our glasses with water. We thank him and wait for him to leave. "Tell me about it. I couldn't come home. At the same time, I guess I'm used to them. That sucks for you, though."

"It does. How's your job?" I ask. I have a proposal for him. My family owns one of the most popular chains of boutique luxury hotels in Europe. My brothers and I are taking over, and we've decided the next logical step is to expand into the US market. I couldn't be more excited for us. When our waiter reappears, I pause. I let him deposit our drinks and salads on the table. "Thank you," I nod to the waiter. "So, I was wondering, do you like your job?"

Marco also thanks him. "My job is okay. You know this. Why the sudden interest in my employment situation? Not all of us were born as heirs to a family fortune. A hotel fortune slash empire. Some of us are stuck with tyrant bosses, with tiny little fingers and tiny little di–"

I raise my hand. "Okay. Okay. I got the picture. Thank you." I pause. "For the record, we're not an empire. An empire would imply worldwide domination, and we're only in Europe... However, if you don't mind working for the empire and helping us achieve world domination, I have an offer for you. I mean, if you want it. We're going to need a right-hand person. I'd like –"

"Yes. Yes, I'm in," he says before I'm even done asking. "What would you need me to do?"

"How do you feel being the food and beverage manager? But that's just to start, I need somebody I can trust, then we'll see about a better job."

"Are you serious?" I nod. "Benefits?" I nod again. "Wow man, I don't know what to say."

"Say yes."

"*Yes!*" We take our drinks up in the air, "*Salud,*" he says at the same time I do. After a few seconds, he asks, "Where is it going to be?"

"We don't have a location yet. As a matter of fact, that's what I was supposed to be doing. Scouting. But I haven't done any work in the past three days."

"What have you been doing in that house these past three days?"

What have I been doing? Besides flirting with a beautiful woman? I'm not sure what to share about her. I mean, sure, I like her, but what are the chances of this going beyond a fling? Once I get the flagship Miami hotel going, I'm probably not going to stick around. Somebody else, maybe even Marcos, will take over and there'll be no need for me. I'll move on to the next city for the next hotel. I pierce a piece of salad and croutons and take my time eating it.

Marcos raises an eyebrow. "It's the tall one, isn't it?" he asks after a few seconds. I pause my next bite mid-air.

"How could you possibly know that?" I ask after I've eaten it.

"I lived with you for over four years. You have a type. Tall. Blond or light brown hair. Pretty face."

"That's not even a type. Half the planet has brown hair."

He gives me a *seriously* look. "Come on. As soon as I saw her, I knew, okay? Also, you didn't stop looking at her."

Was it that evident? "Fine. Yes. Her name is Alma." I honestly don't want to have this conversation right now. This thing with her is too intense. I can't help myself. It's moving too fast, but at the same time, not fast enough. Which I know makes no sense but that's the best way I can explain it to myself.

"Did you tell her who you are?" I shake my head no. "Did you tell her about your family?" Another shake. "Did you tell her why you're here?" I don't even bother to answer this one. "Lucas. You spent three days with a woman, who you allegedly like and you haven't told her anything about you. What do you think is going to happen when she finds out?" he asks.

"Does it really matter? We had a fling. Grownups have flings. Doesn't mean anything. Besides, we haven't decided who will head the US expansion— it could be me or one of my brothers. I might not even be in Miami. I might end up in Asia or South America, who knows."

He shakes his head. "I know you. I know you're a good person, and you mean well. The thing is, technically, you're her competition. If you like her and you end up moving here, she's going to hate your guts. I mean, you do realize that, right?"

Hearing him say it out loud, it strikes me that he's right. As a matter of fact, I requested the US so that I could lead the US expansion and spend some time in Miami. I take my job and my family very seriously, but I do love this city. At the time, it seemed like a great idea. The thing is, I didn't count on meeting her. "Fine. I'll think about it. Maybe I'll talk to her, just on the off chance that I do end up in Miami."

The rest of the meal is great. We catch up on everything, both personal and professional.

When we stop at his house, I take over his office. I make a couple of important calls and send a few emails. I also catch up on emails from my assistant and make sure my family is alive and well.

By the time I return to the bed and breakfast, the house is quiet. I go up to my room, change, then go to bed. It takes all of five seconds from the time I'm in bed, alone, before I start wondering if she's in the room next to me.

I realize I *want* to see her. I *want* her in my arms. *Fuck it.* Without thinking about it, I get up from bed and knock on her door.

Chapter Ten

Lucas

I knock on her door gently. A few seconds later, she opens in a t-shirt and underwear. At least, I think she has underwear, but I can't tell. *Okay.* I put both my hands on the door frame and give her a once-over. I really can't help it. I clear my throat. "Hi," I say.

"Hi," she replies. She's kind of holding but leaning on the edge of the door.

Now what?

"I'm sorry. Are you busy?"

She shakes her head. "I was earlier. We did a tour of the house and the back of the property. The house is fine, but we're going to redo some of the gardening. I was just looking at the videos and making some notes."

"I see. Can I come in?" She moves out of the way so that I can enter the room. I walk a few feet and turn.

"Your friend seems nice. How was your dinner?" she asks as she closes the door.

"Dinner was nice. I haven't been in Miami in a while and

we had a chance to catch up." I look at her. She has no makeup, and her hair is up in a ponytail. She is simply beautiful.

I fix on her luscious lips and walk towards her. When I glance at her mouth, she glances at mine. Unexpectedly, she pushes forward, brings her head up and kisses me. Our lips barely connect, quick and electric, before she takes a step back again.

I take a step forward.

We stare into each other's eyes for a couple of seconds. I stare at the most beautiful hazel eyes ever created. I can't help *but* pause. At the same time, I want more. Without thinking about it, the tip of my fingers run over her neck softly. I gently touch her neck dimple with my thumb, then my hand slides behind her neck, and I pull her close. I run my fingers up and down the nape of her neck. My other hand slowly slides down her back, resting on her waist. Unconsciously, I tilt my head and kiss her, gently at first, then I deepen the kiss. When our chests connect, I can feel her heartbeat. A warm and fuzzy feeling catches me off guard.

After a few seconds, I walk her backwards towards the bed. When we reach it, I slowly take off her shirt. She helps me take off mine. I hold on to her hips, and her hands pull me as they wrap around my neck and cheek. Kissing her is delicious. It's like anything she does or doesn't do, consciously or unconsciously, is designed to draw me in. The feeling overpowers all of my senses. I have no idea what this means but the realization is both unsettling and so right. I can't stop wondering if she can feel this. It occurs to me, there's only one thing to do, make her mine. So I do.

The next day, I wake up to a phone buzzing. I quickly find my cell and read the message. It's my office telling me that the conference has been canceled and that I should come home and regroup. When I put the phone down, I realize that I'm alone in bed.

I look up, and she's nearby getting dressed. It's six AM.

"Hi," she smiles at me. Approaching me, she gives me a quick kiss then goes back to getting ready. "Everything okay?" she asks.

"Yeah. It's already morning in Spain. That was my office telling me to come back home." Her face falls a little, but she recovers quickly and turns her back to me. "Are you going somewhere?" I ask.

She turns to me again, as she attempts to put earrings on. "Yes. We're reopening today. Soon the plywood is coming down. We have some guests coming in at eleven am. Early check-ins. I've been stuck here for three days. I need to go home, check on my things, wash clothes, you know. I mean, I'm sure you have to do the same." She pauses and shakes her head. "Probably not, since you don't actually live here and your house hasn't been through a hurricane... you know what I mean." She's flustered and looks adorable.

I stand, put on pants, and turn to her. She glances at me through a mirror, a worried expression on her face. I walk in her direction and stand in front of her. "Alma, it's okay." Finally, she stops fidgeting. She takes a deep breath, and I do the same. "We had a great time. Maybe next time I'm in town, we can do it again... without the hurricane part." The last comment makes her smile and she nods. "I'll get out of here. Maybe I'll see you later? Tomorrow?"

She nods again. I kiss her, intending for it to be a quick kiss, but when our lips connect, I can't. I hug her waist and I kiss her deeper. She wraps her hands around my shoulder, and it feels like I'm leaving something behind with her. I don't know what it is, but I can't shake the feeling. On the other hand, this isn't real life. This isn't *my* life. I have to go home.

Once I'm out of her room, I go to mine. I take a shower, and get ready as quickly as I can. I decide the best thing is to check out and go home. I pack my things and put them away, then I grab my luggage and head downstairs. Half of me is disappointed that she's not around to say goodbye. The other half is grateful; I don't do drama. At the same time, if she were, I might be inclined to kiss her again and that would only confuse things. We had a great time and now it's done.

When Leyla checks me out, I take an Uber to Marcos' house and I spend the whole day there.

In the morning, since it's still afternoon in Spain, I catch up with my assistant and set up meetings with a couple of business partners. A business does not run itself. It's the middle of the afternoon, nighttime in Spain, when Marcos comes in with whisky. It occurs to me the last time I had whisky was with her.

While we drink, we catch up on work and personal things. The next morning, I catch my flight home. *It's over.*

Chapter Eleven

Alma

Lucas left without saying goodbye. Half of me is offended. The other half was relieved that we didn't have a big drawn-out goodbye. We had a great time, and I'll probably never see him again. Which is fine–

"*Alma.*"

When I hear my name, I turn. "*Madre.*" *Mother*, I say. I stop and I watch her as she looks around the kitchen.

"Not bad."

"Thank you. What are you doing here?" I ask as I walk in her direction.

"I heard you guys finally opened it."

I can't help wonder who the fuck told her. At the same time, I do realize we have a website and she could have very easily searched for it.

She stops in front of the kitchen island and places her purse on top, then looks at me as I stop across from her. She's legit checking me out. I'm sure she finds this whole thing, probably me in general... *deficient*. "Okay. You proved your point. We got it. Now it's time to come home," she announces.

"I am home."

"You know what I mean."

I refuse to engage. *Do not engage. Do not engage.* Oh, fuck it.

It's infuriating to talk to my parents. I scratch my forehead, take a few breaths and think for a second. "Okay. I appreciate that you came by but I honestly don't have time for this. We've already talked about this. Several times. I'm not moving back home and I'm not marrying one of your friends' sons. Okay Mother? I have a business, a job and an actual life. More importantly, I'm happy."

At my reply she's shaking her head. "Happy? Why would you want to be here and work? when you can have it all? You could join the board, host galas— you could do so much good."

"Is that an actual question?" I pause. "Once again, my life."

She sighs. "*No seas terca.*" Basically, she's calling me *stubborn.*

"Mother–"

"Can you please not call me that? It's Mom or better yet, *Mami. Seguro ya se te olvidó hablar en Español.*" She wants to know if I forgot to speak Spanish. *Of course, she does.* Maybe I'll tell her I can't speak it, just to spite her a little.

"I can speak Spanish perfectly–" before I can continue, all of my friends file into the room and stand with me. We all stare at my mother across the kitchen island.

My mom looks at all of us and shakes her head. "Alma. Give me a call. We need to talk about this *in private*. You need to come home."

"Not likely. Once again, for the twentieth time, we're starting a business. I'll be sure to let you know if I ever change my mind." My mother grabs her purse and after another head shake, she strides away in her heels.

Ummm, a little more head shaking and maybe a neck

vertebra will get loose. *Maybe. If we're lucky.* Don't get me wrong, I don't want her to die or anything, but if a neck vertebra takes her out of commission for a year... or three, I won't complain.

"Alma, your mom has issues. Just tell her straight up to leave you alone," Julie advises.

"Don't you think I have?"

"Alma, don't get this the wrong way but sometimes your mom is terrifying," Maria says. "She has those cold serial-killer eyes. I worry she's going to send a hitman after us."

"A hitman?" I repeat. A second later, we burst into laughter. "She doesn't know any, we'll be fine," I say after a few minutes. After I thank my friend for having my back, and we head back to work.

At least I don't think she does.

Chapter Twelve

Alma

It's almost the end of August and it's hot and humid as hell. At the same time, I'm not complaining, it could be worse. *Like a hurricane. Or the zombie apocalypse.* Thankfully, none are coming our way so I'll take that as a win.

For Labor Day, I'm planning a pool day with our guests. I'm making treats and decorations with a red, white, blue theme. I searched for fun cocktails and outdoor games. It'll be an amazing fun day. I love that our guests enjoy it and appreciate it. For the Fourth of July, we did something similar and some of our younger guests posted about it on social media.

The truth is, the last few weeks have been crazy but in a good way. After a string of cancellations, due to the hurricane, we then had a string of reservations, also due to the hurricane. Or rather, the videos about being in an empty bed and breakfast, in the middle of a storm and alone with a stranger.

There are now at least fifty theories about who the owner of the voice is. Thankfully, none have even come close to his identity. Famous actors are in the lead. Thankfully, so far, none of those actors have claimed it. It would be very awkward if any of them did. As a matter of fact, some have even denied it, which truth be told, has only added fuel to the controversy.

At the end of the day, *I* spent three days with a complete stranger. It feels like something you do when you're in college backpacking through Europe or something. I've asked myself if maybe the whole thing was a dream. My friends are fast to remind me they met the guy, so I know he's not a figment of my imagination.

Unless, I'm a ghost? I mean, it happened to Bruce Willis in *The Six Sense*, so maybe it can happen to others? Unfortunately— or fortunately depending on the day— every time I'm in the kitchen, I can see his face, smell his scent and hear his laugh and it's both a blessing and a curse. At this point, I'm pretty sure I'm not a ghost, so, again #winning.

The last time we were together, something happened. *A connection.* For a second, I had a crazy thought that Lucas was the one. At the same time, he can't be. He left without even saying goodbye. The worst thing is, he didn't share his phone or an email, nor did he ask for mine. If he were *the one,* wouldn't he at least want to contact me? Otherwise, what's the point? *Right?*

I know that it *feels* like he's important, but actions speak louder than words. It was a fling. He doesn't live in Miami. He's made no attempt to contact me. *Yet,* I can't seem to let go of the memory, the conversations, his body on top of mine and the way he looked at me.

I take a big breath. In and out. Again. *This too shall pass.* It has to.

After I make breakfast and we serve it to our guests, I head to our main desk, and somebody else cleans the kitchen. Usually, after breakfast we have a bunch of check-outs. We'll clean and prep the rooms, and between two PM and four PM, we'll welcome a new set of check-ins.

Today, for some reason, by two PM I'm beat. I need to stop thinking about him. It's not healthy, not to mention, I'm wasting a lot of mental energy.

I go to the little house and do some work alone, and think about a nap. This is one of the advantages of having four partners; there's always somebody around to take care of guests.

I return to the big house by five PM and start preparing snacks. Wine and cheeses for our guests and maybe some sort of entertainment, when Leyla comes into the kitchen. "What are you doing here?" she asks, pausing in front of me.

"Working?"

"Why?"

"Ummm. Because it's my job? I own this? Or a fifth of it?" I say quickly. What is going on? Am I about to be fired? Oh God, on top of everything? That would suck. *Wait, can partners be fired?* Must research that. "Why are you asking?"

"You don't know, do you?" She pauses. "Lucas is here. He checked in a few hours ago." She looks at her watch. "He checked in at like two PM."

My heart drops, but then at the same time wants to leap to the sky. *Okay. Okay.* This is unexpected, but good. *I think.* I take a few deep breaths. A part of me can't help but wonder if he came back for me. At the same time, it can't be. He made no contact for weeks. *Weeks.* If he was interested in me, he surely would have done something sooner. I'm not interested in being his Miami side chick. Actually, if that's why he came back, we're going to have a big problem.

"Alma?" she asks. "Did you hear what I said? Are you okay?"

I focus on her. "Yeah. Yeah. I heard. I'm good."

"He asked for you. We told him you were taking a nap. He had a ten-hour flight and said he would do the same, then come find you." She cocks her head. "Are you sure you're alright?" I nod. "Are you going to go and say hi?" She raises an eyebrow.

"I don't know if I should."

"My friend, you definitely should. I'll finish here." She comes around, behind me and moves me out the way by the shoulders, then turns me in the direction outside of the kitchen. "Go," she says into my ear, and I take off, like a person who wants to win first place at a race.

Chapter Thirteen

Alma

I take off jogging, then running, up the stairs. When I get to the second floor, I realize I don't know his room number. I run back down and go towards our reservation desk. Maria holds her hand high. In between her index and middle finger, is a piece of paper. "Thank you." I grab it and open it as I run up the stairs a second time. I realize it's actually room number one, on the first floor. So, I turn back running down the stairs. I'm almost at the landing when I slip and fall. *Ow. That's going to leave a mark.*

This time around, Lucas is actually in our biggest and most expensive room, so I turn and go that way. As I jog across the living room, a couple of my friends look at me like I'm crazy. Another two smile at me in encouragement. I run down the hall and stop right outside the room and catch my breath. *What the hell am I doing? Ack.*

I knock softly a few times and nothing. I wait. *Oh, screw it.* I start knocking faster and harder, non-stop, with both hands. I turn back, and I see two heads at the end of the hallway. If my friends didn't think I was crazy, they surely do now. A few seconds later, the door opens. *Finally.*

Lucas is wearing jeans and a cotton hoodie with the Sunny Beach University logo. A lazy smile spreads on his lips. I grin, then force myself to stop smiling. "Hi," I say with my eyebrows pinched in, and a serious face. "Hi. Did I wake you?"

"You did." He covers his mouth as he yawns, then runs a hand through his hair. His piercing blue eyes are clearing as the seconds pass. They take my breath away, and I think about the first night I laid eyes on him. "It's fine," he says with another yawn.

"Sorry. Not sorry. I heard that you were here, and I wanted to come say hi. *Hi*. Actually, I need to talk to you. Should I come back later?" I say quickly and wait.

His eyes narrow. "Nope. You're not going anywhere." Unexpectedly, he reaches for my shirt and pulls me inside, then closes the door. I can't help but squeal in delight. With the door now closed, he leans on it. When he pulls me and wraps his hands around my waist, I put my hands around his shoulder. "I'm on vacation," he says with a sexy half-grin.

That was *not* what I was expecting, but okay. "Are you? Good for you." I say. "And this is your vacation attire?" He nods quickly then kisses my neck. "You look like a college student." I can't help saying it. He really does. I can feel his smile. "And you came here? What about if there's another hurricane?" I joke. He looks at me and shrugs. "The zombie apocalypse?"

"You're funny."

I clear my throat. "So, for how long are you in town?"

"Ten days. Actually, a week. You have me for a week."

I have him? Do I have time to psychoanalyze that statement? I look at him. I'm about to say something when he glances at my mouth. I can't help but glance at his, and in less than a second, we're kissing like crazy.

Yes, I do realize we're falling into bed without a lot of conversation, again, but I can't deny that the vibes and the chemistry are incredible, can I? We have seven days, plen-ty of time to have a conversation or two or three. Plen-ty. Besides, you never know when the next zombie pandemic might really happen. *Carpe diem* or FOMO or something.

When he deepens the kiss, all thoughts leave my mind, all that's left is a delicious feeling running through me.

I am in so much trouble.

We wake up in the middle of the night. Exhausted and starving. I make a quick plate of fruits, cheeses, crackers, and wine and bring it to the room. While we eat and catch up, we have a short conversation about the theories regarding his voice in the hurricane videos.

Lucas thinks the whole thing is both hilarious and stupid. At the same time, he doesn't want me to reveal his identity just yet. Fine with me, the mystery is helping our social media, which in turn is helping our bookings. "What should we do then? I ask."

"I say leave it alone," he replies, grabbing a piece of cheese.

"Are you sure?"

"Yes. I'm only going to be here for a week. I don't want drama. I didn't even tell my friends I was coming."

We're sitting on the bed and I look at him. "Oh, so this is a secret trip or something?"

"Or something," he says. When he winks at me, I stifle a laugh.

I take a few days off work, we go to the beach and spend a couple of days basking in the sun, eating awesome food and having... *private* time. Unfortunately, that's about as mean-ingful a conversation as we have. *Why do I do this to myself?*

Now I'm going to spend the next few weeks thinking about the conversations I should've had.

Fine, I admit it. I may have completely lost my mind. The thing is, I've never been so drawn to anybody like that in my life. I can't explain it. I can't justify it, and to be honest, I don't want to, so why fight it? After seven amazing days, he flies out.

*****

"Please tell me you used protection," Maria says as she sits down across from me. Lucas left this morning. Now it's nighttime and we're all gathered in the little house having drinks.

"I won't dignify that with an answer." I eat a couple pieces of fruit and completely ignore her. She looks at me and waits. "Okay, fine. For the record, yes. I'm stupid but not that stupid."

"Good girl," she says. "Now what?"

I take a sip of my wine, then grab a piece of cheese. "I have no idea."

"You didn't learn anything new about him. Did you?" I raise an eyebrow. "So he's still a stranger?" she asks.

When she puts it like that. "Was I supposed to interrogate the guy?"

"I don't know. What is your gut telling you?" *My gut?* If she only knew.

This whole thing is crazy. He's still basically a stranger *but* my body has kind of decided that he might be the one but that's an opinion based mostly on great sex. My heart is on the fence and my brain agrees with it. And that's just inside. Outside, there's four different opinions on what I should be doing. I'm being pulled in several different directions and I don't know who to listen to.

I take a big drink of my wine.

"Alma. I know that we give you a hard time, but you really need to talk to him. Can we at least all agree on that?" When they all nod in agreement, I decide they're right. I need to talk to my— wait, what do I even call him? I can't call him a one-night stand... that ship has sailed. He's not my boyfriend. Playboy? Play-toy? Gigolo? *Ack!* The word that keeps coming to mind is lover. Let's stick to lover.

"Alma?"

I look up. "Yes?"

"Did you hear us?"

"Yes. I will make sure next time I see him, whenever that is, that I get at least some basic information."

Insert face-palm right about here. It occurred to me that I have no idea when he's coming back. Why didn't I ask? *What is wrong with me?*

Chapter Fourteen

Alma

It's mid-September when he returns. This time, we need to have a conversation. Yes, I know I said that the last time but I've been thinking, at the very least, I should ask if he's single, or married or divorced. Kids? *Oh my God. Why haven't I asked?!*

We're in bed, and I just need to know. I sit up in bed unexpectedly, startling him. "Hey, I'm sorry to do this to you right now but we need to talk," I start. After a few seconds, I turn on a side lamp. I cover it with a shirt to dim the glare. *I'm not a complete monster.*

Lucas groans, then grabs a pillow and pushes it behind his head. "Now?" I nod. "Okay. Sure. What do you want to talk about?" he asks, as he's yawning.

When he gives me his full attention, I clear my throat. "Are you single? I mean I assumed you were, but– oh my god. You're married, aren't you? With five kids?"

When I say this, he bursts into laughter. I wait. "Did you have a nightmare or something?" he asks, still smiling.

"That's not funny. This is not funny." I pause. "Please take me out of my misery. Are you?"

His smile is dimming when he says, "Not married. Not divorced. No kids." He pauses. "Correction. Not yet, but eventually, yes to marriage and kids. No to divorce."

"Oh, thank God." I take a breath and put my hand on my chest. We're making progress. I really don't want to be the other woman. The thought of that is horrifying. It's worse than the zombie apocalypse, it's literally bad karma for life. "Now that that's out of the way, what exactly are we doing here?"

"What do you mean?"

"I'm going to be completely honest, I don't want to be your Miami fling. Like we only hook up when you're in Miami, then you go home and you do God knows what. What will happen is this: you'll go home and fall in love while I'll still be here, thirty years down the road, waiting for you year after year... all of my friends will get married... while you come once a year to cheat on your wife, maybe I'll cheat on mine... I mean, I know I'm exaggerating but I just need to kno–"

He covers my mouth with his index finger. "*Stop*. Nobody's cheating on anybody. I get the picture, and I agree. I don't want to do that either and I don't want to sit at home thinking you've met Mr. Right, and I'm going to have to come back here and have to fight for you. Jail would really suck."

The unexpected revelation catches me off guard. "Fight for me? Isn't that a little dramatic? *Medieval, even?* I mean, free will and all." I raise an eyebrow and pause. "Look, if you meet somebody, just tell me. If I meet somebody, I'll tell you. The end."

Lucas gazes at the ceiling and shakes his head. Looking back at me he says, "To be completely honest, I don't like the thought of somebody touching you. Call me old-fashioned but I kind of want you to myself."

"You want me?" I repeat.

"Of course, I want you. I think about you almost every hour of the day. Why else do you think I keep coming back?"

"Awww, Lucas. I think about you too." When I say this, he places a gentle hand on my neck, pulls me towards him, and kisses me.

"Then let's put a label, be my girlfriend." I nod. *"Done.* Problem solved in five seconds. I think I broke a record." We grin at each other. "But seriously, you don't have to worry about me getting engaged in secret, and I don't need to worry about guys hitting on you."

I think about this for a second. "First of all, was that a question? It didn't sound like a question. It sounded like Mr. Cocky was back actually."

He raises an eyebrow. "Did you want me to ask?" I nod. "Do you want to be my girlfriend?"

"So, it'll be a long-distance relationship? You realize I don't even have your phone number or an email. I've never seen a picture of your family. I don't know where you live. I don't really know anything about you."

"You know stuff about me."

"Do sex things count?"

"Hell, yes."

"Lucas! Be serious. I'm talking about meaningful things, stupid things, like what's your favorite color? Your favorite food? Do you watch TV? What's your favorite show? Things normal people know about each other."

"I could say the same thing about you by the way. I mean, besides your obsession with zombies, I don't know that much about you either." He sighs. "Give me your phone." I turn back and grab my phone and hand it over. He takes it and a couple of minutes later hands it back. "Done. Now you have my phone number, my email and my home address. Send me yours."

"You gave me your home address!?" I ask. He nods. "Why

would you give me your–." I groan and let my head fall on his chest. He kisses the side of it.

"I thought you wanted my information. What? Talk to me."

"I don't want to sleep with you and call you my boyfriend just for show. I want to have a relationship. How's that going to work? You don't even live here."

"What would happen if I did?" He looks at me. "Confession? I might. I'm trying to get transferred here. It takes time to plan a move across an ocean, and there's a million permits for work that need to be–"

"Are you serious? You're moving to Miami? With a job."

He grins. "Yes. With a job and everything. And I think now I have a girlfriend too." He gives me a lopsided smile. "At least I hope I do," I grin back and we kiss. "Now, my favorite color is green. What's yours?"

The question makes me laugh. "Blue, like the sky," I pause. "And I'm not obsessed with zombies."

He moves his head sideways. "You kind of are... but it's okay, it's cute. It's one of the things I love about you." We kiss again, and then he shows me pictures of his family. His brother's and his parents. I only have a couple of old pictures of mine but I pull out a few digital newspaper articles with current pictures of them. We lay in bed next to each other, showing each other pictures. Pictures of vacations, friends, places we've visited and more.

Lucas tells me a little bit more about his company's plan for expansion. They want to move into the US market. Slowly, starting in a few key cities like Miami, New York and LA. He'll be in charge of the whole thing. He sounds excited, which makes me excited, both for him and from us. Not to mention, what this could mean for our relationship.

By the time he leaves, I have mixed emotions. I'm sad that

he's gone but I also feel much better about this whole thing, *and* I officially have a boyfriend. #winning.

Chapter Fifteen

Alma

Even though we're in the fall season by October, because this is Miami, one can barely tell. Sometimes, summer melts into... more summer.

Although we don't see each other, we call and text and we try to Zoom regularly, but mostly, we email each other daily. I'm surprised to find out that Lucas is pretty funny over text and email and makes a lot of jokes. It's a new side of him.

Lucas: *One of my employees asked me for time off, then she told me she needed it so that she could recuperate because she was going to get bionic boobs.*

Lucas: *I thought I should go see you but then I remember you're on a different continent.*

Lucas: *Today I saw a guest walking through the lobby of one of our hotels. He had a bright yellow suit. I can't decide if he looked like Pokémon or Tweedy Bird.*

I can't help but laugh at the texts and emails. When Lucas returns at the end of October, for the first time, he doesn't stay with us. Half of me is surprised. The other half is, thankful. After we talked it over, I realized I can do my thing, he'll do his thing and we'll get together after hours. This might be the best idea ever.

In our case, we're deep in the middle of planning our second reopening. We'll launch officially in mid-November when the chances of hurricanes, storms and a zombie apocalypse are very low and the weather is generally awesome. While I work at the bed and breakfast, he has work meetings. We still don't know where his hotel is going to be located but as long as it's far from mine, we'll be okay.

We spend time together, but it's different. We meet daily after work and for the first time, he comes to the house I share with Christy to spend the night with me.

In addition to visiting my house and staying over for the first time, we also have dinners at local restaurants, hang out with our friends or stay home and cook, like normal couples.

I met his best friend Marcos and a few of their college friends. We hosted them at the bed and breakfast for an impromptu barbecue and pool day. While we eat and drink and bask in the sun, I get to see a different side of him. His snobby facade disappears around his friends and he smiles more. He made jokes, some more stupid than others, to make them laugh and laughed at all of their jokes.

To be honest, it reminded me a little about me and my friends. Even after years apart, anytime we would see each other it was as if no time had passed and we were back in college. The day is awesome and relaxing and when my friends liked his friends, I knew it was going to be okay.

This time, by the time he leaves, I feel like we have a real chance. Like this could be a real relationship that could go all the way. The more time I spend with him, the more I find myself falling for him. The realization is both scary and exciting. I can only hope he feels the same.

My birthday is coming.

October twenty-third and twenty-fourth are Christy and Leyla's birthdays. Mine is about a week later, on November first. *Yep, it's the day after Halloween.* As a zombie lover, there's no way to beat that, so I don't even try.

Lucas left, and I didn't tell him it was my birthday because it's just another day. *Nobody cares.* Besides, he had round-trip tickets and I didn't want to make him go through the trouble of changing them for me.

Christy is an only child and during our college years, Leyla's family sometimes hosted parties for us. For the last few years, while working on cruises, birthdays were regular days whose only purpose was to add more numbers to the number of years I've been on this earth. Nobody *really* cares.

Last year Jason, Leyla's brother, and Christy's new boyfriend hosted the triple party at Alex's house. They invited me and made me feel included. All of their *familias* were there. Mine wasn't.

This year, the plan is similar. Alex is hosting the birthday party. Their families will be there. Mine won't.

When the day of the party arrives, I get ready and head there with my friends. I honestly did not feel like coming, but they convinced me. When we arrive, the house is already half-full with people. Friends from college, their families, and friends we know from working and living in Miami.

Julie, Alex and her brother Ben are gracious hosts. They keep asking if I need anything or trying to feed me and to be honest, it's sweet that they care. I *know* that they care. Maybe I'm just feeling emotional because Lucas left, and my family is a no— show, again.

Less than an hour later, Julie pulls my hand and leads me

across the house. I have no idea where she's taking me. *Until I see him.*

Lucas and his friends are here, as are his parents. They have flowers and gifts. I jog to him and when he catches me and hugs me tight, I stay in his arms for a couple of minutes. I don't want to let go. When I do, his friends hug me and kiss me. His mom envelops me in a big hug and tells me how happy she is to meet me. As it turns out, Lucas never left Miami. He hid in the hotel for a couple of days so that he could surprise me.

For the rest of the night, they keep me company. Lucas is never far away, holding my waist or my hand when we're standing or caressing my shoulder with his thumb when we're sitting.

When they sang happy birthday, it occurs to me that he's here and I'm not alone. My friends and partners and their partners are all here. The people that love me are here. *It's the best feeling ever.*

He tells me that he'll only be around for a few more days. Apparently, Alex shared that it was my birthday and invited him. Lucas confessed that he wanted to surprise me. At the end of the night, I leave with him.

I wake up in the middle of the night with his arms around me. My back to his front. When I try to move, he snuggles into my body and it feels as if my body is being wrapped by an invisible thread. When I slowly turn around, and we face each other, he gently moves a clump of hair from my face, then his arm wraps around my back. I open my eyes and we're gazing at each other. I can't get enough of him.

His hand on my neck, he gently guides my face up. He nudges his nose against mine and kisses me softly. It's a slow build-up. Every touch, every kiss, every caress is an amplifier and causes everything to get warm and relaxed while at the same time, the anticipation builds. The feeling just spreads everywhere, and our heartbeats synchronize.

When he looks at me, I feel a warmth in my soul. I realize, while this between us might have started as a one-night stand, we're way past that. *We're falling for each other.*

Chapter Sixteen

Lucas

I surprised her for her birthday and it was awesome. My parents were on their way to Los Angeles and had a layover in Miami. All it took was a bit of rescheduling. Luckily my parents loved her.

After a couple of days celebrating her birthday, both in private and public, it's time to go back to business. Before I go home, I have been invited to a business networking event. "Hey, you still haven't told me. Will you come with me to the party?" I ask from her living room sofa.

"Why?" she asks from the kitchen.

She's walking my way when I say, "Because I want to go and I want you to come with me. You've been working nonstop."

"I can't believe you're telling me I've been working too much. What about you?"

"See, all the more reason to go. Go with me. We'll have some fun and close some business."

"Business? Is that the only reason?" When I don't answer, she says, "You know what, I think I'm going to pass. I have no interest in being on display so that you can close some business."

She sits on the couch next to me and tucks her legs under her. She's sitting sideways, her elbow on the back of the sofa, and her head resting on her palm.

I look at her. "Alma, it's a business mixer, which means there'll be a bunch of *business*people. You'll have a chance to promote your *business*." When I say this, she pauses. I can see the wheels turning. She knows I'm right. She should be thinking like a businessperson. "You're a businesswoman now. Also, can I just say how sexy that is?"

"Of course, you think that's sexy." She beams at me and I grin back at her. "But you're right, I am excited about being a business owner. Okay. Fine, I'll go with you and make some power moves." When she winks at me, I can't help but kiss her.

She's one of the strongest people I know. She survived a shitty childhood and didn't let it define her. Instead, that made her adaptable. She's fun and kind and committed to her business. She's also incredibly creative, whether that's wine tasting, painting or hosting small events. Every day she has ideas for things she believes will generate extra income. It's sexy as fuck to hear her talk and making moves and coming up with plans to grow her business.

A few hours later, she's finally ready and when she comes out to the living room, I stop in my tracks. I can't help but gaze up and down over her body. She's wearing an emerald-colored strapless dress. It highlights her curves and falls just above the knees. She's also wearing black heels and a small black purse. She's sexy as hell. "What do you think?" she asks, giving a little twirl.

"You look gorgeous, Alma."

She beams at me. "Thank you. I guess I can still clean up

nicely from time to time." I turn around and grab a red velvet box sitting on the coffee table. "What's that?" she asks.

"I got you something. I want you to wear it tonight." Opening the box, I let her admire the delicate necklace. It's a pear-cut white diamond and emerald layered tennis necklace with matching earrings.

She gasps softly. "I can't accept this, Lucas."

"Don't you like it?"

"Of course, I love it but it's too much."

"No, it's not. Come on, turn around."

"Lucas–"

"I'm not taking no for an answer." She makes a low growling noise in frustration that makes me chuckle, but turns anyway. She casually puts a hand on the necklace as I clasp it on. After I do, I can't help but kiss her shoulder. When she turns and thanks me, I wink at her. "You're welcome. Ready?" She nods.

Half an hour later, with a hand on the small of her back, I guide her toward a pricey penthouse in Brickell, the financial district. The views of the bay and the city are amazing.

Soon, several people are approaching us. I introduce her to a few people and she smiles at me. I can sense the switch being flipped. This is Alma the business person. When she glances my way, I can't help but give her a flirty smile.

I get wrapped into a conversation but I keep my eye on her. It's amazing how I can pick her out of the crowd every single time. Anytime I look at her, she senses me too and looks up. This time she's confidently talking with a group of men, commanding their attention. She's sexy as fuck and I get to go home with her at the end of the night.

An hour goes by but I keep my eyes on her the whole time. Finally, I'm alone and I walk towards her. I can't help but put my hand on her waist and kiss her shoulder from behind. The person she's talking with excuses herself.

"*Hola preciosa.*" *Hi beautiful*, I say from behind close to her ear, just for her.

"*Hola guapo.*" *Hi handsome*, she teases and turns to face me. "I love your sexy Spanish accent."

I grin at her. "Having fun?"

"I kind of am, actually. I'm getting ideas and I've invited at least twenty people to check out our place."

"Aren't you glad you listened to me?" I tease.

"Have I told you lately how smug you are?" At this, I laugh. Suddenly, her face pales and she pauses. "Are you ready?" she asks, just as I notice a couple walking our way.

"For?" I ask.

She eyes me with concern, then shifts her gaze and I follow when she does. "Lucas, these are my parents, Mr. and Mrs. Rodriguez," she says as a very well-dressed couple approach us. *Sorry*, she mouths as her dad shakes my hand, followed by her mom.

"Alma, can we talk to you in private?" the woman says dismissively.

"Mother, whatever you have to say, you can say in front of Lucas."

I stare at the older woman. I can't help but notice that her updo is so tight, and her forehead is being stretched so far back, that she reminds me of a beluga whale.

"We need to talk." When someone approaches us, her parents plaster on fake smiles. A few minutes later, the stranger leaves. "Can we be frank with you?" her mom asks, this time looking at me.

I take a sip of my drink and focus on her. "Of course."

"I'd like to know what your intentions are. At her age, our

daughter cannot afford to waste time or play games with men that only want to have sex with her."

"Mom!" Alma whisper.

"*Señora*. I'm not playing games," I tell them.

"So, you plan to leave your family? To come to Miami and work and take care of our daughter?" She asks.

"I don't understand where you're going with this. Besides, whatever happens should be up to Alma. Not you or even me."

"We know you're not from Miami. You have your own family business to take care of." She pauses and gives me unblinking, focused eye contact. "The truth is, we have certain... *expectations* for our daughter. We're getting old. We need her to come home and help her brother."

My first thought is, I need to investigate these people. Second thought? This lady just met me. *Is she trying to intimidate me? The fuck.*

I'm serious when I say, "Good thing your son is married. I'm sure your daughter-in-law can manage just fine." After a pause, I add, "Besides, Alma has started her own business and as you can imagine, she is extremely busy. You don't really expect her to leave her business to help with yours, do you?" I say and glance at both.

Her parents look flabbergasted. "Moving forward, I do expect you to respect *her* time and *her* business. *Con permiso.*" *Excuse us,* I say as I gently grab her hand and pull her away.

Alma stares at me wide-eyed as we walk away. I have a feeling nobody talks to her parents that way.

I'll have to let them know, at some point, that this type of behavior will no longer be tolerated.

Chapter Seventeen

Alma

We had the best time on Halloween. I decorated the common areas and made treats for our young guests. I also bought pounds and pounds of chocolate and candy. For the first time, we opened the doors to the community.

Maria and Alex spend the day almost having heart attacks. To be honest, I enjoy antagonizing Alex. This is payback for his strict shoe ban while the remodeling of the house was going on. He only allowed us to wear closed-toe shoes. Maria just can't help it.

Alex was worried about dirty little fingers on the house he lovingly renovated. When a little kid starts to lick his hand and glances at the wall, Alex looks just about ready to pass out. Just for fun, I text him fake pictures of the walls covered in chocolate, followed by pictures of gallons of paint. On the other hand, Maria made a list of one hundred things that could go wrong involving hotels, kids and chocolate. I honestly have no idea how she came up with so many.

Me? When not standing by the door, I go around the house dressed as a fairy, giving candy to all the kids I could find. I think I made at least fifty new enemies off their parents. On the other hand, the kids love me. We had a great time. *Best. Day. Ever.*

It's mid-November, and we're officially opening again. We invited local celebrities, business owners from the area and anybody we could think of. We also invited press and local hospitality professionals.

We get up bright and early and head over to the bed and breakfast, minus Leyla. As it turns out, Carlos is proposing to her, and she has no idea. Their families are here, and my partners and I are in charge of rounding them up and taking them to a second-floor balcony. When Carlos texts us that they're on their way, we do just that.

We watch them from a balcony while we take pictures and videos. She looks beautiful and so happy. Afterwards, we had a lovely catered breakfast. Carlos took care of everything. It's the perfect little break.

Soon after breakfast, I gather my friends for a quick cheer. I can't believe we actually made it. I ask all of my partners and their boyfriends, also Ben and Mikaela, who are very much part of the team, to put their hands in the middle of a circle. Lucas is behind me, a hand on my waist. When I look back at him, he winks at me. "Ready?" I ask, looking at my friends. "On three. One... two... three..." We all scream, "Goooo team!" Our laughter is infectious.

When the circle dissolves, someone pulls my hand. Before I know it, I'm being enveloped in a hug with four other people; it's my friends and partners. I take a deep breath and hug them back. I love them and this is going to be awesome.

Soon after, people start arriving and our opening day gets going. Not to mention we have guests that need tending to. At the end of the day, we're exhausted but we're also booked back-to-back for weeks. Not only do we have people asking about reservations but others have asked about booking our backyard for small private parties and weddings.

It's crazy to think that in less than three years I went from being homeless and, living on a cruise ship, to owning a business with my four best friends. I have a successful business, an amazing boyfriend and I'm surrounded by people that love me. *Life is good.*

The next day, I work all day but leave early. Lucas invited me to dinner at one of his favorite restaurants to celebrate. We clean up, and we look amazing. Actually, I look nice, he looks gorgeous.

Before dinner, Lucas asks for champagne. *"Felicidades,"* he says, raising a glass. I return his grin. *"Salud."*

"Thank you."

"I'm very proud of you and I have no doubt you guys are going to do great. It will to take some time, but you'll get there. You should be very proud of yourself."

"Thank you. I am," I repeat after I take another sip.

"I spoke with Jason and he told me he's coming home in January. Christy is moving with him. I was wondering, what are you going to do?"

This is an excellent question. Jason has been working out of state for the past ten months and they've been having a long-distance relationship. Christy told me that they're planning to move in together in January and frankly I haven't given it much thought. "Ummm... I don't know yet. I guess I'll have to find a place of my own."

"How do you feel about looking at places together? I mean, no pressure but I'm going to need a place to live too."

I consider this for a few seconds and frankly, I don't hate the idea. "You know what, maybe. Let's talk about it more."

While having dinner, sunset is falling over the bay. We take some pictures together as well as pictures of the sunset.

When a waiter passes by, Lucas asks him to take a picture of us.

When I see it, I can't help noticing that it is a great picture of us. *The best one yet.* With the sunset and the bay behind us, we look happy and so in love. Lucas smiles and then kisses me.

I inhale deep and take it all in. I'm falling in love with my boyfriend. This feeling I have right now is everything.

On the way back to the hotel, Lucas tells me I should post the photo of us. It almost sounds like he's ready to make it official. I agree. Let the whole world know. I guess this is as official an announcement of a relationship as one can get in this day and age.

We agree to post it on our personal social media accounts and on the one for the bed and breakfast. The one for the bed and breakfast, simply says, *"la voz misteriosa,"* the mystery voice, with a wink-eye emoji. I know our followers have been dying to know who the voice belonged to. It'll be fun to see their reactions.

When we get to the hotel, we put our phones away. We spent the night together, and it's amazing. The next day, I wake up to several 911 texts from Julie. She's asking me to meet her at work as soon as I can.

Apparently, whatever she needs to tell me can't wait. As long as the house is not on fire and the zombie apocalypse hasn't started, (which she confirms is not the case,) I think we'll be okay. I go back to bed, and when I wake up, Lucas is getting ready to leave.

He sits in bed, next to me. "I have to go to a meeting, but I want to talk to you about something. Will you meet me at this address at 2 PM?" he asks as he hands me a piece of paper.

"Sure. I'll get ready to leave too. I have to go and do a few things."

He kisses my shoulder. "You can stay here. You don't need to leave."

"I know, but they need me at work. I'll meet you there later." He nods, then kisses me deeply, and hugs me.

As I get ready, it occurs to me that, life is really great. It's wonderful what happens when you have a successful business, a hot boyfriend and sex on a regular basis.

Chapter Eighteen

Alma

By the time I return to work, I'm floating on air. I go directly to the little house. Julie and Leyla are waiting for me. I head to our conference table. "What's going on, you guys?" I ask as I sit across from them and I put my purse on the table. They don't say anything. "You guys?"

"I have something to tell you. I feel shitty because you're so happy, but I'd rather tell you the truth," Julie starts.

"O-kay." I take a deep breath and look at them. "You're scaring me. Whatever it is, please tell me."

"Have you checked our social media accounts since yesterday?" To be honest, I was too *busy* with Lucas to log into any social media pages. I nod. "Yesterday, you posted the picture of you and Lucas. The picture started slowly, mostly our followers I guess... but around midnight, it started going viral."

I raise an eyebrow. *That's an odd time.* "Midnight our time? Why that time specifically?"

"I thought this was odd too. I read some of the comments and, some were in Spanish. Then I realized, it was five or six AM in Spain. So, I looked him up."

My stomach is somersaulting. For some reason, right about now, I really wish I could turn into a mindless zombie. I have a feeling I'm not going to like what's coming. "And?" I ask.

"He's one of the heirs to a family fortune in Spain. A hotel fortune." she says quickly.

For a few seconds, I'm relieved. I've known his family is in the hotel industry; he never hid this. "I know he works in a hotel; I know it belongs to his family. He's already told me all this. I mean, he didn't tell me he was an heir, but that's not a deal breaker for me."

"Actually, they own one of the most popular chains of boutique luxury hotels in Europe. It's been all over hospitality news that they're about to expand into the American market."

I stare at them, "Yes, but we've known this is happening."

"Alma, you don't understand. Yes, we knew the company was expanding into South Florida. The problem is, according to the press release that his company put out this morning... they're looking into a couple of locations in Coral Gables. They're narrowing it down soon."

When she says this, I pause. That can't be right, can it? It must be a mistake. "In Coral Gables?" I ask. They nod. "That has to be a joke– why would he– unless he–"

"That's not all."

"Julie, you're killing me."

"I know, and I'm so sorry. I actually worked briefly for his company while I was in Spain. I never met him in person, but he's one of the most eligible bachelors in Spain. He's handsome and he's not just a rich white guy, he's a *real* rich white guy. He's a billionaire. The Spanish press is going to go wild when they find out who you are."

"What does that mean?" I ask.

"We're thinking the press is going to show up here at some

point. They'll want to know who you are and your relationship with him," Leyla says.

Not a zombie apocalypse but a public relations disaster. *Got it.* "Okay. Okay. Assuming that's the case, do we have a plan?"

"We don't, but we have an idea. Alex is going to send Joanne tomorrow to help us put out a statement if we need it." When Leyla says this, I feel better. Alex has a small business and for our openings, he lent us Joanne, who's part of his public relations team. She wrote press releases, coordinated interviews and helped us write short speeches. She's very capable, and I know we're in great hands.

We make a plan, and on the professional front, I feel great. On the personal one, by twelve PM, I'm reeling. The more I think about this thing with Lucas, the worse it sounds. The truth is, I can't wait for two PM.

On a whim, I get ready and go to the address he gave me this morning.

Chapter Nineteen

Alma

The security at the gate rivals the Pentagon, but they finally let me through. I quickly realize it's a huge mansion on the bay. Based on what I know about the ridiculously overpriced South Florida housing market, I know the house probably cost a few million.

I park and head towards the doors. Lucas opens it before I reach it, a huge smile on his face. "Hey, you're like an hour early. The food is not here yet. Is everything okay?" he asks. I walk past him.

I can't help but notice that the house is mostly empty, and the beautiful furniture is sparse. I stop walking and turn to face him. "I need to talk to you."

"Sure. Come on," he says walking past me, his smile disappearing. "What's up?"

I follow him to the back of the house, to the kitchen. He pulls two bottles of water from a mostly empty fridge and gives me one. "First, who's house is this?" I ask as I look around. The house is gorgeous. I focus on a huge set of doors that have the most amazing view of the bay. "Lucas, who lives here?" I ask again. I turn around and stand across from him. There's a literal island between us.

"I do. Or will. I just bought it."

"I didn't know you were looking to buy a house."

"I wasn't, but I got a good deal on it so I went for it," he grins. "Actually, that's what I wanted to talk to you about. I bought this house for us."

O-kay. This is awkward. "Right. Of course, you did."

"I thought you would be, I don't know.., happier?"

I put the unopened bottle in front of me, on the kitchen island. "To be honest, I'm currently kind of homeless, but if I'm going to move, I'd like to have a say in it. Maybe the location? I think it should be a joint decision. You know, like a couple?"

"You sound mad. Are you mad at me because I bought a house?" I don't answer. "I'd like to know how you feel about me. *I* think about you all the time, I'm developing feelings and I'd like to move forward wi–"

"Lucas, frankly, while I'm surprised about the house, I can't talk about it right now. So, we'll come back to that wild news in a few minutes. First, I need to ask you something, and I need you to be honest."

"Okay."

"Why did you let me post that picture of us yesterday?"

"What do you mean? What does that have to do with anything?" He pauses. "I thought you wanted to. Reveal the mystery voice? Like your followers wanted?" he says casually and shrugs, then takes a drink of his water.

"My followers? Do you really care about my followers?" I'm pretty sure he doesn't. He despises social media. "By any chance, does it have to do with a big announcement *your* company made this morning?" He turns white as a ghost and I know I'm on to something.

"What have you heard?"

"A lot and not enough. I just need to know. Was it a coincidence, or did you know the company was making that announcement?"

"I knew."

I feel like a bucket of cold water has been dumped over me and hell has frozen over. "Second question, you told me that you were looking for a location for your hotel. The press release mentioned a specific location. Are you looking at locations in Coral Gables?"

"We're looking all over South Florida. We haven't made a decision yet."

"*Please* cut the bullshit. Are you looking at a location in Coral Gables, where *my* brand-new hotel is located? *Yes* or *no*." He doesn't answer. "Why wouldn't you tell me something like that? Out of all places in Miami, why there?"

"Because our hotels are luxurious, and that's a luxury area. It's not personal."

"It's not personal?" *Not personal?* Is he freaking serious? I walked out of a career in the cruise industry. It's years of planning, my friends and my life savings. It's personal to me. I take a deep breath. "You do realize that we're competition?"

He shakes his head. "We're kind of not."

"Is this why you went to my hotel when we opened? To check out the competition?"

He crosses his arms and looks down. "No offense, but my family has been in the business for generations. I don't need to check out the competition. There's no competition."

My mouth opens. Right about now, I wish I had something to throw at his head. "No competition? You snobby, arrogant prick."

He places both hands on the kitchen island and looks at me. "I'm the arrogant prick? What exactly are you angry about? Yes, I'm wealthy but you grew up wealthy too and as you already know, having money makes up for a lot of things. Besides from where I'm standing, one of the reasons your hotel is booked back-to-back has to do with some of *your* connections. I mean–"

"I'm angry because you've have been coming to our hotel and you're probably using it as a case study to learn the local market. You asked me not to post any pictures of you. How convenient is it that you agree to post a picture with me the day *your* company announces their huge expansion? You don't expect me to think that it was all a happy coincidence, do you?"

"I already admitted it wasn't a coincidence. Come on, let's not play games, you've been benefiting for months from the buzz of the videos and the pictures and the whole mystery voice. How's that any different than me agreeing to post a picture, which by the way, will probably go viral, thus increasing the buzz about both my and *your* hotel even more... All of this publicity for free— and you're mad because I agree to post a picture that will bring publicity for a project *I'm* doing?"

"I'm not mad about the picture!" I say louder than I probably need to. "Of course, you should benefit too, I mean, it's only fair. I'm mad about the fact that we're about to be in competition! That apparently, you've secured a site close to ours. A fact that you conveniently forgot to share!"

"Alma, I don't need to spy. To be perfectly clear, I didn't even mean to go to your hotel. I don't actually make my own reservations. One of the secretaries did. I *was* there working. Of course, I'm happy that I met you. You're amazing. I really like you, and I think this relationship has potential but the fact is, we're an old and *massively* successful brand. No offense, but we won't need to steal marketing strategies from a group of girls fresh out of hospitality school who make videos to promote their little hip bed and breakfast."

Offense taken. "Oh my God! You're an ass. You're not getting the point! And we're not fresh out of college. You know this, you prick." I turn and start walking. "And by the way, your house is tacky."

"Alma... Alma..." he calls after me, but before he can say anything else, I walk away.

I get a few texts and calls from him apologizing and wanting to talk. I guess he did get the point, but ultimately, I turn off my phone.

Chapter Twenty

Alma

I barely sleep. I wake up at the break of dawn to a phone call from Maria freaking out. There are reporters outside our bed and breakfast.

Christy and I get ready as quickly as we can and head over to the bed and breakfast together. On our way there, we call everyone. When we arrive, we have to fight our way around reporters and media representatives blocking the doors. This is not how I expected the day to start. I remind myself that it could be worse. They could be zombies trying to eat me. On the other hand, I suppose, in a way they are.

An hour later, we call for a meeting in the little house. Alex and his PR person, Joanne, arrive shortly after. I'm relieved when she quickly gets to work. All kinds of rumors are flying around, including a disturbing one that he's buying us out.

"Are you guys, okay?" Alex asks. Christy and I nod. "Can somebody please tell me what's happening?"

"Lucas is the heir to a hotel empire. Think Hilton or Marriott but in Europe. They're expanding into the US," Julie begins.

He leans on the table and crosses his arms. "Elaborate. What does that have to do with anything?"

Julie looks at me. "He's also a billionaire and one of the most eligible bachelors in Spain. The news broke overnight in Spain that he's with Alma. The picture they posted at dinner going viral. To top it off, his company released a statement that they're expanding to the USA. Specifically Coral Gables."

"Of course, they are. Where is he?" Alex asks, looking at me. "Full disclosure, I might wring his neck."

"You won't have to. We had a fight. I have no idea where he is."

Alex is staring at me when he says, "Call him. Tell him to come over. He needs to talk to the press and get these people out of here."

"Alex, I love you like a brother, but we're not calling him. We're taking care of this ourselves. We have nothing to do with his hotel," I say.

He looks at all of us. "Are you guys sure about this? You guys want to take on an old massive company? I will support you, but they have a lot of money. This could turn into a PR nightmare."

I look at my partners. "I don't think we want to, but we have her." I look at Joanne and she smiles at me. "When Joanne does her thing, we'll read the statement, then we'll move on. We haven't done anything wrong."

We spend the next few hours doing research on his company. Also, writing and rewriting a press release. I keep telling myself that it'll be fine, while at the same time, mentally kicking myself in the ass for not asking him more questions about his hotel and putting my friends in this predicament.

Unexpectedly, somebody from his company's public relations department contacts us to coordinate a strategy. Joanne is the only one that speaks to them.

Finally, we have the perfect statement. After we make copies, Joanne walks out and distributes it to those outside, then sends it electronically to a bunch of other media people.

Additionally, she gives everyone a time for a live press conference at five PM, and we spend the rest of the morning rehearsing our statement and agreeing on the answers to common questions.

A few minutes before three PM, I get an envelope and flowers delivered. It's from Lucas. To begin with, he's directing us to his company's social media pages.

While my friends run around and project the YouTube channel on our big TV, I read the note. *I'm sorry. I am an arrogant prick.*

When I look up, Lucas is on screen.

Chapter Twenty-One

Alma

Lucas seems to be in a house. I think it's his friend Marco's house. I take a deep breath and we all wait for him to start. The first thing I notice is that he looks tired, and his eyes are dark. I can't help but wonder if he slept.

"First of all, I want to clear some of the crazy rumors I've been hearing out there. We have not made an offer to the owners of Sunny Beach Inn and at this point we have no interest in making one. Sunny Beach Inn is a beautiful place in a great location. We were lucky to stay there back in July and we have nothing but praise for the gracious owners."

"Second, yes, we were looking at locations in Coral Gables but as you all know, our company operates big luxury hotels, and we couldn't find a large enough location to accommodate us..." I'm sure that's bull. There are probably a lot of places that can accommodate them. I take a deep breath and look at my friends. *Well, at least he didn't bash us. Yet.*

"Next, I'm happy to announce that we have secured an amazing location on South Beach, right on the water. We're excited to start remodeling soon. We're sure we can bring the unparalleled luxury that we're known for throughout Europe to South Beach."

When he says this, we all look at each other. I think my friends are just as relieved as I am by the news.

"Finally, I'd like to ask all members of the press to please respect Ms. Rodriguez' privacy. Like all of you, she's trying to do her job. They have guests to serve, and that's hard to do when there's twenty random strangers aiming cameras at your faces. Ms. Rodriguez was not aware of the details of our project, and rightly so, as she does *not* work for us. The nature of our relationship is private, and as such, I will not share any details and I will not be commenting on it."

"To wrap it up, if you have questions about Sunny Beach Inn, please contact their PR representative. If you want more information on our plans, you'll find everything on our website. Thank you."

After a pause, there's a clip in Spanish. When he's finished, the screen goes black. I don't say anything. I can't. I don't know where we go from here.

"Well, all things considered, that wasn't too bad. We should be happy he didn't say anything bad about us. On the contrary, he said we were gracious," Leyla says. "Joanne? That's good, right?"

Joanne is furiously writing notes, but she nods. A few minutes later, she looks up. "I just decided something. We're inviting him over."

The five of us stare at her. A second later all hell breaks loose. For a few minutes, we're all talking over each other. The five of us all agree, for different reasons, that we don't want him here.

Finally, Joanne raises a hand and we stop talking. "Guys! He went on YouTube alone. He wants to help you. Instead of starting a back-and-forth, we'll coordinate everything, then this will be over. That's what they want and that we want, right?" My friends look to me. I nod, then they all nod too.

Fine. Let's finish this.

By four PM, we get ready to face the press. *Literally.* The podium is set up outside the bed and breakfast, under a nice shade and far away from our main door.

Right as we're getting ready, Lucas and Marcos show up at the little house. We quickly agree on our statements. He keeps glancing at me. I have a crazy need to talk to him. Like my body will stop functioning until I do. I close my eyes and take deep breaths. I don't know if I can do this. I can't be this close to him.

A few seconds later, one of my friends takes my hand. I look up at Maria and I nod. "You're okay," she tells me. After a few more minutes she pulls me and we all walk out together. I don't let go of her until we're outside.

We spend the next hour answering questions from a bunch of strangers. Lucas is repeating a lot of the things he's already said. We also reiterate many of his points: we're not for sale, he was a gracious guest, and we're happy for them. Their expansion will attract guests from Europe, and that's a good thing for all the hotels in the area. He answers many questions about his company. Thankfully, we all agree on a *no comment* rule on anything personal.

Lucas is standing opposite of me, at the end of the line, but I swear I can smell him from here. I'm standing next to Maria, Christy and Leyla. Julie's currently speaking. *Almost over. Almost there.*

The hour is almost up, and unexpectedly, Maria turns to me and speaks in my ear. "Are you going to let him go?" I look at her in surprise. Out of all of them, she's the most cautious of my friends. This is something I would expect from Julie, not her. "Are you?" she asks again.

"We're in the middle of a press event. What do you want me to do?" I whisper.

"I don't know, but maybe don't let him go?"

"You're telling me now!? Are you serious?" I whisper-scream.

"Now is not the time," Christy frantically whispers from my other side.

"It's the perfect time," Maria says. "I mean, how many times did he say he hated social media? The guy went on YouTube for you. *Live.*"

"Don't you think I know this?"

"Then do something!" *Crap.* I know she's right, but the timing is horrible.

Julie thanks everybody for coming, and we start dispersing. I focus on Lucas as he talks with a few people. Soon, he starts walking away from us. *He's not coming back to the house with us, is he?* I glance at Maria. "*Dale!* Go!" she hisses.

Without thinking about it, I turn and go after him. I can feel the cameras following me. *Oh fuck. Oh fuck.* "Lucas!" I call when I'm right behind him. I can hear the click of cameras behind us. He turns. "Can I talk to you?"

He glances at the crowd behind me. "Sure. Come on." Without asking, he grabs my hand and pushes his way through all the people trying to take pictures and video. He's opening up a path and I'm right behind him.

I'm well aware of the questions being thrown at him, at us but neither of us stops to answer or cares at all. Finally, we make it to the gate. He guides me in, closes the door, and then grabs my hand again. Thankfully, the press doesn't follow but I can hear the flashes of cameras behind us as we walk the path and step inside the little house.

"Are you okay?" he asks once we're inside and he does a quick glance over.

I walk in and stand a few feet away from him. It feels like we're an ocean apart. I nod. "You?"

He releases a breath. "Yes. I wanted to apologize for everything. You were right. I should have told you everything from the beginning. I knew my family wanted the hotel in Coral Gables and I didn't say anything. I thought it was business but I realized yesterday, it was more than that for you. I'm so sorry."

"I'm sorry I called you a prick yesterday. I didn't mean it."

"I deserved it. The truth is, you're right, I can get a little cocky sometimes. I need you to put me in my place from time to time."

"Are you really moving it to South Beach?" I ask. He nods. "Why?"

"Look, I don't want to be your competition. Not professionally, anyways. I told my family it wasn't going to work. You could say it was a last-ditch attempt but thankfully, I've found a nice location and they went for it. I'm hoping that you can forgive me. I volunteered to lead the renovation of the new hotel, and in a few weeks, I'll be moving to Miami. The truth is, I want to be where you are. I'm falling in love with you."

When I start walking forward, he does the same and we embrace each other midway. We kiss and my heart beats again. "I'm falling in love with you too," I confess. "Whether there's a hurricane or a zombie apocalypse, there's nowhere I'd rather be than in your arms."

When I say this, he gives me a lopsided smile and when we kiss, I know as long as we're together we're going to be okay.

Epilogue

Lucas

Unlike the previous time, we went to look for houses together. We searched for a house that had the location, size, condition and budget that we wanted for a value that she deemed acceptable. It was exhausting. I could have bought us any property she wanted but she refused. Then I figured, if we can survive house hunting we can survive anything.

In the end, we went for a three-bedroom, three-and-a-half-bath house. It's in a gated community, near the water. I would have preferred a bigger house but she's right, it's the perfect size for us. It's actually the perfect starter house for two people who have never bought a house with a partner before. The fact that I get to share the experience with her is priceless. She's just... *joyful* and makes any holiday or event or date fun.

Going home to her is the best part of my day. She makes me laugh with her crazy zombie obsession and her sense of humor. She's kind and generous and she'll do anything for her friends. She has integrity and grit. More than that, he has no problem putting me in my place and I can't believe I found her over four thousand miles and an ocean away.

As the first anniversary of meeting her approaches, it occurs to me that we're not getting any younger. I really, really love and I want to make sure she knows this, so I've decided I'm going to put a ring on it. I managed to convince her and her partners to take a few days off and I take them off to an exclusive hotel in Punta Cana, a beautiful beach in the Dominican Republic.

On the second day, when I get down on one knee. with the sunset behind me and all of our friends around us, she says yes. *I love this woman so much.* When she hugs me and kisses me, I almost can't believe how lucky I was to find her.

About the Author

Ida Duque writes sweary, sweet with heat, romantic comedies with a Miami flair. Actually, if she's being honest, it's more like loud, crazy Miami-infused romcom. Her books feature smart sassy women who love life, family and each other and are hoping to find true love. Also, there's kissing...lots of kissing!

A native of a beautiful island in the Caribbean, these days Ida lives in South Florida with her husband and two kids, one of whose future plans include becoming "the boss of Miami." Seriously. Ida's loving every minute of raising her but will welcome parenting tips on dealing with aspiring dictators. There are currently no playgroups in their area organized for fiercely independent kids also interested in political machinations and autocracy.

Find Ida Duque on the web!

www.idaduque.com

Check out Ida's other Sweet with Heat Romantic Comedy

The Humor of Love

The Academy of Love

Coming in the fall of 2023: The Sunny Beach Inn Series. A complete series of six short romantic comedies with Miami flair. You will meet all of the characters featured in this story and see them fall in love.

Obsessed with My Boss

Ashley Zakrzewski

Chapter One

Michael Dalton was not easily intimidated. Well at least he could hide the fact that he was intimidated by someone's business savvy quite well - to the point that few people would notice. His practiced smile easily threw most people off any line of questioning and easily hid any personal discomfort he felt in any situation in his personal life or in business.

At his father's urging he had taken a variety of roles at Dalton Tech after finishing his MBA. His latest stint was as VP of Marketing. It was the worst of all of his assignments. The department was filled with fresh college graduates who all seemed extremely excited to discuss every detail of their projects with him, in private. The most egregious offenders made no secret of their true intentions.

He wasn't looking forward to today. Saturday - it was another in their series of special project meetings concerning the joint venture with Roscoe Technologies. All the usual players were in the room.

Michael spotted a cute blond with glasses making her way into the conference room narrowly missing the swinging door.

She grabbed an empty seat directly across from him at the table.

"Who is she?"

"And come to think of it, where is Roscoe, he's typically obnoxiously early. I never beat him here," thought Michael as he scanned the room again.

Next another surprise walked through the door, one Eric Carnegie the CFO. "I don't think I want to know why Eric is here. The projections must be really over budget - and it is probably all my fault."

"Good morning everyone. Let me thank you again for making time on the weekend to attend this very important project coordination meeting. I'm going to be lead us all in a team-building exercise before we hear a technology status update from Heather Farchild."

There was an audible groan throughout the room over the words 'team-building' exercise. Next everyone started to whisper about just who was Heather Farchild. Heads were turning left and right to see who just might be this 'Heather Farchild'.

Eric looked in the direction of the blond women and said, "Heather, could you introduce yourself to the group before we get started."

The blonde sitting across from him rose from her seat and cleared her throat, "Good morning, I'm Heather Farchild, I'm stepping into Mark's shoes today, well, not his actual shoes, because well, who would want to step into someone else's shoes. "

A low rumble of laughter rounded the table.

Eric caught Heather's eye and she paused and started again. "Well, I'm the VP of New Product Development at Roscoe Technologies. I'll be sharing the technology status update - well Eric, uh Mr. Carnegie already told you that. Thanks and great to meet you."

Heather sat down abruptly and begin to type something on her tablet.

"Well, that was interesting," thought Michael. *"I am definitely not the most uncomfortable person in this room today. Maybe this team building exercise won't be too bad after all."*

"Our team building exercise today is called 'Hidden Talents'. We've all been working together over the past three months, but how well do we really know each other? I'm confident that if we can all get to know each other a bit better it will allow us to be more open to ideas and generate solutions to the many technical challenges of the project. I'd like us to go around the room and share a hidden talent or skill with the group."

There was another wave of whispers around the table.

"Well, Michael, why don't you start us off. Care to share your hidden talent with the group? Oh and let's introduce ourselves and give our role in the organization for Ms. Farchild."

So much for not feeling intimidated.

"Ok Eric, I'd be happy to start us off. I'm Michael Dalton and my current role is VP of Marketing. So, a hidden talent, that is a bit of a challenge Eric. "

Michael felt twelve pairs of eyes trained on him as he racked his brain for an acceptable response to his question.

"I enjoy baking. Well, I'm good at it too." Michael stammered, "My hidden talent is baking and my best dish is pie."

Michael wondered if it was only his imagination, or had all the women around the table simultaneously leaned in his direction, their mouths agape.

"I love pie," muttered Heather below her breath.

"Thank you for getting us started Michael," added Eric. "Fred, why don't you continue."

Fred was the Technical Project lead. Michael watched as Heather perked up as Fred talked about his hidden talent of building model rockets. *"How could that be a hidden talent? He has a degree in Mechanical Engineering for God's sake."*

The assembled staff continued with introductions and hidden talents. He was surprised to find out that Elaine from finance loved salsa dancing and went to competitions up and down the West Coast with her boyfriend. To be honest he didn't think that straight-laced Elaine had a boyfriend, let alone did salsa dancing. But along with the secret salsa dancers there were knitters and painters and others whose hidden talent was simply playing an instrument in their high school marching band.

Who was he to talk, he barely made it through high school - let alone playing an instrument.

The room was buzzing with numerous side conversations and was filled with energy.

"Thank you all for sharing your hidden talents with us. Now we can move on to the technical presentation. Ms Farchild, I'll give you the floor."

"Thanks Mr. Carnegie. If you'll all login to your project portal."

A hand went up from the group, "Ms Farchild?"

"Yes Fred, do you have a question?"

"You didn't share a hidden talent Ms. Farchild."

"Oh, I guess I didn't. But I'm not really a part of the project team. So let's get started on the technology update."

Eric looked in her direction, "Ms Farchild, we'd really like to hear about your hidden talent too."

"Okay, if you insist."

"So, I grew up in Vegas and my Mom worked in the gaming

industry. That's just a fancy name for the casinos to those of you here in Mornington - away from the strip. Since she was working multiple jobs I frequently had to hang out at the casino after school. Bottom line, I can count cards."

Fred chimed in, "Counting cards?"

"Have you heard the line, 'Don't bet against the House because they always win' Fred?"

"No, I haven't."

"Well, that doesn't apply to me. I will always win. And, I may possibly be banned from a large number of casinos. Moving on. Let's start with the software report from our outside consultants who have been working on the beta testing of version 11.5."

Michael would normally be tuning out during Roscoe's project updates, but Heather's animated voice and mannerisms kept his attention. She had definitely made coming to the office on a Saturday worthwhile.

Michael thought, *"How can I convince Roscoe to send her to all the project meetings instead."* He knew it would be a tall order to sway Roscoe, but it seemed like the best course of action. There was something about her...

Chapter Two

Michael walked briskly through the marble floored lobby of Dalton Tech. He waved hello to Jim at the main security desk and headed towards the executive elevator. Michael was surprised how much he enjoyed to peace and quiet of the building early in the morning. After years of waking in the afternoon it felt good to arrive early and hit the ground running.

"Morning Janice, is my father in? I know I'm not on his schedule, but I figured it was early enough that I could catch him before he dug in for the day."

"Of course Michael, you know your father's schedule is always open for you. He's on a call with the London office. Do you mind having a seat for a few minutes until he wraps that up? It should only be a few minutes."

Michael plopped down in the chair beside Janice's workstation and picked up the framed picture on her desk to get a closer look. "Sure thing Janice. How is your new granddaughter doing - is this a new picture?"

If the way to a man's heart was through his stomach, the

way to a grandma's heart was to ask about her grandchildren. The time passed quickly as Janice regaled Michael with her granddaughters' latest tricks, pulling up a album full of pictures on her computer.

Roscoe Dalton finished his call and popped out of his office to see his son and EA leaning close together, chuckling as they looked a picture of Janice's granddaughter covered in ice cream. "Well, look who's here at the office. This is early, even for Michael 2.0. What brings you to my office son?"

"Morning Dad, and I'll have you know I'm in my office most days by 7:45 am, but this is extra early even for the new and improved me. I had something I wanted to discuss with you if you've got time," Michael said as he rose from his seat.

Roscoe Dalton would never tire of seeing his son so engaged in the company business. These past few years since he'd finally closed the door on his playboy ways had made him so very proud.

"Sure thing son, let's talk. Janice, can you hold all my calls and push my 9 am meeting back if we're not finished up by then."

"Of course Mr. Dalton. Good to see you Michael."

Michael made his way into his Dad's office and took at seat at small conference table that overlooked the city skyline.

"So Michael, what's up. Is there a situation with the marketing team that you need my help with?"

"No Dad, all good. I just wanted to talk with you about accelerating the timeline of my rotations. With your agreement, I'd like to take over as the lead executive for our joint venture with Roscoe Technologies, and once we launch I'd like to become acting COO. This would allow you to slow down a bit. I know Mom would like that. I've enjoyed my time in the department, but I think I'm ready to move on to the next challenge."

Well, that's not the only reason. I'm hoping that this will mean a chance to meet up with Heather from Roscoe Tech again. But there is no need to mention that now.

"You continue to impress me with your dedication Michael. All good reasons, you can definitely take over the lead on the joint venture, but I will need the board's approval to move you to COO."

Roscoe rose and poked his head out of the door, "Janice, can you call Eric and see if he's available to come up and meet with us."

Eric joined them a short while later and the worked through a transition plan for Michael's new role.

"Damn proud Michael, you've really made your mark here at the company," added Eric. "I think you should check in with Heather Farchild over at Roscoe. Remember, she was at our project session a few weekends ago."

Oh I remember. I am very anxious to meet up with her again.

"Yes, I think I remember her, didn't she give the technical update, the day you asked everyone to share their hidden talents?"

"That's right, Heather will be a great resource. It is too bad that Roscoe snatched her up before us. Maybe you can charm her and convince her to come to work for Dalton Tech. Graduated summa cum laude with a masters at nineteen"

Gulp. Nineteen?

"That is amazing. How old is she Eric?"

Eric stood and shook Michael's hand, "I believe the ripe old age of 25. And you know Michael, don't hesitate to call on me for anything else you need as you get up to speed on the project. Congratulations and good luck."

"Thanks Eric, and you to Dad, for having faith in me. I'll make an appointment with Mark to let him know about the changes in person and see if he can put me in contact with Heather."

He could hardly believe how easy it was to convince them to go along with his plan. *"I guess actually coming in to work on time and not getting arrested for public intoxication every month really improves your credibility."*

His father called out to him as he was leaving, "Oh and Michael, don't forget Libby's secret birthday party on Sunday afternoon. We're counting on you to bring one of your famous pies for dessert."

"I haven't forgotten, I'm on it. I'm baking a test pie from one of her recipes this weekend. I'll see you then Dad."

Michael was buzzing with excitement as he entered the lobby of Roscoe Technologies and approached the security guard.

"Morning Sir. My name is Michael Dalton and I have..."

"Welcome Mr. Dalton I see that you have an appointment with Mr. Roscoe. I just got the alert on my smart wearable. Here's your badge, take the blue elevator up to the Executive floor."

Wow, that was quick.

Once Michael reached the top floor of the building he stepped out into an empty foyer. He looked around and knocked at the door to Mark's office. There was no answer so he stepped through open door. The room was overflowing with disassembled equipment and computer, and tables covered in tools and parts.

How can he get anything done in here? I'm going to have a stroke with all the beeping and blinking.

The office looked empty. "Mark, are you in here? It's Michael."

Mark Roscoe popped out from behind a rack of equipment wearing an odd looking hat and what looked to be an artificial hand. He reached out to shake Michael's hand, "Good to see you Michael," and then realized what he was wearing, "Oh, sorry, I get so wrapped up in my projects. I forgot I was still wearing this." He slipped the glove off his hand and placed it on an hand manikin in the center of the cluttered work table.

"So Michael what brings you by? Are you finally ready to take me up on my offer of a helicopter ride over the city?"

"No, Mark, maybe another time. I'm here to let you know that I've moved into a new role at Dalton Tech, Acting COO. I'll be taking over for Eric as the main point of contact for the joint venture rollout."

"Well that will be just nifty Michael. Congratulations. We should celebrate. Do you want to go to lunch? Wait, it's only 9am, too early for lunch. How about brunch?"

"Thanks for asking Mark, but I really just need someone to give me some guidance in understanding the final project milestones."

"I can do that Michael. How about tomorrow? I'm free all day."

Nope, tomorrow is Saturday, and I refuse to spend it with Mark Roscoe.

"That is so kind of you Mark, but I was hoping that you could connect me with..."

Michael turned as he heard someone enter the office. The very person's name he was about to utter was coming through that door, not looking where she was going. She smashed squarely into Michael's chest. Heather wobbled as she struggled to keep her balance. He reached out to anchor her with his hands.

"Oh... Sorry, I didn't see you there."

She looked up and smiled for a brief second and then frowned as she realized who it was that she had crashed into.

"Mr. Dalton. I didn't see you there."

Their position was strangely intimate with her hands on his chest and his hands on her shoulders. In a different setting they could be slow dancing.

"Please, call me Michael, it's really nice to see you again Heather."

Before she could move out of his grasp, a tall black man barreled through the door behind her.

"Heather, why didn't you wait for..."

And in the next moment the man bumped into Heather, which pushed her yet again solidly into Michael's chest.

"Sorry, again." Heather slid her hands up Michael's chest, and muttered, "boy you're solid under this suit." She regained her composure and took a large step backward to remove herself from their awkward embrace.

Mark chimed in, "Heather, great, you're here, Michael was just telling me he's the new acting COO at Dalton Tech, very exciting, but a bit unnerving since we are so close to the product rollout."

"Okay Mark, I'll take care of upgrading his access on the project portal," answered Heather.

"Cool. After I get Michael his new access badge and give him a quick tour of the R&D lab I thought you could check in with him on the deliverables, for the rollout. He's you new point of contact."

Why does she look so surprised. I'm pretty adept at technology. I didn't even talk that much at the last project meeting. Obviously my reputation precedes me.

"I'll show Michael to your office once we're done."

"Mark, I really don't need a tour right now, can't I just talk with Heather now?"

"Don't be silly Michael, I don't mind giving you the tour myself."

There would be no escape.

Mark slung his arm around Michael's shoulders and walked him toward the elevator. Before the doors closed Michael was able to catch one more glimpse of Heather. She was smiling and gave him an odd wave as if she knew how he felt being dragged off by Mark Roscoe for a boondoggle tour.

Now that they were alone, Ellis turned to Heather and said, "why didn't you tell me you knew Michael Dalton? Let me just say, the pictures DO NOT do him justice. He is so tall and damn, he fills out his suit in all the right places."

"I hadn't noticed. Well, of course I noticed when I was pressed up against him just now. But I don't know him Ellis. I only met him once at a project meeting a few weeks back. We didn't even speak, well not to each other. Can you believe that he bakes? Apparently his specialty is pie."

"A man that can cook, that's someone to bring home to Momma."

Heather laughed, "As if Ellis. I'll just be emailing him about the project milestones, there is no way he actually wants to spend any time with me."

"Well he did seem happy to see you just now. Could you tell if he was really happy to see you when you bumped into him?"

"Ellis!"

Chapter Three

As luck would have it Mark was called away to an important phone call that shortened the grand tour. Michael had been ready to feign a sudden illness before his reprieve. Mark had pointed him in the direction of Heather's office.

He was nervous. Michael stood in front of the door willing his hand to knock.

What do I have to be nervous about?

He knocked once, then a second time, and there was still no answer. "Heather, um, It's Michael Dalton, may I come in?"

After the third and final knock he grabbed the handle and slowly eased the door open. What a sharp contrast to Mark's space. Everything was neat and orderly. The blinds were open and light was streaming into the space. Heather was standing beside her desk, illuminated by the bright sunshine.

No wonder she didn't hear me knock, she's wearing earphones.

Heather must have spotted whatever she was looking for, she moved closer to the shelf and rose up on her toes to attempt to reach something at the very top. She slowly maneuvered one large bin out of the way and reached higher.

You shouldn't be standing here watching her. It's creepy.

In slow motion, the large bin she had just moved shifted and began to slide out of the shelf toward her head. Without thinking Michael closed the space between them and reached up to catch the bin and push it back into place on the shelf. He grabbed Heather's arm with his free hand to steady her. She flinched at the sudden contact and turned around with a look of surprise to again find herself chest to chest with one Michael Dalton.

Heather flushed as pulled out her ear buds, "Michael, what are you doing here?"

I thought she was taller.

"Thanks for catching that bin before it fell on my head. I'd hate to have to fill out another incident report for my own injury," she smiled, "The head of HR joked that if I got 3 in one month they'd need to send me to remedial safety class."

Realizing again that they were standing in very close proximity Heather said, "We're going to have to stop meeting like this. Oh, I know we'll need to meet about the project, but I will have to stop bumping into you, like literally bumping into you all the time."

"You can bump into me anytime you'd like Heather."

Focus Dalton, this is business, you shouldn't be telling her you enjoy having her bump into you, even if you in fact did enjoy it.

Heather cocked her head to the side, "Okay." She took a step back to her desk and slipped on her shoes. "I thought Mark was taking you on a grand tour. I figured it might be weeks before you were seen again."

Michael chuckled, "luckily Mark got called away so we had

to end our tour early. I'm here to review the project milestones, that is if that still works in your schedule."

"Of course. I was looking for my spare tablet. Figured it would be easier for you to have a fully configured device to access the portal. Ellis is always putting things on the top shelf, stupid tall people. Would you mind grabbing it from the bookshelf?"

Heather pulled out the top folder from the stack on the conference table and logged into the laptop. "Let's start an overview of the milestones between now and the launch, then I'll show you how to access everything through the portal, using the tablet."

With their close proximity Michael indulged himself in the opportunity to admire her up close. He'd known she was attractive after their first meeting, but up close she was breathtaking. Michael struggled to focus. He strained to keep his eyes on the laptop. His eyes kept wandering to her lips, and down her neck and...

"As you can see we're on track to meet our projections, with a bit of wiggle room at the end. Any questions?"

"No, it makes sense. This project a great match for the strengths of both Dalton Tech and Roscoe Tech. We've got the manufacturing expertise and supply chain, you've got the technical talent and venture capital."

"Yes, that is exactly right. Talking just like a COO."

Good job Dalton, maybe you've impressed her a bit.

The time passed quickly and soon the conversation slowly shifted towards more personal topics.

"Have you always been interested in technology?"

"I've always been fascinated by how things work. My Mom though was not pleased. I took everything apart, and many times I couldn't get things put back together."

"What about you, did you always know you wanted to work at your family's company?"

"That would be a no. I took the long way around. Luckily my family was supportive when I finally decided to buckle down and complete college. I'm very grateful."

Heather smiled softly, "You should be proud of what you've accomplished."

Michael was smitten. She said such kind things. He couldn't help himself, he was grinning back at her like an idiot.

With a loud rumbling sound, Heather's stomach alerted them to arrival of lunchtime. "Hungry?" he asked. "It is after 1 pm. Can I take you to lunch? Or we could order in, I know there is more to review."

"Lunch would be great. I know a great deli, close by. They have great pie."

After a short walk they arrived at the *Sit and Eat Deli* and slid into an open both along the front of the deli near the windows. Michael pulled out the menu and handed one to Heather.

"Don't need it, I always order the same thing, Reuben on Rye with extra cheese and pickles, and of course pie. I typically get the special."

Michael scanned the menu and decided it was best to get the same thing as Heather to save time. The waitress was headed there way, "Hey Heather. It's been awhile, how have you been? Will you be having your usual?" as she placed two glasses of ice water on the table.

"Yes Tonya, and a cup of coffee please."

"And for you handsome?"

Heather laughed and Michael looked up in shock, "I'll have the same, except just water for me. Thank you."

"Don't worry, she calls every man in here handsome. Well you are handsome. And not just relative to all the senior citizens in here. You do stand out." Heather stopped her babble by taking a long drink from her water glass.

"Good to know that you think I'm handsome Heather."

Heather choked on her water.

"She called me sweetie for months until I insisted she call me by my real name."

With the awkward moment behind them Michael and Heather fell back into an easy banter. Soon their food was delivered. Heather grabbed her paper wrapped sandwich oozing with cheese with both hands and took a hug bite. She closed her eyes and groaned. "Oh baby, it has been too long. I've missed you."

Now it was Michael's turn to choke as he watched Heather enjoy her sandwich. She licked her fingers between each bite.

Michael froze, he could not stop looking at her mouth. He was jealous of a sandwich.

She looked up, "aren't you going to eat?"

He took a hefty bite of his sandwich.

"I told you this place was great. I'd eat here every day, but I know that wouldn't be a good idea. Remember to save room for the pie."

Awhile later Tonya returned to refill their drinks, "So, did you save room for dessert?"

"You know I did Tonya. What's the special today?"

"Heather, you are in luck, the special is French Silk today. Should I bring you a slice? We have mint chocolate chip ice cream too."

"Yes please."

"And for you..."

"Nothing for me, thanks."

"Michael, if you think I am going to share my pie, you are sadly mistaken."

Why couldn't he stop grinning. Everything she did made him want to jump across the table and kiss her senseless.

"Okay, okay. No sharing. What are the other options?"

"We have apple and cherry every day, the cherry pie has a crumb topping today."

"Cherry."

"Coming right up... handsome."

Michael shook his head at Tonya's remark, "not to talk shop, but how much more do we have to review when we get back? I may need a nap after all this food."

"We should probably review the full schedule and action items for the launch. But we've still got three months, it can wait. I've probably bored you to tears already."

Michael was just about the refute her assumption when his phone rang. Summer was calling. "Excuse me a moment. I need to take this."

He turned in the booth so he was facing away from Heather.

"Summer, what's up?"

"Hey Michael, where are you? I stopped by your office and they said you've been out all day."

"I had a business meeting at Roscoe Tech."

"And congratulations by the way, COO, I'm impressed. So I guess I'll see you on Sunday."

"Yes you will. I really can't talk now, I need to get back to my lunch date. Bye Sis."

"Date. Michael, what date?"

Michael hung up the phone. You had to use the word date, didn't you. He knew that Summer would not let this go.

When their dessert arrived, Heather dug in with gusto. "Mmm, I love pie."

"This is..." Michael choked out, his mouth overflowing with cherries and crumb topping.

"Perfect, I know. You bake, what do you think? Isn't it the best you've ever had?"

"You've never tried mine."

"Thanks for lunch Michael."

"It was my pleasure. So what's next on our agenda?"

"As it turns out I've got few urgent emails to handle, would you mind if we continued this another time. I'm sure we can coordinate the remainder of the work via email. No need to meet in person."

"Heather, I don't..."

Heather moved to the credenza along the wall and picked up a pile of folders and walked it over to Michael. "Homework. I know I said everything was on the portal, but there are a few background reports that you might find helpful - they're easier to read on paper."

"I've sent you my contact info via email, with my personal cell, call me anytime. Well not anytime, you know, but I'm available, " Heather paused.

"Glad to know you're available Heather. Thank you so much. I'm on track now. Have a good weekend."

"Goodbye Michael. Same to you."

He was running out of options. He couldn't delay her any further, it was time to man up.

"Heather, you like pie, and um, I'm testing out a new recipe this weekend, um I'm a bit worried since it is a new recipe, it's for a birthday party, and I could use some help, um...."

He stopped talking and paused, looking at her expectantly.

"Huh? Was there a question in there somewhere Michael?"

He swallowed. This wasn't hard, just ask her.

"Would you be available to taste test my pie, tomorrow afternoon, that is if you're available?"

He smiled and tried not to look too anxious as he awaited her response.

"Will there be coffee?"

"Of course."

"Count me in. Happy to help. Just text me the time and address. That will give you time to read the background reports and see if you have questions."

"I'll text you as soon as I'm back to the office. See you tomorrow Heather."

Breathing a sigh of relief, Michael was out the door.

Once he had left Heather pondered, "What was that? geez, you'd think he was trying to ask me on a date or something."

"Nah, can't be, or could it. No."

She typed a quick IM to Ellis. "Got a minute - need your advice."

Chapter Four

"So let me get this straight. You had a meeting, then he invited you to lunch, and then as he was leaving he asked you to come over to his house and taste test a new pie recipe, on a weekend?" asked Ellis as he paced back and forth in front of Heather's desk.

"Yes, that about sums it up, just like the last three times you said it," commented Heather, "But Ellis, what do you think he meant? Was it a, 'I've got more questions about the joint venture so stop by,' or was it 'I'd really like to see you again, so stop by?'"

"Has he sent you the text with the address and time yet?"

"No, not yet. It must have been a mistake. That makes the most sense."

A ringing phone demanded attention. "Crap, it's Mark again, he's called three times in the last hour, I better answer."

"Heather Farchild speaking. Oh Mark, hi. Yes, I'm still here, but I was about to head out shortly. No, Michael Dalton isn't still here, he left a couple of hours ago. Yes, we reviewed most of the project. Yes, I'll follow up with an email and confirm the next meeting. Ok, we can host it here. No Mark, I don't know where you left your power glove," Heather covered the receiver with her hand and whispered to Ellis, 'He loses everything,' "Yes, I'll look around. Have a good weekend too. Bye Mark."

"Still Heather, he took you to lunch, did he flirt with you?"

"No, well, at least I don't think so, no worries Ellis, sorry to get your hopes up of inviting me and my potential new boyfriend over for dinner. "

Her phone buzzed. It was a text alert.

"Was that your phone?"

"Yes."

"Why aren't you checking - it could be the text from Michael."

"It isn't, I know it isn't. I'd rather not look. It was silly of me to get my hopes up."

"Give me your phone - I'll look."

"No."

"Come on Heather, aren't you the least bit curious?"

"I'm surrounded by all these conflicting messages. It has been such a strange day. I just need the weekend to get back on track. I'll just look and get this over with."

Heather turned her phone over and read the text. She placed the phone back on her desk. Obviously confused by the message, she picked it up again and frowned at the screen.

"Sorry Heather, I thought for sure it would be from Michael."

"But Ellis, it is from Michael."

"What does it say?" She turned the phone to Ellis and he read the text aloud, "Hey Heather, Thanks for all your help today, feeling better about the project. Looking forward to seeing you 2moro, 3pm - 7381 Lowe Dr, Unit 3B. Bring your appetite. M"

"Bring your appetite?"

"So, you texted her to confirm your invitation and her reply was 'K', nothing else, that seems odd Michael."

"I know Summer, I thought she was interested, I thought we really hit it off at lunch, but I guess I was wrong."

Michael enjoyed his and Summer's regular Saturday morning coffee meet up. They both could attest that it was a huge improvement from the gatherings in their younger years. Back then they met for hangover brunch that was never before noon.

"Wait, is this the same person you had lunch with yesterday when I called? Your lunch date?"

"Yes, but lunch wasn't a date, it was just lunch."

"But you used the word 'date', you wanted it to be a date, didn't you?" Summer smirked.

Summer was like a dog with a bone. Michael covered his face with his hands.

"So when do I get to meet her?"

"Summer,"

"Okay, okay. Michael, can I just see the text? Please. I am much more adept at social media than you. Let me help you figure this out."

"Summer, no worries. I've got to bake the pie for Libby's birthday celebration whether or not she comes over. I'm a big boy, I can handle rejection."

"Yesterday felt like a turning point in my life. Up until now I've been surrounded by people who think they know who I am but they don't. Most of them haven't forgotten who I used to be. She's different Summer. She treats me like, she treats me like I'm a worthwhile person."

"Who happens to be the COO of Dalton Tech, a Fortune 500 company. Don't sell yourself short bro. Now, give me your phone."

Michael hesitated as Summer held out her hand, "The phone, please."

Michael scrolled down and found the text he had sent to Heather the previous day, and then handed his phone to his sister.

"Well, that explains it."

"What? My text was fine."

"Yes brother dear, it was fine. If you were inviting Mom over, but not a girl you are trying to ask out on a date. I have so much work to do."

"You think I should I text her again?"

Clothes were strewn everywhere. Heather had pulled most of her potential outfits for the, date, but maybe not a date, from her closet for review with Ellis over FaceTime.

"Ellis, this is too hard. What do you mean that I need to look dressed up, but casual? Flirty, not trashy. Why am I doing this again? It's got to be a business thing, a favor," as she spoke to Ellis's image in her phone.

"You are doing this because that very hot man invited you over to his place. He's cooking for you. You owe it to yourself to see what happens. What is the worst that could happen? I say you need to step up your game Farchild," Ellis replied.

Heather groaned, "The worst that could happen. Well, for starters, he just wants to ask me more questions about the project or maybe this is just to thank me for helping him. Then I show up all casual, but dressed up and flirty and boom it crashes and burns when his place is filled with pictures of him and his supermodel girlfriend."

"Calm down. Let it go and focus on what you are going to wear."

"Okay, I think my best bet is the skinny jeans, with boots, and my pink button down. I look good in pink, right?" as she held up the pink button down in front of her t-shirt.

"Paul, what do you think?" Ellis called to his spouse who was off screen.

"Looks good to me."

"Are we done here? I need to clean up this mountain of clothes or I won't have anywhere to sleep tonight."

Heather looked up at her phone to see Ellis grinning, "Don't even say it. I know you are thinking it. I'm hanging up now. See you on Monday."

"Wait Heather, just one more thing. You're going to wear your hair down, aren't you?"

"Ugh, really."

"Trust me, you'll thank me once Michael is running his hands..."

"Enough Ellis. Bye."

Heather ended the call and flopped down on the mound of clothes on her bed. "Well, I guess I have to take another shower, thanks Ellis. This is going to be such a huge waste of time. Good thing there will be food."

Heather wasn't sure what to expect as she parked her car on the street and walked up the stone path to Michael's townhouse. To be honest, it was a bit more understated than she expected for Michael Dalton, he was a billionaire after all.

"Here goes nothing."

She peered through the frosted sidelight windows. "At least it looks like someone is home." Heather held her breath and pressed the doorbell.

Michael opened the door.

"Heather. You're here. Hmm, you look nice."

Really, that's all you got, you look nice?

"So glad you could make it, come on in." Michael stepped aside to wave her into the foyer. Heather followed the aroma which led to the kitchen where she could see two pies cooling on the center island.

"They smell heavenly. What kind of pie is it?"

"Sour cream and raisin."

Heather frowned, "that sounds like a really odd combination."

"You'll have to trust me, Heather. I used an old family recipe. I promise it will taste great. Well I hope it will. That's why you're here, to test out for me. I just pulled them out of the oven, so they need some time to cool. Would you like some coffee while we wait?"

"Sure."

"How do you take your coffee, cream and sugar?"

"Yes please."

Michael busied himself preparing the coffee and Heather moved into living space that was just beyond the kitchen. Her eyes drifted to all the artfully hung photographs that adorned the wall. She paused to study a family portrait featuring Michael wearing his cap and gown, surrounded by his family. Immediately to the right was a picture of Michael and a young woman, both with wide smiles taken in what looked to be a tropical location.

"There's the girlfriend," Heather muttered to herself, her shoulders slumping.

"That's my favorite picture of Summer and I."

"You make a beautiful couple."

"Couple, no. Summer is my sister."

"Oh."

"Here's your coffee, what don't we go out on the back deck." Michael passed her a steaming mug and ushered her towards the french doors at the back of the room.

"What a beautiful view."

Oh yeah, a very beautiful view. You took the words out of my mouth Heather.

"Yes, yes it is. I enjoy the peace and quiet most of all."

Heather stepped up to the back railing and Michael joined her. "Michael, have you had time to review any of the project materials I gave you? I figured you must have some questions."

"I've started reading them, but no, no questions so far."

The breeze picked up as the sun slipped behind a cloud. Heather shivered. "I'll be right back." Michael popped back into the house and returned a moment later carrying a fluffy green afghan. He wrapped it snugly around Heather's shoulders.

"Better? You looked a bit chilly."

"Yes, thank you."

Next he moved alongside Heather at the railing and let his arm lean up against hers.

Another gust of wind blew sent Heather's hair swirling around her face. She laughed and pulled it back into a temporary ponytail with one of her hands. "This is why I should have worn a ponytail. Mornington is so windy all the time."

"We should probably head back inside, I bet the pie is cool enough to eat by now."

By the time Heather had pulled off the afghan, folded it and laid it over the arm of the couch Michael had returned with two plates. They sat down on the couch and he passed her a plate.

"Are you sure I'm going to like this?"

"I am confident you will. Libby's recipes are always foolproof."

Michael held his breath as Heather took a bite. She closed her eyes and murmured something he couldn't quite make out. "So, what's the verdict Heather?"

"I don't know how to describe it, it's tangy, but sweet and creamy. It's almost like caramel. Great job. A plus to you."

Michael broke out into a wide grin. "Phew, I was worried there for a minute."

He dug into his pie too, and they fell into easy conversation. Michael mentioned Libby's surprise birthday party, which wouldn't really be a surprise. He knew his Mom would take her out shopping so that they could have a big reveal on their return. Libby knew everything that went on in their house, but she never let on that she knew about any of her many 'surprise' birthday dinners they had over the years.

Feeling more confident Michael inched closer to Heather as he placed his plate on the coffee table.

Remember what Summer said, 'Don't sell yourself short.'

He slid closer still, until their legs were touching. Michael reached out to take her hand, intertwined their fingers, and lifted them to his lips.

Surprised by his gesture, she asked, "you don't have any questions about the project, do you?"

"No," he leaned closer.

"You meant to ask me over for a date?"

"Yes," he leaned even closer. Heather eyes went wide with realization.

He lifted his hand to her cheek and brushed his thumb across her lips. Heather's eyes fluttered closed.

Michael closed the distance between them and pressed his

lips to hers gently. Seeking permission to kiss her again, he released her lips to meet her now open eyes.

She was smiling.

This was all the permission he needed. He dug both hands into her hair and captured her mouth possessively. Heather reached her own hands up to encircle his neck and pull him even closer.

In a practiced move he pushed forward, pressing her body down into the couch as his other hand skimmed up her leg to palm her ass.

Heather squeaked in surprise.

Michael kissed along her jaw to reach her ear, eliciting another gasp from Heather. He moved down to her neck and then back up to capture her lips again.

He was on auto-pilot. And then it dawned on him. He was moving too fast. But damn, it felt good and she seemed to be enjoying it too.

Michael stilled and peeled himself from their embrace. He offered Heather a hand and pulled her up as well.

Heather was beautifully flushed and it took all of his self-control not to pull her into his lap and continue what they had started.

"I know this is all happening pretty fast, but just so there is no confusion, I like you Heather, and I'd love the chance to get to know you better, outside of the project we're working on together. Would you like to have dinner with me?"

She nodded, "when?"

―――

Michael arrived promptly at 5 pm on Sunday afternoon at his parent's home, pie in hand, for the birthday festivities. Soon he was standing in the darkened dining room, along with his Dad and sister waiting for the arrival of the guest of honor.

It wasn't long before they heard their approach. Mikayla turned on the lights and on cue he shouted, 'surprise' along with the others.

They all sat down to enjoy their dinner, and the special dessert courtesy of Michael.

After the meal, Libby enveloped him in a tight hug. "Thank you for the pie, that was very sweet of you to bake that for me."

Summer stepped up and slid her arm around his waist, "so Mike, does that big smile on your face mean that your girl showed yesterday despite your abysmal dating skills?"

"Date?" questioned Libby. "You did not tell me you were seeing someone Michael."

"Summer"

"Don't worry Libby, I'm on it. Once I meet her I will fill you in on all the details. Won't be long before I meet her. Mike hasn't smiled like this in years. So, when are you going to see her again Mike?"

"Next Saturday, for dinner."

Summer was right, he hadn't felt so happy and optimistic about his future in a very long time. He could handle all the teasing she could dish out today, nothing could spoil his excellent mood.

Chapter Five

"Sis, I told you, It's just dinner, I'm taking her to that Italian place down by the water. The food is great and it will be quiet. Off the beaten track."

"Mike, really. Don't you want to impress her? You should make a reservation at a swanky place. Or better yet, invite her over to your place and cook her dinner."

Michael scrunched his eyes as he listened to his sister ramble on about the need to impress Heather on their first date. He just knew that Heather would not be impressed by a fancy restaurant meal. The idea of cooking her dinner was tempting, too tempting in so many ways.

"Summer, I need to get back to work. I promise I'll think about what you said. Talk to you soon."

"Okay Mike, that's all I ask, think about it. I can't wait to hear all about the date next week."

Summer had suggested, well, informed him that they should get together for lunch on Monday instead of their normal coffee meet up so she would hear all about their date. "Grill me, more like it."

Michael leaned back in his chair and closed his eyes again and thought, "She's probably right, I should take her somewhere elegant, refined."

Michael's phone rang again, and for a minute he was worried it was Summer calling back to push her first date agenda. He was in luck, it was only Ted.

"Hey Ted, what's up. And for that matter what are you doing up at this early hour."

"Mike, just because I run a nightclub doesn't mean that I always sleep in late. This is a business call."

'A business call?"

"Yes, Mike, It pains me that you've already forgotten our discussion."

Michael racked his brain to remember what Ted was talking about. "Between this new job and thinking about my date with Heather I am really not paying attention."

"How about you refresh my memory Ted."

"Remember, you said you would make some time to check out the club and talk marketing strategy, this weekend. I want to hear more about how my business is, didn't you say, 'uniquely suited for video marketing'. Well and of course catch up with Laurel and I, have a few drinks. Saturday night."

Now he remembered. Ted didn't even know that he had taken on the new position at the company, and now he had a date that he was definitely not going to cancel. It was time to punt.

"Yeah, Saturday night. I remember. Look Ted, something's come up. I won't be able to make it on Saturday. Can we reschedule?"

"Something's come up, what the hell does that mean? Please don't tell me you'll be working all weekend."

"No, it's not work, although I have taken a new position,

I'm acting COO, I'm really trying to focus on our joint venture project with Roscoe Tech."

"*Geez Mike, do you have to spend the weekend working with that Roscoe guy that you told me about?*"

"No, not exactly. I have a date."

"*A date? Woo Boy, that is so good to hear. Back in the saddle my friend. Hey, why don't you bring her by Verdant on Saturday. I'd love to meet her. I know Laurel would too.*"

"I don't think so Ted. It's our first date, I don't think a club would be the best choice. I'm going to take her to that Italian place down by the waterfront. The food is great, and everybody likes Italian, right."

"*Buddy, you are so out of practice, Verdant would be the perfect place for a first date, booze, dancing, and lots of dark corners. You know as my silent partner I can hook you up with the one of the best tables in the club.*"

"Thanks Ted, I promise I'll think about what you said, that would be fun. I've got to get back to work. Talk to you soon."

"*Soon my man. Just text if you want me to reserve a table in the VIP section for you, is it Saturday night, right?*"

"Yes, Saturday. Go ahead and reserve a table, just in case. Thanks Ted."

"*I've got you covered, what are friends for. Hope to see you Saturday.*"

Ted was right, the club would be fun and there would be booze to loosen things up. The dark corners, that was both a pro and a con. *"That just doesn't seem right for a first date."* Heather doesn't seem like the kind of girl to be dazzled by someone flashing wads of cash in a trendy nightclub, but you never know, she's young, maybe a night clubbing would be right up her alley.

They were here. Sitting at the table. Staring at each other. The uncommonly attentive staff seemed to sense each time they would initiate conversation with one another and immediately approach to check on how thing were going or refill their water glasses.

"If one more person stops by this table before our food arrives I will..."

Before Michael could complete his thought, the Maitre d arrived at their table, "Mr. Dalton, I do hope you are well this evening. The Sommelier wanted me to inform you that he's found your selection, but he'll be just a few moments while he decants the wine. The Cabernet's need to breathe... It should only be a few more minutes. We so appreciate you joining us here this evening."

"Fine. Thank you, Nicolas," Michael practically grunted in response. "We're in no hurry. Tell him to take his time," he added with emphasis, looking the man straight in the eye.

"Of course Mr. Dalton. I'll leave you and your dinner companion to your conversation."

Heather added, "Finally. I said that out loud, didn't I. I'm sorry, I just get the feeling like the staff doesn't want us to talk to each other, like it will screw with their quiet ambience."

Michael grinned, "I completely agree. Can I tell you something Heather?"

"Of course."

"I didn't really want to take you here for dinner."

Heather frowned, "I'm confused, why are we here if you didn't want to take me to dinner Michael?."

"No, no, that's not what I meant. I had a different restaurant in mind. There is this great Italian place down by the waterfront..."

Heather finished his sentence, "Cafe Nostra."

Michael grinned broadly, "You know it. They make the best baked ziti."

"I love Italian."

"I know, doesn't everybody. How about we get out of here and get some real food? I'm starving and I'm really not in the mood for sea bass and quinoa."

Heather stood from her chair, "You don't need to ask me twice, let's go."

Michael rose as well and dropped the starched white napkin from his lap onto the table. He grabbed Heather's hand and ushered them past the gaping wait staff and stunned Sommelier holding a decanter of red wine. He paused as he reached the Maitre D, and pulled two crisp one hundred dollar bills from his billfold, "This should cover it, if not, call my office on Monday and I'll take care of any balance."

Leaving the man speechless, Michael and Heather hurried out of the front door of his establishment. A quick stop at the valet and they were on their way towards the waterfront.

"I hope we can get a table, it is Saturday night, maybe you should just bring me home Michael. We can try again next weekend."

"Have faith Heather. I know they'll have a free table."

Michael pulled into a parking space and hopped out quickly to circle the car and open Heather's door, "Ms. Farchild."

Heather blushed and slid her hand into his as he helped her out of the car. Michael stepped alongside Heather as they walked towards Cafe Nostra. Things were finally back on track. High expectations, here we come.

Chapter Six

"How far is it to the car?"

"No valet here, but it's just a short distance. Do you want to wait here? I can go get the car and pick you up."

Heather groaned, "I am so full."

"You said you needed to eat my last ziti. I warned you to save room for the cannoli."

"I know, I may be entering a food coma, you may have to carry me." Michael moved to hoist her into his arms, "Wait, no, I wasn't serious."

"Okay. I just hate to be responsible for you sliding into a food coma and injuring yourself."

Heather laughed, "Very funny, but you are responsible Michael. Coming here was your idea. An excellent idea I might add," as she bumped into him playfully.

The dinner had been perfect. They arrived just in time to grab the last table out on the patio overlooking the harbor. The view was amazing with the sun setting over the water. The staff let them linger over coffee as they cleaned up the nearby tables.

Michael was carefully carrying a bright pink box which

held the prize cannoli that Heather had requested to enjoy tomorrow. He had marveled at how she ate her dinner with gusto. *"You need to remember she likes red wine, and cannoli for when you cook her dinner."*

After a short walk they reached the car and Michael handed her the box so he could open the door of the car. He held the door for her and his eyes moved down her body as she slid into the smooth leather seat. The slit of her dress opened revealing an expansive section of her thigh as she maneuvered into the seat.

Not wanting to continue gawking he stepped back to close the door softly. The drive back to Heather's apartment was quite short and Michael was sad when he pulled up in front of her building.

Heather moved to exit the car, but Michael grabbed her hand, "Heather, hold on a second. I've got something for you."

He reached behind his seat to pull out a small box tied with a ribbon.

"Here you go. Open it." said Michael as he handed her the box.

Heather smiled, but hesitated, "You didn't need to get me anything. Dinner, and my extra cannoli are quite enough."

"Humor me."

She pulled the red ribbon from the box and opened it to reveal a navy blue stress ball. "Is this a stress ball?" questioned Heather as she turned it over in her hands.

"Yes, it has both the company logos, we created a bunch of promo items for the joint venture when I was heading up the marketing team."

"Great, thanks."

"Ok Dalton, you got the restaurant right, but not the corny post date gift. You'll just have to send her some flowers next week to make up for this," he thought.

"That's very sweet of you Michael, I can always use another tool to release my stress," said Heather as she blushed a bit and leaned in to kiss his cheek. Michael was at an odd angle and she caught the corner of his mouth instead. Surprised, Heather began to pull away, but Michael turned towards her and reached up to cradle her face.

"Heather," he whispered as he pressed his lips to hers and then shifted again so he could deepen the kiss. Before long they were both breathless. Michael stroked his thumb across her lips.

"I guess I should walk you to your door."

Heather nodded, unable to say a word. Michael hopped out of the car once again to help her out of the car. They walked hand in hand up to her door.

Heather pulled out her keys and said softly, "Would you like to come in?"

Michael paused willing himself to think before answering. *Yes, I would really like to come in and stay to cook you breakfast tomorrow morning.*

He leaned forward to give her a chaste kiss, "Thank you for the invitation, but I should probably head home."

"Oh, okay" said Heather, looking a bit deflated.

"Heather, you've got to know that I really want to come in. But if I do, well, just like I said last weekend..."

She smiled, "I know. Dinner was perfect Michael, thank you again."

"Goodnight Heather, I'll see you again soon," and he turned to walk back to his car.

That was a pitiful goodbye.

He stopped and then spun around to race back to a very startled Heather. Michael swept her into his arms for a toe-curling kiss. The pair clung to one another while they caught their breath.

"Wow, that was quite a goodnight kiss. I said that out loud, didn't I," added Heather.

Michael broke out into an even wider grin and kissed her again, dipping her back until she squeaked again.

"When can I see you again? Are you busy tomorrow? How about breakfast?"

"Breakfast?"

"Heather, I'd love to come in and stay to cook you breakfast tomorrow. But since I'm a gentleman, I'll settle for taking you out for breakfast tomorrow, or brunch or coffee." Michael felt a bit ridiculous with his pleading, but every time he was around Heather he became a desperate hungry man.

"Tomorrow, coffee, sounds perfect. I can meet you at 9 am at Bean."

"It's a date," and with one final peck on the lips Michael was truly on his way home, with a spring in his step.

As the joint venture project accelerated into its final stages, Michael and Heather were each working longer and longer hours. They both tried to check in with each other, a coffee here, a lunch there. But the oppressive schedule meant absolutely zero date opportunities.

First Michael invited Heather over for dinner. The night of their date Heather got stuck coding to fix a major obstacle in one of the software modules. He was disappointed. Heather was even more disappointed - Michael had made pie.

Next Heather invited Michael to join her for a symphony performance of the music of Star Wars. Michael had to cancel due to a last minute trip to London. He'd needed to go in Eric's place - Eric - who never got sick - managed to get the flu. She was disappointed. Michael was even more disappointed when he got a glimpse of the dress Heather had chosen to wear to the concert when she face-timed him on the way to the concert.

Flashbulbs were going off in quick succession as the four men entered the ballroom and approached the podium. Dozens of reporters lined sides of the room, a few were crouching down in front of the first row of chairs.

Roscoe Dalton moved to the podium flanked by Eric Carnegie, Michael and Mark Roscoe.

"Thank you all for coming. For those of you who don't know me, I'm Roscoe Dalton, CEO of Dalton Tech. I'd like to introduce my son, Michael, who'll be making a short statement, followed by Mark Roscoe, CEO of Roscoe Technologies. Following our statements we'll take a few questions."

Roscoe stepped aside and turned to shake Michael's hand as he moved to the podium.

"We're here to update you on Dalton Tech's joint venture with Roscoe Tech. This project brought together the manufacturing expertise of Dalton Tech and the technical vision of Mark Roscoe and his team at Roscoe Tech."

"I'd like to officially introduce Mark Roscoe, the innovative inventor who spearheaded our efforts."

Mark Roscoe took Michael's place at the podium and began his presentation.

The ballroom adjacent to the press conference space had been transformed into a shimmery wonderland of twinkly lighted ficus trees and cozy tables with mylar balloon centerpieces featuring the logos of the two companies. Michael grabbed a flute of champagne from a passing waiter as he scanned the room for Heather. He spotted Roscoe across the room in the midst of a crowd of people to the left of the open bar. Then he saw her.

She was wearing the dress that had left his mouth watering when he was in London. The red halter top dress accented her shoulders. His eyes traveled down to her shapely legs.

Heather shifted to gain some separation from the crowd that had gathered around Mark. She was really done talking about the joint venture. Heather had already heard all of Mark's party jokes three times over. Luckily she caught Michael's eye from across the room and smiled lifting her hand to wave him over.

"So a neutron walks into a bar and asks, "How much for a drink?" The bartender replies, "For you, no charge."

The assembled group broke out into a chorus of loud laughter right as Michael reached Heather's side. Michael lid his arm around her waist and pulled her further away from Mark's admirers. He leaned in to kiss her cheek, "Hey you."

"Hey yourself. Did you just get here? Great party by the way."

"Thanks, but this is mostly the work of the marketing team. They are so much happier without me in charge. But I did just arrive, are you having fun?"

"Free champagne, plenty of food, and now you're here. I'm good," as she leaned into his embrace.

"I'm pleased that the project is moving to the manufacturing stage, and I can't believe I'm saying this, but I'm actually going to miss the weekly project meetings."

"Admit it Michael, you are going to miss seeing Mark every week. I'm sure he'd clear his Saturdays to meet you for lunch."

Michael laughed, "There might be someone else that I've grown accustomed to seeing every weekend. Someone who is so busy and important that I can't even make it onto her busy schedule."

Heather bumped his shoulder, "I know it's been hectic, but now that we're done with the launch our schedule will calm down. You owe me dinner and pie mister."

A pounding baseline filled their ears as they entered Verdant. Michael leaned over to yell into Heather's ear, "This way, Ted is expecting us."

Michael pulled Heather by the hand as they wove through the throng on people on the dance floor to reach the velvet roped entrance to the stairs that led up to the VIP section. A tall and impressively broad man dressed in black stood guard over the entrance with his arms crossed.

Ted Teddy appeared behind the man and clapped his hand on his shoulder while he said something into his ear. The man nodded and quickly moved the rope to let them through.

He retreated up the stairs. Michael and Heather followed. Once they reached the top of the stairs and stepped into the significantly quieter VIP space, Ted greeted Michael with a hug, "Michael, man, great to see you. And you must be Heather. I've heard so much about you."

"Yes, that's me, Heather. Heather Farchild. And what exactly have you heard about me?"

Ted opened his mouth to speak but was stopped as his girlfriend appeared at his side. "You must be Heather, ignore Ted, I do most of the time. I'm Laurel by the way, great to meet you."

Laurel and Heather left the two men to slide into a booth near the back wall of the room.

"Buddy, she is hot. Where did you meet her?"

"Ted, don't let Laurel hear you. Remember, I met her at

work Ted. We've been working together on the joint venture. She works for Roscoe Tech."

"Looks and brains. Well done. So what are you drinking tonight my man, scotch?"

After a couple rounds of drinks Michael felt warm and relaxed especially with Heather tucked in close to his side. His arm was slung loosely around her shoulders allowing his fingers to trail from her shoulder and down the smooth skin on her exposed arms in a rhythmic pattern.

"Heather, did you grow up in Mornington?"

"No, I'm a transplant, by way of Vegas and then Boston, where I went to college."

"Vegas," Ted smiled, "Mike and I took many awesome trips to Vegas, good times," he winced as Laurel poked in him the side to halt his trip down memory lane.

"So do you like to gamble? I would love to have add a few tables here at the club, especially up here for my VIPs, but too bad we can't."

"Well technically you could offer card games, as long as there was no betting."

"Sounds good - I think I've got a deck of cards in my office. You guys up for a friendly game?" Without waiting for an answer Ted rose from his chair and left the room.

Laurel chimed in, "you don't have to play, Ted can be a bit over excited sometimes. Too much energy. Maybe I can convince him to head downstairs for a dance."

"I'd love to play, but I don't think it would be very fair."

"Fair," Laurel questioned.

Michael piped in, "If I remember correctly from the day we met, you said you always win."

Laurel looked incredulous, "that's not possible."

Ted returned to their table, deck of cards in hand. He signaled the waitress who approached their table. "We'll need 4 shot glasses, and a bottle of vodka."

"What do we need shot glasses for Ted?" queried Michael.

"Heather said we can't bet, but we can make the game interesting. Winner of each round takes one shot, and the losers take two."

Heather responded, "Okay, sounds fair to me."

Michael was annoyed, "Heather, we don't have to play. It's been a long day."

"I'll play, but no shots for me, I'm your designated driver Ted, and tomorrow is a work day," answered Laurel.

"Everybody set, here we go," said Ted as he dealt the first round of cards.

Michael wondered if Heather had been honest about her hidden talent after she lost the first two hands of poker, one to Ted and one to Michael. Then Heather easily won the next two rounds. Michael felt woozy. Ted was getting annoyed.

"You are good Farchild. Why are you so lucky?"

"It's not luck, it's skill."

Michael couldn't focus. Heather easily balanced her cards in one hand and stroked his leg with the other. She placed her cards down on the table for a moment and leaned in to whisper in his ear, "You doing ok?"

Michael choked out a "yes, I'm fine."

Of course I'm fine, you're pressed up against me and rubbing your hand up and down my leg.

Next Heather laid out her cards, "Full house, can you beat that Teddy?"

Ted scowled and threw his cards down, "No, obviously I can't," and he refilled the shot glasses from the now mostly empty bottle. He downed the shot and refilled both his and Michael's for their second one since they had lost the round.

Heather stood up and wobbled a bit, pressing her hand onto Michael's shoulder for support. He rose next and pulled Ted into a brief hug. Michael grabbed Heather's hand to lead her down the stairs. They reached the entrance where the bouncer said, "Mr. Dalton, your cab will be here in a few minutes."

"Thank you."

"Ted is a good host. Maybe a bit of a sore loser. It was nice of him to call us a cab. I am in no condition to drive," as she swayed again in Michael's arms, sliding her hands up to encircle his neck.

Once they were settled in the cab Heather moved closer and pressed her lips to his neck. He shuddered. Leaning down, he captured her lips. She sighed as he tilted her head to deepen the kiss. The cab came to an abrupt stop in front of Heather's door.

"Would you like to come in?"

Michael grinned and seized her lips again, "Lead the way."

Chapter Seven

Michael stretched in bed. Why was his head pounding? He fought the urge to roll over and go back to sleep. He squinted in the bright morning light that was streaming through the sheer pink curtains.

"Pink curtains?"

It was quite apparent that he was not waking up at his townhouse. The memories of the previously night cascaded through his mind.

"Would you like to come in?"

"Lead the way."

Heather had offered wine, but he didn't give her much of a chance to reach the bottle. Michael boxed her against the counter and pulled her close. He slid her hair to the side to reveal her bare shoulder and pressed his lips against her cool skin. She turned in his arms and slipped from his grasp, bottle of wine and corkscrew in hand. He smiled as he remembered her giggle as she darted up the stairs.

Looking around the room he spotted the telltale signs of the previous evening's activities. A half empty bottle of wine on the dresser, her heels by the door, his jacket and shirt slung over a chair and her bra hung over the bedpost.

Michael leaned up on his elbows to get a good look at his bed partner. Her back was exposed, but her face was hidden by a halo of still damp blonde curls.

The shower...

I should wake her up and we can get started on round three...

Michael reached out to caress her back but paused. *No, it would be better so much better to wake her up after I've made her breakfast. Yes, we'll need food.*

He slipped on his boxers and pants that were lying pooled on the floor beside the bed and headed down the stairs to the kitchen. There wasn't much to work with in the fridge, but there were eggs - he could make an omelet.

Coffee. Must make coffee. Heather loves her coffee.

Michael was not surprised when he found the coffeemaker on the countertop preloaded and ready to go. He hit the start button and went in search of mugs.

Vrrmm, Vrrmm. His pocket buzzed. Michael ignored it and continued his search of the cabinets. It didn't take long before his phone was ringing again.

Michael pulled the phone from his pocket to see a photo of Summer filling the screen.

"Hey Summer, what's up?"

"Mike, oh my God. Why haven't you been answering your phone? I've been calling for hours."

"I was sleeping. I know it's a weekday, but I gave everyone on the project team the day off to recuperate after the launch party. What's wrong?"

"It's Dad. Mike, he's in the hospital, intensive care. They're preparing him for surgery. You need to get here as soon as you can."

"Surgery, Summer, slow down, what happened."

"Heart attack. It's bad Mike. I'm scared. Even Mom is scared, and you know she never gets upset. You need to hurry. We're at Starling General."

"Ok Summer. I'll be there as quickly as I can. Tell Mom I'm on my way."

The coffee maker dinged.

Michael groaned. *Heather. I can't make her breakfast. I don't even have time to say goodbye.*

He hurried up the stairs and stepped quietly into Heather's bedroom. He grabbed his shirt and jacket from the chair, slipped on his shoes, and shoved his socks into his pocket.

Michael allowed himself one minute to gaze at Heather who was still curled up in the bed fast asleep. He dropped his head and turned to leave. Michael dashed down the stairs and was out the door.

Heather woke with a start at the sound of a slamming door. Still disoriented from the abrupt awakening, she sat up in bed and looked around.

Empty bed, clothes gone. Heather fell back into bed and pulled the covers over her head.

Heather was up to her eyeballs in computing power, multitasking between her tablet and workstation. She was happy to be back at the office. It was just what she needed - a huge distraction.

The door to her office swung open and Ellis Thompson entered, skidding to a stop in front of her desk.

"Heather, did you hear the news?"

"No, what news."

"About Dalton Tech."

"Dalton Tech?"

"Just turn on the TV, try channel 43, I think the press conference is about to start."

She rose to reach the remote on her conference table to turn on the TV. The camera was focused on an empty podium surrounded by microphones.

The announcer said, *"We expect the press conference to begin shortly. Michael Dalton, acting COO will be making a statement, look, he's arrived and is approaching the podium."*

Heather's legs buckled, seeing him again, even on a TV screen was too much. She pulled out a chair and sat down.

"Thank for you coming. Our PR team is handing out copies of my remarks. I will not be taking questions. They will be available to answer your questions following my statement."

"My father, Roscoe Dalton suffered a heart attack late Wednesday evening."

Heather gasped.

"He is currently recovering at Starling General following open heart bypass surgery. His condition is stable and he is expected to make a full recovery."

As the camera zoomed in for a close-up and Heather could see dark circles blossoming around his eyes. He looked weary and appeared to be wearing the same clothes he had worn to the post launch reception.

"In the interim I will be taking on the role of CEO. Eric Carnegie, our current CFO has also agreed to act as liaison between myself and the board as well as facilitating the ongoing work with our joint venture with Roscoe Technologies."

Ellis chimed in, "I guess we won't be seeing much of him around here anymore. Uh, sorry Heather."

"My family and I appreciate all of the support we've

received, but ask for privacy during this difficult time and for my father's upcoming recovery."

"Well, at least he had a good reason for skipping out."

"*I want to assure the Dalton Tech Board, our stockholders, our employees and customers that you have my full commitment to the company and its success. Thank you.*"

Michael left the podium and was ushered off the stage to a waiting limousine

"Hey Heather. I know that you and Michael were getting close. This is awful news. Wait, did I hear you say that he had a good reason for skipping out?"

"Yes, no, it's not important." She turned off the TV and returned to her desk. Heather spun her chair to look out into the grey sky.

"Oh no you don't, Heather. Spill. Now that I think of it, you disappeared during the reception and you weren't at work yesterday."

She turned back to face him, eyes full of tears. "So, Michael and I went out to a club after the reception."

"A club, wow, that's exciting news. Did you get to press up against that gorgeous hunk of a man on the dance floor?"

"No, but we did a lot of drinking."

"And then..."

"He came over to my place, and he might have spent the night, but left without telling me in the morning or even leaving a note. But strangely enough I think he made coffee before he left."

"Heather, he spent the night? Please tell me he didn't just pass out drunk on your couch."

"No. But I don't want to talk about it."

"Don't you think you should call him and see how he's doing? He looked pretty worn out at that press conference. He needs a hug."

"Ellis, obviously the whole sleeping together thing was a mistake. We were never serious, just a bunch of lunches and coffees. Just one real date."

"I think you're wrong Heather. Having someone to lean on in a relationship is what gets you through the tough times. I don't know what I would do sometimes without Paul to keep me grounded, he's my rock."

"You and Paul, that's something special. We will just agree to disagree about Michael. Look Ellis, I have to get back to work. Mark is going to be barging in here any minute about damage control after that announcement. I know we're good, but you know how he gets."

Three Weeks Later

Summer stepped off the executive elevator to greet Janice, her Dad's, well now Michael's EA.

"Hey Janice, how's the big grouch today?"

"Summer, good to see you. The same I'm afraid. He's here when I arrive, and still working when I leave"

"I was really hoping you'd get him to crack by showing him that cute video of your granddaughter carving pumpkins. So can I go right in, or do I need an appointment?"

"You know you never need one, but let me buzz him, that way he'll bark at me instead of you."

Janice picked up her phone and hit the intercom button.

"Yes, Janice, what is it?" Michael growled.

"Michael, your sister Summer is here to see you, I'm sending her in."

"Tell her I'm not available Janice..."

Janice hung up before he could finish. "Good luck Summer, you'll need it."

Summer opened the door to her brother's office. "Geez Mike, you don't need to bite the woman's head off."

"Summer, it's good to see you, but I don't have much time. I've got to get through these financial reports before my 2 pm meeting with Eric."

"Mike, let's go grab some coffee. You sound and look like you need a break. Mom and Dad say hello by the way."

Michael pushed back from his desk and rubbed his face with his hands.

"Summer, I can't maybe another time."

"But Mike, It's only 10 am, your meeting isn't until 2 pm. Just give me an hour."

"I won't be very good company."

"You are always good company. And now that I think of it, how are things going with you and your lady? I know your first date was a big success, even though you totally ignored my awesome dating advice."

Michael's focus had returned to the papers on his desk, "Nothing to tell Summer. It's over."

"It's over. Mike. I know it was a touch and go with Dad for a few days, and then really stressful for another week or two, but he's doing so much better, he's getting stronger every day. When is the last time you talked with her? I'm sure she'll understand."

"It's been too long Summer, she's not going to want to see me or talk to me again after what I did."

"This sounds like a perfect opportunity for me to again bestow upon you my sage dating advice. Come on Mike, let's just go get some coffee." Summer continued to plead and cajole but she was unsuccessful and left his office, slamming his door closed, "no luck Janice. But I'm not giving up yet. Keep me posted."

Janice smiled with understanding, "see you later Summer."

The mood was not much better over a Roscoe Technologies. Ellis was annoyed that he had been unable to spur Heather to pick up the phone, or text or stop by to see one Michael Dalton. She was focused on her work, putting out fires related to the joint venture, but there was no spark, no jokes, no babbling.

He couldn't stand it anymore. It was now or never. Entering her office in a rush, Ellis moved quickly to shut her laptop and then jump back.

"Ellis, what are you doing," as she reopened her laptop and scowled in his direction.

"Let's go get some coffee, and a snack, I'm hungry."

"That's fine Ellis, take a break, I'll keep working until you're back."

"No, you need to take a break, Heather."

"No I don't," as she continued to type.

"Heather, this is an intervention. I miss you."

"I'm right here Ellis. Nothing to miss."

"Have you taken my advice, about calling Michael?"

"Ellis, do we have to talk about this again? I'm over it, I've moved on, it was fun while it lasted, but it's over."

Ellis was deflated, she was unaffected by his perseverance. He needed another plan of attack.

"How about if I go get some coffee from Bean and then once I get back you can take a short break?"

Heather didn't look up from her work and answered, "Sure Ellis."

Ellis headed out and muttered to himself, "Okay, but I still don't believe you. I'm going to get those blueberry scones you like and I won't share them."

Bean was bustling. Summer had taken one of the few open seats at the counter near the cash register. She took a long sip from her chai latte. A very tall black man approached the cashier.

The barista greeting him, "Hey Ellis, good to see you."

"Hey Kimberly, what's good today? Do you still have any blueberry scones left?"

'You are in luck, there are two left, one for you and one for Heather. Come to think of it, why isn't Heather with you. I haven't seen her in a while. Don't tell me she's found another coffee shop."

Summer's ears perked up.

"She's not here, nose to the grindstone. I knew that your blueberry scones might tempt her to take a break."

"So two cups of French roast, with room for cream, and two scones. It will only be a minute."

Summer turned to the man and introduced herself. "Excuse me."

Ellis turned towards her and smiled, "Hi, how are you doing..."

She extended her hand to him, "Summer, Summer Dalton."

Ellis's eyes went wide, "I'm Ellis Thompson and you're Summer Dalton, wow, great to meet you. I work over a Roscoe Technologies, we're working on a big project with Dalton Tech. Oh, I was sorry to hear about your Dad. I hope he is doing better."

"Thanks for asking, he's at home doing his rehab, but it is hard to get him to actually rest."

"I heard you talking about a friend, Heather was it?"

"Yes, I'm picking up some coffee, and well scones for both of us. She's been in such a funk. I can't get her to wake up and smell the coffee and give Michael a call..."

"Michael, yup... and you're Summer Dalton, his sister."

"Yes I am Ellis, and I am so glad to meet you. We have so much to talk about."

Chapter Eight

Summer Dalton: Get her to the spot by 10:05 at the latest.

Ellis Thompson: Roger that, t-minus 30 and counting on my mark.

Summer Dalton: What? Just make sure she leaves on time.

Ellis Thompson: Got it, fingers crossed. I will get her to the dropzone.

Summer Dalton: Dropzone? Keep me posted.

Michael sat at their normal table with a view of the street so he could watch for Summer's approach. She had been unbelievably persistent about restarting their regular Saturday coffee dates. He smiled - that was new - it was probably time to smile more and work a bit less on the weekends. Summer was right, their Dad was recovering and everyone at Dalton Tech had gotten used to the idea of him being CEO. Eric had been such a great resource and cheerleader. He had arrived extra early and was already done with his first cup of coffee. Summer wasn't scheduled to arrive for another 10 minutes. Michael headed up to the counter for a refill and to place Summer's order.

Meanwhile, at a nearby intersection, 1 block north of the 'drop zone'

Heather was struggling to keep up with Ellis' long strides as they crossed the street.

"Ellis, slow down, why are you walking so fast?"

"I don't want to be late."

"Late, late for what? I'm pretty sure they'll still have coffee no matter when we get there, they sell coffee all day. These promised heavenly pastries better meet my very high expectations after this walk. Moderate pace my ass."

"I promise you, it will be so worth it, for both of us."

The pair continued their brisk pace down the sidewalk. Heather bobbed and weaved around numerous pedestrians and dogs in her attempt to keep up with Ellis.

Heather looked down for a moment to avoid hole in the sidewalk when, "Oh," she crashed right into Ellis who had stopped abruptly and was bent over, holding his side and wincing.

"Uh.. Heather, you'll have to go... without me... I can't ... have to rest..."

"But Ellis, I can just wait here with you while you rest."

"No!"

"No? I really don't mind."

"You... just go on... I'll catch ... up ... in a bit."

Heather tilted her head in confusion. "Okay, if you say so, but if I don't see you down at the coffee shop in 10 minutes I'm coming back."

"Thanks Heather," he sputtered as he continued to breath heavily. He sat down on the ground and hung his head between his knees.

Heather patted him on the back. "Okay, rest up, see you soon," and she was on her way.

"That was so weird. I thought he was an Olympian. Geez, he is really out of shape."

Ellis hopped up from the sidewalk and moved behind a nearby tree until he saw Heather round the corner. With Heather out of sight Ellis pulled out his phone.

Ellis Thompson: The package is on its way.

Summer Dalton: Package, oh, you mean Heather. She better hurry, Michael is probably already there.

Ellis Thompson: She will, I told her about the chocolate croissants, she's power walking.

Summer Dalton: So Excited

Meanwhile, back at the coffee shop - otherwise known as the 'drop zone'

Summer was late, where was she. Michael shot off a quick text, and there was no reply. *That's odd. Maybe I should stop by her apartment, just in case we got our signals crossed.*

He rose from his table to return his cup to the counter. Michael poured Summer's still warm chai latte into a to-go cup and started towards the door.

Little did he know that Heather was approaching the coffee shop.

Ellis was crouching behind a large potted shrub when he saw Michael exit the coffee shop.

Michael went through the door and narrowly missed bumping into a mom tugging a small child by the hand while pushing a stroller. As he passed the toddler dropped a stuffed bear and Michael stooped to retrieve it for the child.

"Damn it, Michael, stand up so you can see her!" he cursed. A passing woman eyed him oddly.

"Here you go buddy," as Michael held out the bear for the child.

In the next moment Heather popped into the coffee shop as the couple exiting held the door for her. Ellis slid to the ground. They had missed each other.

Ellis Thompson: Mayday, Mayday, the package has missed rendezvous point.

Summer Dalton: I know he was there - he just texted me. What happened?

Ellis Thompson: The parachute did not deploy

Summer Dalton: Parachute?

———

Summer Dalton: Hey Ellis, I have another idea.

Ellis Thompson: What you got

Summer Dalton: Can you get Heather to the R&D lab at Dalton Tech - Thurs 3 pm

Ellis Thompson: I'm on it. How will you get Michael there?

Summer Dalton: I'll request a tour, he loves when I take an interest in the company.

———

"Heather, isn't this week scheduled for your girls in STEM field trip? "

Now that the joint venture was up and running smoothly, Heather had returned to coaching the 'Girl Code' STEM group at Bennett High School. The group met weekly and we working on a number of robotic machines and vehicles to enter in the upcoming regional NASA robotics competition. Just for fun they had monthly field trips, mostly to local technology companies to broaden the girls to all kinds of math, science, and technology - not just robotics.

"Yes, it is field trip week. I was going to double dip and bring them to see our product development lab again. There are a few new kids in the group, so hopefully the rest won't be disappointed."

"Why don't you bring them on a tour of the demonstration factory in the R&D lab over at Dalton Tech? That would show them a real world use of robotic technology."

Heather thought for a moment, she was a bit hesitant to set foot over at Dalton Tech, but there was no chance that she'd run into Michael - he never came to the lab - he was eighteen floors up in the executive offices - a safe distance.

"Good idea Ellis. I have to message the team, but could you check in with Fred over at REVIEW to set up the tour, Thursday at 1 p.m.?"

Ellis broke into a wide grin, "happy to help." He sat down at his workstation to send an email to Fred, but looked at his phone and stopped to share the good news with his partner in crime.

Ellis Thompson: All set, she'll be there Thurs 1 pm
Summer Dalton: Sweet!

To be honest, Heather was a bit surprised at how excited the girls on her team were about the visit to REVIEW. Sure, they were all top students and loved building things, but the constant bevy of whispers and giggles coming from the group behind her was unnerving.

A tall girl in the back of the group leaned over to her friend, "Do you think we'll see him? I mean he is CEO."

Her friend sighed, "doubtful, we're touring the R&D lab, not the executive offices."

"Do you think Heather knows him? Or maybe we could press the wrong button on the elevator…"

The group finished checking in at the security desk and approached the bank of elevators. "Okay girls, we're heading up to the 20th floor. Half of you go with Mr. Thompson, the other half with me. I know that you'll be on your best behavior. We won't be able to go into the clean room, but they have a great viewing portal in the lab."

The two girls slipped into the elevator, a bit annoyed that Heather was standing right in front of the floor selection buttons.

Summer entered the main lobby of REVIEW and caught a glimpse of Heather and the group of teenage girls getting on the elevator.

"Just in time," as she hurried to catch the next elevator on her way to meet her brother.

Meanwhile on the Executive Floor

"Janice, I'll be back in a couple of hours. I'm meeting Summer to give her a tour of the R&D lab. Text me if anything urgent comes up."

She was quick to answer, "of course Michael, I'll be in touch for anything urgent. Have fun."

Janice smiled and shot off a quick text to Summer indicating that he was on his way and she would not be texting him about anything - nothing would be urgent enough to stop this important meeting.

Heather and her group arrived on at the R&D lab floor and headed through another security checkpoint.

Ellis moved ahead of Heather, "I'll sign them in, why don't you wait here for Fred," knowing full well that Michael Dalton would soon be stepping out of one of the elevators.

"Okay, sounds good. Fred should be here any minute," as she pulled out her tablet to quickly check her email.

The elevator opened and out stepped Fred Harrington, the Technical Project Engineer for the joint venture. Summer was right behind him.

"Heather, hey, good to see you. I was so happy to get your call. I've missed seeing you since we turned the project over to the manufacturing team." and they turned together to head towards the robotic manufacturing exhibit.

Ellis Thompson: Where are you?
Summer Dalton: Just got here, Mike will be right down.
Ellis Thompson: I'm so excited
Summer Dalton: Me too, sparks will fly

Summer slid her phone back into her purse. The elevator dinged and Michael stepped out of the elevator. "Summer, you're already here," as he pulled her into a tight hug.

"This is so exciting Mike."

"Really, Summer, I was surprised when you called about wanting to take a tour. I didn't think that technology was your thing."

"You've stepped up to take on a bigger role in the company. It's time I did the same, and this is a great way to start."

Michael led them past the security desk and down the hall.

Summer picked up her pace as she caught sight of the end group of girls turn the corner towards the lab.

"Summer, slow down, why are you rushing?"

"I told you Mike, I'm so excited."

The pair reached the R&D lab and Summer moved over to the large picture window which now had a view of the group of a dozen teenage girls gathered around row of computer monitors.

"Mike, wow, that is quite impressive," as she worked to gain Michael's attention. He stepped towards the windows and Summer held her breath, waiting for him to notice Heather. She wasn't much taller than the student in her group, she kept leaning over and disappearing from view.

One of the girls standing near the back of the crowd sensed that someone was looking through the window behind them and turned around. Her mouth dropped open and she tugged on the sleeve of the girl next to her.

"It's him," she whispered. Her friend turned and broke into a wide smile. The tugging and whispering cascaded down the line until most of the group was staring at Michael and Summer - well mostly at Michael.

"Summer, I think we're disturbing the group that's in there now, let's hang back a bit." Michael took a step away from the window, Summer reached out to stop him.

"No, we should stay here, better yet, let's go inside so we can hear the presentation, I'm sure they won't mind."

Am I imagining it or are those girls moving closer to the window?

He wasn't. Soon the majority of the girls were practically pressed up the window, unashamedly looking him up and down.

I feel like a piece of meat.

Michael gave an awkward wave to the assembled group.

Summer was overjoyed, they were so close, he'd notice Heather any second and then she could sit back and watch their reunion. She caught Ellis' eye and have signaled with a double thumbs up.

She was so busy reveling in their success that she didn't see the security guard approach.

"Mr. Dalton, sorry to interrupt, but I have a phone call at the desk for you. It's Eric Carnegie, he says its urgent."

Summer's eye went wide. Ellis was shocked and waved his arms, signally Summer to do something. But Michael quickly turned on his heels to follow the security guard. Summer grabbed his sleeve in a vain attempt to stop him, "But Mike, can't it wait for a few minutes, you can call him back. I really want to go in and see the lab, now."

"Summer, I'll only be a second."

It was in that moment that Heather chose to turn around to see her STEM team looking out the window.

She scolded them, "Girls, pay attention, come back over here and get away from the window."

Summer hovered in the lobby to wait for Ellis' arrival. She saw him converse with Heather and watched as she lead her teenage charges out the front door.

"What happened, we were so close?"

"He got a phone call, he is so damned responsible now. The old Mike would have blown it off."

"I guess we need to try again."

"Yes we do."

"So what's the plan."

"We call in the big guns."

"The big guns?"

Summer pulled out her phone and scrolled through her contacts.

"Hi Mom, it's Summer, I was wondering if you are free for lunch tomorrow?"

The lunchtime crowd at the Mornington country club restaurant was buzzing. Summer saw her mother from across the room at the usual table positioned off in an alcove overlooking the 1st tee.

As she reached the table she leaned in to kiss her mother's cheek, "How are you Mom? Dad still giving you trouble?"

"Of course, I can't get the man to properly rest. Do you know he asked his doctor if he could play golf again, and the doctor said yes, if he rode in the cart."

"That sounds like Dad. Without going to work each day he's got to be bored out of his mind."

"Yes, but deep down he knows it is time to retire. He was grooming Michael to take over, the heart attack just sped up his schedule. He is adjusting, slowly. So, why did you ask me to lunch dear? You could have just stopped by the house if you wanted an update on your Dad."

"Mom, I need your help with an important project. I'm having a bit of trouble pulling it all together."

She smiled, "Of course, how can I help?"

Summer didn't normally ramble, but once she started talking about Michael and Heather, how they had met and why the insanely stupid reason that they were no longer together she couldn't stop. Next she explained the great lengths that she and Ellis had gone to over the past few weeks to arrange an accidental meeting. Mikayla listened with attention and Summer was sure that her mother was ready to step in and help reunite Michael with her future sister-in-law.

"I don't think you should do anything else."

"Great, so you'll help. I knew you would."

"No."

"No?"

"Summer, Michael is a grown man, he can handle his own love life."

"But Mom..."

"Let them work it out on their own Summer. Have faith, if it is meant to be, it will work out somehow. Maybe he just needs a bit more time."

"More time. It's been a month since they..."

"They what Summer?"

"Uh... since they went on a date. That is too long, he needs to call her before someone else snatches her up. She's special Mom, you should hear the way he talks about here. Wouldn't the media just eat up a story of true love? I know it would help the company's image," Summer added in desperation.

"Let it be Summer, let's enjoy our lunch."

Summer was dejected. This was not the answer she had expected or desired.

Chapter Nine

Michael tugged at his bow tie as he entered the ballroom at the Grand Hotel for the yearly fundraiser and award presentation for the Mornington Civitas club.

Why are these damn ties always too tight.

The room was filled to bursting with the well connected of Mornington in their dress to impress best. White gloved waiters weaved through the crowd with canapés and glasses of champagne. As Michael stepped onto the space he grabbed a glass from a passing waiter and chugged it down.

"Easy there buddy, somebody might think you don't want to be here."

Summer appeared at his side, the light reflecting off her beaded gown.

"Mom rope you into coming too?"

"No, I'm here in Dad's place, he was supposed to present the Humanitarian of the Year award and also, pass along REVIEW's donation."

"Lucky you, yes, CEO Michael Dalton. You look the part. I

guess I'll see you later. Good luck with your speech bro. I'm off to check out the dessert table."

Michael walked past the many food tables and scanned the silent auction offerings in an effort to kill time and avoid having to strike up a conversation with any of the chipper party goers. There were so many people. Michael spun around to make space for a throng of passing guests, but he bumped into someone and turned around again to say, "Excuse me..."

The rest of the room faded as his eyes connected with a pair of familiar blue eyes that belonged to Heather Farchild.

"Michael, hi. It's good to see you.... again."

"It is good to see you too Heather."

Heather shifted to put some space between them, "how is your Dad? I hope he's better. I've heard a few things, at the office, through the grapevine..."

Michael reached up to place his hand on her shoulder, but quickly rethought the gesture as too personal and removed it. "Thank you, he is better, he's made quite a bit of progress in the last few weeks. That's why I'm here. I'm standing in for him to present an award."

"That right, congratulations on being named CEO."

Michael lost focus for a moment as he stared into her eyes. *How did I forget how beautiful she is. It's now or never, isn't it.*

"Would you like to dance?"

"Dance, yes, uh, no. Two left feet."

"Heather, please," as he held out his hand.

She accepted his hand and they walked to join the swaying crowd on the dance floor, "okay, but fair warning, your feet will be at risk."

"I'll take my chances."

As they began to dance Michael pulled back, "Heather, I'm so sorry."

"Michael,"

"Please, let me finish Heather."

Michael leaned closer to speak directly into her ear and they continued to sway. "I wish I could go back and change what I did that morning. I woke up and I wanted to bring you breakfast in bed, but then Summer called. She was frantic. She'd been trying to call me for hours."

"That makes sense Michael. Who wouldn't rush out when their family needed them? I understand."

A presence invaded their moment, "Excuse me, Mr. Dalton, could you and your partner look this way?"

Heather turned toward the voice and was greeted with a blinding flash.

Not wanting to lose the momentum of their conversation, Michael paused and said, "Why don't we take a break and find somewhere quiet, where we can talk."

He led her across the room and followed a cool breeze through a set of open french doors. There was a chill in the air, a glimpse of the change in seasons. The night sky was filled with stars and Michael and Heather walked to the railing to take in the view of the city lights.

"Beautiful, isn't it," commented Heather.

"Breathtaking." Michael wasn't talking about the view of the city.

An uneasy silence fell between the pair as neither one appeared ready to restart their conversation. But soon the silence became unbearable and they both turned to each other and said, "I've missed you."

Heather smiled and stepped closed to Michael. She wound her arm through his and threaded their fingers together as they leaned on the railing.

"I missed stopping by to bring you coffee, I missed going out to lunch, I've missed everything. I can't believe I was so stupid to throw that all away."

"Michael, let it go. You haven't thrown it all away. Let's start over," as she pulled her arm away and stepped back. She extended her hand to Michael, "Hi, I'm Heather Farchild."

He broke into a wide grin, "It's great to meet you Heather, I'm Michael Dalton."

"Would you like to go to dinner with me?"

Heather leaned forward to reply, "just so you know Mr. Dalton, I don't put out on the first date."

They both laughed, but then noticed their proximity and they both began to lean in for a kiss.

A young woman approached the pair and cleared her throat, "excuse me, Mr. Dalton, so sorry to, uh, interrupt. I'm Becky from the Civitas organization. I just wanted to remind you that we'll need you in the ballroom to make your presentation in about 10 minutes. Can you follow me back inside so we can get everything in place?"

Michael pulled back from Heather, but kept his arm secured around her waist. "Becky, thanks for the reminder. Just give me a moment and I'll meet you there."

"Of course Mr. Dalton."

"I guess duty calls," said Heather, looking a bit disappointed at another missed connection.

"Yes, it does. But you'll stay right. Not to listen to my speech, but so we can, talk some more and maybe check out the silent auctions, there's plenty of food."

Heather rested her hand on his cheek, "I'm not going anywhere, well, except to get some wine. You never know how long those speakers might talk..."

Michael took her hand and led her back into the ballroom, "Sounds good, so I'll catch you by the bar once I'm finished. I promise my presentation will be short and sweet." He squeezed her hand and was off.

As if by chance, or luck, at opposite ends of the ballroom,

Summer and Ellis were both witness to the sight of Michael and Heather as they parted ways and headed in separate directions.

Summer exclaimed, "This can't be happening," as she made her way to intercept Heather.

"I need to stop her," Ellis said as he too began to push through the crowd from his side of the room.

Ellis reached her first and grabbed her arm, "Heather, you can't leave yet."

Summer arrived a minute later and grabbed her other arm, "please Heather - give Michael a chance to explain."

"Ellis, What do you mean? I'm not leaving."

The determined look on Summer's face was replaced by a huge grin, "You're not?"

She extended her hand, "Hi Heather, it's nice to meet you, I'm Michael's sister Summer. I am so happy to finally meet you."

A thunderous round of applause filled the room as Michael posed with the winner of the Humanitarian of the Year award. He caught Heather's eye from across the room as he made his way over to where she was standing. It took him awhile to reach her since there were many hands to shake along the way.

"Summer, I see you've met Heather," as he stepped beside her and slid his arm around her waist, pulling her in close.

"Yes Mike, it's about time I met her," added Summer.

"I don't disagree."

Heather spoke up, "and Michael, you remember Ellis Thompson from Roscoe Tech."

Michael extended his hand to Ellis, "of course. Good to see you again Ellis."

"Mr. Dalton, let me say it is great to see you again too."

Michael noticed that Heather was not holding a glass of wine. "Heather, did you not make it to the bar, should I get you something? Red wine?"

"I'm good, Summer and Ellis wanted to make sure I wasn't leaving for some strange reason," as she turned and looked at the pair who appeared a bit uncomfortable.

"Well, since I'm finished with my obligations for the evening, I could give you a ride home, if you'd like," Michael questioned.

"I'd love that."

Michael didn't need to be told twice, he took Heather's hand and was off towards the door.

"Well, that was rude, they didn't even say goodbye," added Summer.

"But Summer, they left, together. Like together."

She broke out into a wide grin and held up her hand to give Ellis a high five. "We did it. They are talking and driving home together. Score!"

Michael's driver opened the door for the couple and the pair slid into the back seat of the limo. "Mr. Dalton, will you be heading home now or will there be a different destination?"

Michael turned to Heather in question, she smiled and nodded.

"Michael, home will be fine, thank you."

Michael felt warm and cozy, but a bit stiff and sore. *"Why is my hand asleep?*

He opened his eyes and recalled that they had fallen asleep on the couch. Despite the tingles coursing through his hand he didn't move and smiled at Heather as he thought back on their conversation from the previous night. They had settled into the couch, kicked off their shoes and shared a bottle of wine.

"Heather, I am so glad that you are giving me another chance, well I hope that you are, I can make you breakfast in the morning, just like I had planned the other night. Or maybe that's too soon, if you want me to call you a cab."

He heard a small snort from Heather - she had fallen asleep.

"So much for pouring my heart out. It can all wait until the morning."

Heather shifted in his arms and opened her eyes.

"Good morning."

"Michael, oh I'm so sorry I fell asleep on you. Like literally fell asleep on you. I'll get moving and call a cab."

She moved to extricate herself up from Michael's embrace, but he grabbed her arm to stop her.

"You're not going anywhere, I owe you breakfast, and additional groveling for forgiveness."

"Michael, you need to let me go."

"Heather, I just got you back, I'm not going to let you go again."

She leaned forward to kiss him firmly on the lips, "Michael, I just need to use the bathroom, I am all in for breakfast."

After a quick bathroom break she met him in the kitchen. He handed her a steaming mug of coffee, "here you go, what do you want for breakfast? You better check your phone, your bag has been chiming."

"I'll be fine with just the coffee. Do you have some clothes I can borrow - so I don't have to do the walk of shame - not that we did anything shameful last night - but I'd hate to have my neighbors see me arrive home in this dress - in the morning. And don't you have your Saturday am coffee date with Summer?"

Heather pulled her phone from her bag, "Oh Ellis."

Michael came up from behind so he could read the texts over her shoulder.

11:22 PM - E: Heather, how did it go?

11:43 PM - E: Hope you got some loving

7:22 AM - E: Heather....hello

8:43 AM - E: Call me later - hope you are getting busy

"Who's E?"

"Ellis,"

"I really don't know what to say about that. Ellis is quite a character."

"Let's just say he is very invested in my love life. Oh, I don't mean that I'm in love with you, he is just.. "

Heather was saved by the chime as Michael's phone began to ring with notifications.

Michael unlocked his phone to see three texts from his sister Summer.

8:47 AM - Sis: Michael, I hope I won't be seeing you at our coffee date today

8:49 AM - Sis: Tell Heather I said hi

8:52 AM - Sis: Call me later - if you ever get out of bed

"So, according to Summer, I have no commitments and am free to make you breakfast."

Heather slid up to Michael's side, "I'm so happy to hear you have no other commitments."

He turned to face her and moved his arms around her waist, "And I am so happy you're here."

Heather smiled and slid her hands around his neck and leaned up to kiss him.

The kiss turned heated as Michael pulled her tightly against his body. He paused, a bit out of breath, "I think breakfast can wait."

Heather smiled and nodded, as Michael pulled her up the stairs to his bedroom.

―――――

It was almost noon by the time Michael and Heather returned to the kitchen in search of sustenance. Heather had found a t-shirt and sweatpants of Michael's to borrow. She stood by the open fridge surveying the possibilities for brunch.

"You've got a lot of food in here for just one person. So many vegetables."

Michael slid up behind her, "vegetables are healthy, and you know I like to cook."

"Do you have anything in the freezer we could heat up? That would be faster. I did work up an appetite," she asked as she moved to pull open the door to the freezer.

Michael stepped forward and used his hand to block her from opening the freezer.

"Michael, why can't I look in your freezer?"

"Heather, just sit down, I'll make us omelets, the freezer is just filled with frozen veggies."

"Why does it seem like you are hiding something?"

Heather appeared to give up and turned towards the stools that sat along the back of the kitchen island, but once Michael relinquished his guard of the freezer door she pounced and yanked the freezer door open.

"What is this Michael?"

He turned to see her standing in front of the open freezer.

"I might be known to stress bake."

The freezer was filled with neatly stacked pies in zip lock bags. Heather pulled out a pie from top of one of the stacks and set it on the island.

"Really, you think, because this freezer is filled with nothing but pie."

"I was considering inviting you over for apology pie, but that didn't happen."

"You know what this means."

"That I need counseling... or a bigger freezer?"

'No, it means breakfast pie!"

The intercom buzzed and Mark Roscoe picked up his phone, "Yes Elaine, fine, put her through."

"Mrs. Dalton, good to hear from you, how is Roscoe doing?"

"Mark, remember I told you to call me Mikayla, and thank you for asking. Roscoe is making great progress in his recovery."

"So what can I do for you Mikayla?"

"I wanted to call and thank you for making sure that Ms. Farchild attended the awards event last week. Did you see the picture in the paper?"

"Yes, I saw the picture. Heather and Michael looked very cozy. Did they get back together?"

"Yes I believe so, they just needed a little push."

About the Author

USA Today and International Best Selling Author Ashley Zakrzewski loves writing small town contemporary romance with some steam. She is best known for her Rough Edges series following the men and women of the Grapevine Fire Department. The series is ten books.

You are able to buy ebooks and signed paperbacks directly from this author on her website. If you would like to keep up with new releases and giveaways, go join her newsletter on her website.

www.ashleyzakrzewski.com

If you would like to see more books in this series or to see what else this author has to offer, you can also go here:

books2read.com/ashleyzakrzewski

Made in the USA
Columbia, SC
24 July 2023